The Plot's the Thing!

As any good author should, she knew the leading characters:

—A cleric's willful daughter bent on taking London's literary world by storm . . .

—A handsome lord who considered all women save one to be flighty creatures concerned with nothing of greater import than gowns and gossip . . .

—A brilliant and beautiful lady whose keen mind was obviously the exception that proved the gentleman's rule . . .

—A charming nine-year-old whose presence soon set the tongues of London society wagging . . .

Yes, the cast of players was all too easy, but for lovely novelist Anne Calder the plot was becoming far too confused. And her vision of herself as a highly successful author capable of maintaining her independence and avoiding the marriage trap, was somehow being replaced by the face of a man whose opinions she could not abide and whose affections might never be hers . . .

The Determined Bachelor

The Determined Bachelor

A REGENCY ROMANCE

by
Judith Harkness

A SIGNET BOOK
NEW AMERICAN LIBRARY

Copyright © 1981 by Judith Harkness

SIGNET TRADEMARK REG. U.S. PAT. OFF. AND FOREIGN COUNTRIES
REGISTERED TRADEMARK—MARCA REGISTRADA
HECHO EN CHICAGO, U.S.A.

SIGNET, SIGNET CLASSIC, MENTOR, PLUME, MERIDIAN AND NAL
BOOKS are published by New American Library,
1633 Broadway, New York, New York 10019

First Printing, February, 1981

  2 3 4 5 6 7 8 9

PRINTED IN THE UNITED STATES OF AMERICA

The Determined
Bachelor

compromise, ... to give them to any master ... the
... his benefit ... my country and my King!"

Lady Dian... ... occupied in twiddling a ribbon ... her

Prelude

For once, Grosvenor Square was utterly deserted. It was that hour of the day—between five and six on a bleak November afternoon—when the inhabitants seemed to have exhausted their enthusiasm for fresh air. The weather was too cold and damp to encourage the usual outing in Hyde Park, and even those few hardy souls who had ventured out at all had long since returned to the comfort of their own hearths. Their more sensible neighbours (those who had not gone away to Scotland for the fox hunting) had stayed within, and were presently deep in afternoon slumbers. The exertions of the evening would not commence for another hour, and the great stone mansions lay silent in the lowering dark. Only a solitary figure scurrying along the glistening cobblestones gave any hint of life. The figure (belonging to a scullery maid hastening back from her mission to the butcher) soon vanished into the servant's entrance at Number Six, leaving the street once more to the silence and the fog.

At Number Twenty-two, a vast stone edifice belonging to the Princess Lieven, the butler was taking his ease beside the pantry window, which afforded a view of the whole square. Rutgers had little to occupy his mind on this bleak afternoon, for his own mistress had gone away on a hunting party some days before. He was therefore absorbed in his own thoughts, which were of no particular interest to anyone save himself, and in contemplating the street, which was notably devoid of activity. He had glimpsed the furtive scullery maid, and let out a contemptuous snort upon seeing the bundle in her arm. How very typical of Number Six, to leave the marketing till evening! Everyone knew that not an edible joint of meat ex-

1

isted in the whole of London past ten in the morning! Only Lord Hargate's slovenly housekeeper could have permitted such an atrocity from the cook. Musing to himself thus upon the shortcomings of Number Six, Rutgers barely noticed the approaching rumble of carriage wheels. When the sound grew louder, he started up, as much from instinct as training, and commenced putting on his coat. But the sudden realization that no coach was likely to stop before his own door made him sit down again. With some curiosity, however, for there was seldom any traffic in the square at this hour, he leant forward to get a better look at the vehicle, just now coming into view.

At first the sight did not excite his interest. It was only a dirty hired chaise, of the type commonly seen at any large posting house, which, from the look of its mud-splattered sides and the exhausted team, appeared to have come some distance. Such was the butler's snobbery (for the most elegant equipages in England daily passed before his door) that he barely accorded it one glance, and this with a little sniff and upward motion of his nose which amply demonstrated his feelings upon seeing so humble a carriage driving in Grosvenor Square. Yet, when this same lowly vehicle passed by the Princess Lieven's mansion and drew up across the way before Number Six, Rutgers could not resist leaning a little closer to the window and screwing up his eyes to have a better look. His curiosity was further raised on seeing the coachman jump down from his perch and commence unloading the numerous trunks and boxes from the roof.

The butler's interest was not all impersonal, for he was forever on the lookout for some new item of gossip which could further lower the estimation of Hargate House amongst the servants in the square. Such was the derision already accorded Lord and Lady Hargate and their staff amongst his peers that the effort hardly seemed worthwhile. And yet Rutgers derived so much satisfaction from hearing them abused, and delighted so earnestly in the critical anecdotes recounted to him by his friends, which could illustrate ever more clearly the utter vulgarity and disorganization of that family, that he could not resist pressing his hawklike nose quite against the chilly glass pane in an effort to get a better view.

Nothing could have astonished him more than the figure which presently stepped down from the chaise. Rather than the vulgar relative he half expected, Rutgers was amazed to see a tall and elegant gentleman alight. From the tips of his glowing Hessians to the multiple capes of his fashionable traveling cloak, he was a picture of masculine elegance. Nor did the gentleman possess that affectation of stylishness in his person and attire which may sometimes fool the eyes of a less experienced observer than Rutgers, who prided himself upon his judgment of his betters. The butler was used to seeing dandies parading in Regent's Park and Bond Street who could not have bought their way into his own mistress's drawing room. It is true that Rutgers would have been delighted to recognize just such a pretender to *tonnishness* alighting before Hargate House, for it would further fuel his argument that Lady Hargate was no better than an overdressed coquette, who could only delight in the company of her own kind. Yet the spectacle before him, though it dampened his spirits at first, only raised them a moment later. The traveler was a Corinthian of the first water—that much one perceived at once. His collars were of just that height, barely grazing the well-defined jawline (for Rutgers, it must be pointed out, had not only the nose of a hawk but the eye of one), which bespoke the best shirtmakers in the kingdom. His leg was slender but well-formed, his neck cloth beautifully knotted, and his gloves impeccable. Nearly upsetting the table beside him, Rutgers managed to see all this, and yet he could not make out the gentleman's features. These were hidden from view by the rakish angle at which his silk hat was set upon his head and the shadow it cast beneath. The butler had all but given up hope of identifying him when the gentleman turned back (evidently to issue some order to the coachman) and his face was illumined for an instant by a candle from within the house.

"By Jupiter and St. George!" was all the butler could exclaim upon recognizing the traveler. "By Jupiter and St. George—it is Sir Basil back from France!"

Chapter I

"What the Devil!" exclaimed Sir Basil Ives, beginning to raise the solid brass knocker, fashioned into the shape of a lion's paw, for the third time. Twice he had knocked, and still no one had come to answer. The vast double doors, with the Hargate arms emblazoned above, remained firmly closed. To the eyes of the weary traveler, who had been jostled over England's worst roads since dawn, they looked as unyielding as the doors of a tomb. Worse—thought he ironically—they looked exactly like the gates to his brother's mind, which had been firmly sealed since birth. Sealed, at any rate, to anything rational, intelligent, or of any import.

Frowning, Sir Basil let the knocker fall and then stepped back to get a view of the upper windows of the mansion. There were candles ablaze in several, therefore the family could not all be abroad. They must certainly have received the message of his return, sent by special courier nearly a fortnight ago from France. Then where the devil were they?

Sir Basil was not ordinarily an impatient man. Indeed, some of the Baronet's most astonishing diplomatic coups had been won by sheer persistence and a refusal to be irritated into foolishness. Impatience was one of those vices which the Ambassador considered nearly as fruitless as it was unbecoming. It had never been known to win an argument nor speed the events of the world, and nearly always resulted in some sort of imbecility. As imbecility was as foreign to his nature as a love of dirty cravats or crimson waistcoats, it was unlikely that Sir Basil would allow himself the luxury of giving in to his impatience just at this moment, when he had nearly attained the object of his journey.

Indeed, all the way from Southampton he had vowed firmly to behave as gentle with his brother as if he had been a poor unfortunate beast, and to avoid at all costs giving in to his natural irritation with him. Lord Hargate's character was so entirely opposed to his younger brother's (being a lover of wine, cards, and every sort of frivolity, which the Baronet abhorred) that it was a constant source of amazement to those who knew them, that they had both been conceived by the same parent. As Lord Hargate was, into the bargain, as foolish as he was weak, it was not surprising that Sir Basil, whose reputation as a brilliant diplomatic strategist was only equaled by his temperance, should avoid any unnecessary contact between them. It had certainly never occurred to the Baronet that he might someday be forced to ask a favour of his brother. And yet that day had come. The favour, besides, was of such a delicate nature, and of so great a magnitude, that the most ingratiating behaviour possible was called for. Reminding himself of this, Sir Basil suppressed the urge to beat his cane against the door. When, after some little while, an ancient butler with eyes still swollen from sleep came to answer the knock, he had managed to press his lips into something like a smile.

"Good Lor'!" croaked the butler upon seeing who it was. His eyes nearly popping out of his head, he stood stock-still, as if incapable of movement. "Good Lor'—I mean to say, it is the young master!"

Sir Basil eyed the elderly retainer with amusement. "Indeed it is, Groves. Though I think you might begin to call me Sir Basil now, if you don't mind. I have been out of knee breeches these past twenty years at least. And do you think I might come in?"

Groves, who had been too amazed to finish putting on his coat, an operation he had neglected to complete before opening the door, stepped quickly back, blushing deeply. His withered old cheeks grew more crimson still when the Baronet stepped past him into the hall and gazed about him with an appraising glance.

"I see your new mistress has not lost a moment in taking up the latest vogue of decoration," ventured the Baronet, having taken in with horror the new crimson wall hangings, an elaborate campaign table with feet in the shape of lion's paws, and some other artifacts of the current rage in exotica.

The butler followed his glance uncertainly.

"Ah, yes, Your Excellency. Things have changed a great

deal in these past years. Her Ladyship was in a great rush to cheer the old place up as soon as your father died, God rest his soul."

"Well, she certainly has done *something*," returned the Baronet dryly, "though I do not know if one could call it exactly cheerful. Is this what every English house looks like nowadays? I shudder to think what Iseleigh would have said, had he seen what had become of his handiwork."

The butler shifted back and forth uncomfortably upon his feet. He held a generally low opinion of the young Lady Hargate, whom he persisted in thinking of as "new," though she had held the title for eleven years. Happy had been the days when Hargate House had been a bastion of masculine tranquility, but those days were now long past, and Groves would not let his master's brother see a hint of his true feelings.

"Ah, Sir—well, well! Ladies will be ladies, will they not? And I have lived long upon this earth without seeing one of 'em who will rest easy till she has made her mark upon every house she enters."

Sir Basil met the butler's eyes for a brief instant, and in their gaze was all that comprehension, which only affirmed bachelors can truly savour, of the absurdity of the female brain.

"Very true, very true. You are looking well, Groves."

The butler, well pleased, made his bow.

"And you, Sir—if I may be so bold—are looking very fit. I trust France has agreed with you?"

"Ah, France! A nation as confounding as the female mind. But we had better not stand about thus."

And with a quick glance toward the waiting coachman, which the butler instantly followed, Sir Basil drew back to remove a fleck of dust from his traveling cape, pull off his gloves, and run a weary hand across his brow.

"Good Lord, Your Excellency!" cried the astounded Groves. "You have not come all this way in a hired chaise! Come on, then, man!" continued he in an outraged tone to the bewildered coachman, who had only been awaiting his orders. "Come along! Don't stand about like an idiot! Bring in the Ambassador's trunks! No! No—" with a doubtful glance at the recipient of these orders—"you had better stay outside. I shall have a footman fetch 'em."

And, snapping back to life, the old butler hastened off in search of the requisite servant. Sir Basil's luggage was soon bestowed indoors, the coachman's fee settled, and the

7

Baronet's outer garments removed. Groves was all agonized apology for having failed to prepare the Ambassador's old apartments.

"I was not told, Sir, that you were expected."

"Not told? How odd. Well, never mind. Only send my things upstairs and see if a footman will not unpack 'em. I have left my own man in Paris, for I shall not be above a few days in London. And do you, if you will, inform my brother I am here. I trust he is at home?"

Grove looked uncomfortable.

"I believe he is resting, Sir," replied he, turning to leave, "but I shall fetch him. And shall I have a bottle of port sent into the library? Very good, Sir. Er, Sir—" the old man paused with an unhappy expression in his eyes.

"Yes, Groves?"

"Things—er—things are not what they used to be, Sir, if you take my meaning."

Sir Basil soon saw what he meant. Passing up the stairs to the library, he glanced into several apartments, so transformed by the industrious Lady Hargate that they were barely recognizable. What had been for most of his youth, and a good deal of his manhood, rooms whose solid aura of masculine serenity had consoled his darkest hours, were now nauseatingly frilled up with every sort of feminine trinket. Scarcely a corner had gone untouched, scarcely an item of furniture unmarred by restless fingers and ambitious upholsterers. Still, he was relieved to see that the library was not much changed. Its commodious leather armchairs were intact, and the vast inlaid desk which had served his father and his father's father before him was still as littered with papers as it had always been in the Baronet's youth. A cheerful fire burned in the grate, and the shelves were still laden with books—though covered, as Sir Basil noticed with a smile, with a thick layer of dust. However, it was sufficient to induce him to pull up a chair before the hearth and stretch out his cramped legs to the heat of the blaze. After twelve hours upon the road, such comfort could hardly but induce a pleasant meandering state of mind. Soothed by the wine, the warmth of the fire, and the solid and familiar surroundings, the Baronet allowed his thoughts to wander aimlessly for a few moments.

How pleasant it was, in truth, to be back in England! His thoughts had been too full of his present troubles during all the journey from Southampton to allow much attention to the passing scenery. And yet the gentle hills and softly inscribed farmlands had done their work upon him. Even in the customary fog of this time of year, it had all seemed lovelier to him than anything in France. Indeed, he had nearly forgotten what a charming countryside it was, and when the carriage had rumbled over Westminster Bridge, allowing him his first glimpse of this fair city, what a pang had been in his heart! How much more splendid and civilized was this to anything in Paris! His first view of Regent's Terrace, and some other of the improvements which had been worked since his departure, had filled him with pride. Say what you would, there was nothing to equal English ingenuity. The French could boast as much as they liked, but their greatest architects could not hold a candle to the best of the British master builders. And, for all their legendary elegance, they were incapable of making a man as comfortable as he was at this moment. What a pity he could not stay longer! But duty called. No, no—he would not stay above a fortnight. Only let him dispatch his present business with success and he would be on his way back across the Channel.

These musings were cut short by the sound of a heavy footstep in the corridor. Recognizing at once his brother's tred, Sir Basil started up. The wide, welcoming smile which he had carefully arranged upon his features was destined to fall almost instantly, however.

"By Jove!" cried he, rising from his chair as the door swung open to admit Lord Hargate. That gentleman being constructed along very solid lines, his figure nearly filled the doorway. Lord Hargate was not so tall as his younger brother, but nearly twice as broad. Across his vast paunch was stretched a waistcoat of a very brilliant shade of blue, threaded through with silver and crimson. His collar points nearly brushed his ears, his cravat was knotted about a dozen times, and his scrawny calves, which seemed every moment in danger of collapsing beneath the immense weight of his frame, were done up in scarlet hose. Hargate had not inherited the same dignity of feature as had his sibling, and across the whole of his wide and almost feminine countenance was spread an idiotic grin.

"By Jove!" cried Sir Basil again, a little more restrained this time, for he had been taken aback by the increased proportion of his brother's figure, and suspected, from the bright flush on that gentleman's cheeks, that he had already imbibed

9

a good deal of wine that day. "How good to see you, Hargate, after all these years!"

" 'Mensely good, 'mensely good!" agreed the elder heartily, staggering a little in his progress toward the Baronet. There were such embraces exchanged as Sir Basil could tolerate, considering the strength of spirits on his brother's breath, and then His Lordship collapsed into the nearest armchair.

" 'Mensely good!" he repeated, beaming foolishly. "And t' what my dear brother, do we owe this honour? I thought you were in France. Paris, ain't it?"

Sir Basil managed to suppress his amazement at this marked indication of his brother's information, or perhaps memory.

"Paris—yes. I have been His Highness's envoy to the French court these last four years."

Lord Hargate looked only half enlightened.

"But did you not receive my letter?" inquired the Baronet, beginning to feel that he was moving in a dream.

"Letter? No, no, I do not recollect anything about a letter. Was there one?"

Sir Basil sighed. Evidently, marriage had done little to improve the powers of his brother's mind.

"I sent a message some days before I left to warn you of my visit. I have been called home on pressing business and hoped I might impose upon you and my sister-in-law for a day or two."

"Ah!" No greater reaction seemed forthcoming, and Sir Basil pressed on:

"Well! You seem very well. I have not seen you since the old man's death. Four years ago, that was."

Lord Hargate's expression suddenly brightened.

"Four years ago! Good Heavens! It don't seem that long! Have you really been away four years? Well, well! I suppose you have."

And as if something in his brain had been given a brisk shake, Lord Hargate suddenly snapped to life. With the keenest interest he demanded:

"What do they feed you in France, eh? I hear the cuisine is dashed good there. But you look slender as a knife, if you don't mind my saying so. Ought to feed yourself properly, you know, old boy. Don't want to waste away to nothing."

Sir Basil smiled dryly. Here was the brother he knew.

"No fear of that, Hargate. I am fed perfectly well."

"Ah! Well, your coat is exceptionally handsome. Did you

have it tailored there? Bit plain for my taste, but a nice bit of cloth, you know. I hear the Frenchies are pretty well with lady's finery, but when it comes to men, they cannot hold a candle to our old Hingham on Bond Street."

Sir Basil responded with a smile that he had never heard the French tailors condemned, and then endeavoured to steer the conversation in another direction. But his brother would not leave off interrogating him about the life at Court, and whether the ladies were very pretty, and what sort of neck cloth was in fashion, and whether the wine was better on the other side of the Channel. Though seeming to have very little curiosity about any more serious matter, these points were of infinite interest to him. Sir Basil would have liked to have got straight to the point—his own point, at any rate—but saw at once that he must humour his brother's curiosity, and providing as many anecdotes as he could muster about life at the Tuileries, he strove to do just that. Having passed nearly half an hour in this fashion, he ventured on to another topic.

"But enough about my own life, Hargate! You must tell me about yourself. You seem prosperous enough, and, I take it, happy?"

Lord Hargate's smile faded. "Prosperous, old chap? Oh, nothing like! I wish I could say I was. But everything is so dashed expensive these days. It is all I can do to keep my poor Louisa properly clad, and the carriages in decent style. Why, it seems to me that Father was never so hard-up as I always feel! Just at the moment, by the nonce, I am particularly out of pocket. Louisa had just done redecorating the house again, and the other evening at White's I was unlucky enough to lose fifty thousand pounds to that cad Marlborough. I cannot fathom how he manages it, but he never fails to rob me, and he is twice as rich as I, at least!"

"Fifty thousand pounds!" Sir Basil could not help crying out, "You lost *fifty thousand pounds* in one evening? Good God, man, you ought not to be allowed in a card room!" *Especially not*, he added to himself, *since you have about as much wit at baccarat as you have at conversation. I cannot blame Marlborough for robbing you, as it is so easy.*

"Ah, but you must not blame me, Basil," Lord Hargate was saying with a whimper, "for I am ever in hopes of making up what I have lost. I have a horse entered at Ascot for the Winter races which I am sure shall more than compensate me for my losses at cards. And in the meantime," he added, brightening, I suppose *you* could not advance me thirty or forty thousand until the next quarter?"

Sir Basil stared back in amazement. Could he believe his own ears? He had not crossed the Channel and traveled in a springless coach all day in order to sign over his fortune to his profligate brother. Quite the contrary. He had come in hopes of being granted a rather generous favour himself. Remembering this suddenly, he managed to turn his shocked expression into a kinder one.

"Oh, if only I could, my dear brother, you may be sure that I would. But if you remember correctly, I received only a pittance of your inheritance from our father's settlement, and have, besides that, a mere nothing from the Crown to compensate me for my labours on the Regent's behalf. A mere thirty or forty thousand pounds must last me all year." This sounding too brusque a dismissal, Sir Basil added hastily, "However, I shall be glad to help you in any other way I can. Marlborough owes me one or two little favours himself, and I believe I may be able to persuade him to forestall his payment for a while, till it suits you to pay."

Lord Hargate looked a little mollified at this. Indeed, his prompt expressions of gratitude were so vociferous and extravagant that they might have repelled his brother still further had not that gentleman a very real desire to make Hargate aware of his indebtedness.

"And your lovely bride?" he quickly interrupted. "I trust she is as bright and gay as ever?"

"Ah, Louisa!" exclaimed Lord Hargate after a moment, for he had not recognized at first this depiction of Lady Hargate. "Yes, yes, she is very well, thank you, although she complains daily of migraines, and tells me she had not felt well this last year. I believe it is the children, you know. She is such a delicate creature, and cannot abide their noisy playing."

"Ah, your dear little children!" Sir Basil fairly beamed at the mention of them. Those who knew the Baronet well would have been amazed to see him look so happy at the mention of children. He was normally no more interested in babies than he was in the cultivation of turnips, but at the moment he had his own reason for seeming to love them and for pressing his brother into a detailed account of his own. "I suppose they are just beginning to talk, are they? And to show their dear little natures?"

As it happened, Lord Hargate was excessively fond of his children, and he now showed himself more than happy to narrate their most recent triumphs in the matter of learning to talk and to play with their dolls. His account lasted for some little while, and at the end of it, Sir Basil (who had endeavoured to keep a rapt expression upon his face during the whole of the lengthy and tedious narrative), declared:

"Why, Hargate, I believe you must be the happiest of men! Fancy having so much to be cheerful about! I wish *I* could boast so much good fortune. The life of a bachelor is very lonely sometimes, and though I have much to occupy me in my work, I admit there are times when I long for a little of these homely comforts which seem to surround *you*. Ah, for the patter of little feet above one's head! What a lucky fellow you are, to be sure."

Lord Hargate smiled his delightful agreement. He had never displayed much perception in the matter of human conduct, and never having interested himself in the ideas of the tastes of his brother, he was not amazed to hear himself thus envied. What could be more natural, after all, than that Sir Basil should wish to emulate him in everything? Through the slow fog of his mind, which was further thickened by his recent nap and the bottle of port he had drunk to induce him into it, began to creep the thin ray of an idea. He had not formerly questioned the purpose of his younger brother's return. It was not his habit to question very much, but rather to take life more or less as it presented itself to him, without any presumption that it could be changed by his own efforts. But his wife, who was of a very different turn of mind, had managed to persuade him that all men should be married, and that any who were not thus happily attached, should be made to do so at once. Having no great ambitions of his own, Lord Hargate had come in the eleven years of his marriage to adopt those of Lady Hargate, and now, staring at his brother, he began to smile ingenuously.

"Oh, I see what you are about, Basil! By Jove, what a splendid idea! You have come back to be married, and wish Louisa and me to find the lady for you!"

Nothing could have been further from Sir Basil's mind. For five and thirty years he had managed to escape the toils of matrimony, and he had no intention whatsoever of sacrificing his blissful solitude at this late date. He had his own reasons for praising the state of marriage, and of parenthood, just now, but they had nothing to do with wishing them upon *himself*. He saw, however, that his diplomatic overtures had been too subtle for Lord Hargate. He had better get to the point at once, or risk venturing still farther into dangerous waters. With a modest expression, therefore, he hastily replied, "I could never impose so much upon you, Hargate. No, no—I fear I must envy you from a distance. I am not worthy of *your* felicity."

"Nonsense, old boy!" came the instantaneous retort. "Nothing could be simpler! Louisa is an absolute miracleworker. She'll have you married off in no time at all, and to some pretty fair young thing, I'll venture! Only leave it to her, and you'll be a happier man in no time."

In vain did Sir Basil attempt to divert his brother's mind from this delightful prospect. Having once seized upon an idea, Lord Hargate found it difficult to let it go. So thoroughly had he been indoctrinated into his wife's way of thinking that matchmaking had become nearly as pleasurable an occupation to him as baccarat. His eyes began to clear, his voice took on a happy, lilting tone, and he even commenced rubbing his hands together in happy anticipation. Sir Basil had little opportunity, in the face of so much goodwill, to make himself clear. Even had he actually blurted out his real feelings and demanded on the spot the very favour he had traveled from France to procure, it is doubtful his brother would have heard him. He saw that he had much better let this little blaze of enthusiasm die down of its own accord before he absolutely doused it with the truth. Determining, therefore, to be as genial as possible, he smiled at the troubles Lord Hargate was already preparing to take on his behalf. The shudder he felt upon even conceiving of himself as throttled by a wife was suffered inwardly, and he even managed to beckon up a grateful smile when, despite all his urgings to remain where he was, Lord Hargate went off in search of his lady, saying that he could not wait to tell her the news.

Sir Basil, left alone once more, stared dolefully into the fire. What a tedious business this was turning out to be! Little had he imagined, when he had received that astounding letter from his solicitor some weeks before informing him that he had been named guardian to a twelve-year-old child he had neither seen nor spoken to, that he might also fall mercy to his sister-in-law's matchmaking ruses. Suddenly the weariness of twelve hours' upon the road overcame him. As he watched the amber and crimson flames flicker in the grate, the elegant lids began to droop a little above the keen gray eyes. That mind, which was said to have outwitted some of the most conniving brains in Europe, found itself powerless in the face of the latest development. How could he persuade his sister-in-law that he wished her not to marry him off, but rather to undertake the care of his ward? It was a delicate matter at best, and one which, exhausted as he was by the aggravations of travel and the accumulated strain of nerves, had better have been put off until another day. But Sir Basil was not destined to be allowed any respite, for in a very few moments the door to the library was again thrust open, and there, in the full glory of her yellow ringlets and the combined arts of every dressmaker in London, stood Lady Hargate.

Chapter II

Louisa Hargate was thirty-two. When she had been in the full flower of girlhood, coddled by a doting father and a mama who would deny her nothing, she had been called lovely. Her beauty was of that type, however, which does not take kindly to the passing years. Her nose was too small and tended upward at the tip, her mouth was a trifle full and nearly always formed into a pout, and those ingredients of beauty which are thought sufficient for a girl of eighteen, consisting of a blooming complexion and shining yellow curls, had not survived her twentieth birthday. Her eyes were large and blue, however, and had they shone with that inner animation of spirit and intelligence which can sometimes make a homely face seem beautiful, she might still have preserved some degree of handsomeness. But as it was, her gaze was as glassy as a doll's, for Lady Hargate's mind was seldom employed in any occupation greater than choosing a gown from one of her closets, and her thoughts were nearly always turned inward, upon herself. In eleven years of marriage, she had made so little progress toward adulthood that she still affected the look and manner of a debutante. The effect, in combination with her style of dress (tending as it did toward multitudinous frills and furbelows and ornamented by innumerable pastel ribbons), made her look like a silly woman, which indeed was an opinion not unwidely held. At the moment of her entrance into her husband's study, however, the usual blank expression of her eyes had given way to an animated sparkle nearly approaching excitement.

Lord Hargate's news, that his brother had arrived from France and was desirous of a wife, had come at the most propitious moment, for Lady Hargate had just been weeping over her misfortune in leading so dull a life, in which nothing seemed ever to occur. She was sick to death, she had informed her maid, of every frock in her closet, and had not even any interest in buying a new one, for what would it avail her? She alone, of all the people of her acquaintance, had not been invited on a hunting party. Though it was well known that Lady Hargate abhorred the out-of-doors and was terrified of large animals, she felt herself absolutely maligned by this oversight of her acquaintances. And, as if that were not enough, it seemed that Lady Huntington had been selected above herself to preside over the membership at Almack's, with My Lady Jersey and My Lady Southington, and that shrew, the Princess Lieven. In truth, it was beyond her capacity of understanding how life could be so unjust and thrust her into so miserable a state of loneliness and ennui.

The appearance of her husband at the door of her boudoir had done little to soothe her. The sight of him, in fact, only served to remind her of her misfortunes. She ought to have listened to her mama and married Baron Orthwaite instead. Hargate was a fat, stupid, unbearable brute, and had made her bear three children, which had nearly killed her. And yet the pain of giving birth had been nothing, she was sure, as compared to the hardships of later motherhood. The mere sight of her children was a daily reminder that she was no longer a girl and that life was every moment slipping through her fingers.

Poor Lord Hargate could hardly have known, as his wife looked sweetly up at him, with tears shining in her eyes, what was in her thoughts. His only desire was to see her look cheerful again, and as he recounted his news, he had the pleasure of watching the tears dry up in her eyes, and her little mouth form itself into a trembling smile. Could this be true? Could Sir Basil actually have returned, and did he indeed wish her to help him find a wife? All at once ideas began to course through her brain. Sir Basil had attained a certain renown in London for his wondrous handling of the French. His name had become nearly as famous as Wellington's among the *ton*. To appear beside him in society could not but add luster to her own reputation, especially if it was known that she was his intimate friend and had been particularly requested to procure him a wife. Only think what envy she would cause amongst her friends! The idea made Lady Hargate as blissful as a lark in June. No sooner had she heard the news than she was smiling all over her face and calling for a fresh gown.

"Only think," she told her husband as they descended the stairs together, "how fortunate we were not to have gone hunting!"

The sight of Sir Basil, if it were possible, raised Lady Hargate's spirits even more. To the delight of seeing a new face was added the satisfaction of remembering how well-formed her brother-in-law's was. He was tall and well-made and had an elegant bearing, and his coat was made out of the best piece of broadcloth she had ever seen. His greeting, which was very gallant, instantly ingratiated him.

"What a splendid thing it is," said he, bowing over her hand, "to see that the passing of four years has gone unremarked by *some*. I fear you will hardly recognize *me*, however, my dear Louisa."

Lady Hargate dimpled prettily and replied that, on the contrary, she remembered him very well. "However, I am sure you have grown much finer since last I saw you, Brother. I must tell you, if you will not think it a vast impertinence, that I have never seen such pretty muslin as that about your neck."

Lady Hargate sank into a sofa, arranging her skirts about her.

"Oh, I am afraid you have caught me out, dear lady," replied the diplomat, resuming his seat, "for I fear I must be extremely travel-worn just *now*. You must forgive me, and only be assured that I should have stopped to change my clothes, only I was in such a hurry to call upon you and my brother that I hoped you would overlook my dusty boots."

Lady Hargate had not noticed any dust upon Sir Basil's boots, but if she had, this pretty speech would certainly have appeased her. Her good humour was increased in the next minutes, for Sir Basil was so solicitous of her health, and had so many things to say to her, that he might almost have been a suitor for her hand. Indeed, it was not long before she had determined in her mind that he was in love with her, or, if not actually in love, yet a little infatuated. Far from being irked by this idea, Lady Hargate found it absolutely delightful. It put her in a better frame of mind than she had been in since the days of her own come-out, and she began to simper and flush in just the same way she had done then.

Sir Basil, we may be sure, had no idea of putting such notions into her head. It had been his intention only to flatter her, and thereby put her in a receptive frame of mind for the favour he had to ask. He saw after a very few minutes that his compliments had done their work. His sister-in-law was regarding him with the roundest eyes, and seemed every moment in danger of toppling out of her chair in eagerness to catch his next words. He had often noticed female attention increased in exact proportion to the flattery they received. It was one of the many peculiarities of their sex.

"My brother," said he after a while, when he felt there had been sufficient compliments on either side and that the real business of his visit might now be embarked upon, "has been telling me all about your dear little children. There are three, are there not?"

Sir Basil was puzzled to see Lady Hargate's face fall at this innocent remark.

"Yes, yes, there are three of them," she replied impatiently, for she was eager to resume the pleasant train of conversation which had just been going forward.

"Ah!" exclaimed the Baronet in genial amazement. "Three! But I suppose you shall have more."

Lady Hargate looked amazed. "More!" she exclaimed, "why in heaven should I want more!"

Lord Hargate, who had been silent heretofore, only beaming back and forth between his brother and his wife without any appearance of understanding them, now began to look uncomfortable and to shift about in his chair.

"Why," continued Sir Basil innocently, "it is well known that where there is an uneven number, there is always the danger that one will be left out of their games."

"Very right, very right," interposed Lord Hargate. "I have often observed little Alex in tears, for being neglected by his brother and sister. Poor little man! And his nurse will never humour him, but makes him go and play in the school room all by himself."

"Nonsense," responded his lady with some feeling. "*I* have never observed anything like! And I am sure I know a great deal more about my own children than you can, my dear. Nurse is very good to all of them, and, in my opinion, spoils Alex far more than she ought. Why, they are altogether much too spoilt. I cannot conceive of having another child, even if I could."

"Oh, to be sure, my love," interposed her husband hurriedly, "no one is saying that you should. Louisa," he added

to his brother with a little cough, "has a most delicate consti-
tution. She nearly died when little Alex was born."

Lady Hargate was very fond of a sympathetic ear. She had
tortured her husband for some time with tales of her misery
during the bearing of her children and now turned to her
brother-in-law with a pathetic look.

"It is very true, Basil. I nearly died. Lord, what a heavy
burden we women are forced to bear! It is beyond everything."

Sir Basil was not anxious to see this line of conversation
progress. Such talk offended his sensibilities and defied everything he had ever been taught to believe about the gentle
courage of motherhood.

"And yet you must love to see the dear little things playing," he said. "You must often long for another."

"Long for another!"

"I mean," he added hurriedly, "if another would appear, as
it were by magic! I am sure you are a wonderful mother,
Louisa. Anyone can see that in your nature shines that
gentleness of spirit, that constancy of good humour, which is
the very essence of motherhood. How they must dote upon
you!"

Lady Hargate was torn. How could she deny these compliments and yet speak the truth? For the truth was that she abhorred children in general, and though she could not help but
love her own, she dearly wished sometimes that they had
never been born. In principle, they were delightful, but in the
actual and persistent reality, they left much to be desired.
They were boisterous and noisy, and never seemed to possess
the charm she would have liked to see in them. It seemed to
her that whenever they appeared they disappointed her by
some rudeness or other, and yet she had not the heart to
scold them. Lord Hargate, whose office it should have been to
censor their behaviour, would not dream of it. He let the
little scoundrels do exactly as they pleased, until sometimes
she was sure their noisy playing and endless tears would kill
her. And yet she fancied herself as a loving and graceful
mother, and was convinced that if only the baby would give
up howling and the elder children were quieter, she should
find them delightful.

"Dear little things," she murmured, imagining them for the
moment clean and pretty and tucked into their beds. "Yes,
yes, how they do dote upon me! Do they not, my love? Why,
I have the greatest desire to see them this very moment! Do

you, my dear, please pull the bell, and I shall send for Nurse."

Lord Hargate obeyed, and Sir Basil expressed his delight at the idea of seeing his young nephews and niece after so many years. Indeed, there had only been two when he had left for France, and he was very eager to acquaint himself with the youngest member of the family.

In due course the nurse appeared and, looking a little surprised, went off to fetch her charges. His lordship, meanwhile, could not resist the temptation to boast about them and to demand that his brother look out for the strong resemblance which existed between himself and the two boys.

"Why, it is nothing of the kind, my dear," responded his wife, smiling at Sir Basil. "You must tell me yourself, my dear brother, if you do not think little Harry is the very image of me! And as to Alex, he is too young yet to be absolutely sure, but I think he has got my eyes and nose, and certainly his figure is nothing like his father's!"

Sir Basil smiled indulgently, and in a moment heard a great clamoring in the hallway. The door was thrust open and into the room rushed a boy and a girl of about six and nine. Behind them, in the doorway, stood the nurse holding the hand of a toddling infant.

"Come to me, my precious darlings!" cried Lady Hargate, and the children rushed into her lap. The eldest child, who wore a dirty pinafore, instantly screamed.

"Harry is pulling my ear!" cried she.

"No such thing," responded the culprit, with a pout.

"Yes he did, Mama! Oh, you wicked boy! I shall pull yours, I shall!"

And with these words, she pushed him out of her mother's lap and commenced chasing him about the room. The little boy, screaming with delighted terror, dashed behind a chair, upsetting an incidental table.

"Naughty, naughty children!" cried their mama. "Nurse, cannot you make them stop? Oh, they have mussed my gown most dreadfully."

The nurse, who was a large, phlegmatic-looking individual, only shrugged and called out half-heartedly for them to stop their nonsense. Neither mother nor nurse were attended to, however, and Lord Hargate seemed delighted by the display. The screaming continued for some little while longer, and then the baby, who had been hiding his face in the nurse's skirts, began to sob.

"See what you have done now, Clarissa!" cried her mother, but making no move either to comfort the youngest child or to put a cease to his sister's antics. These were only brought to a halt when she accidentally fell across her uncle's legs, and, sitting up rubbing her knee, stared back at his astonished gaze.

"Enough of your playing, my little darlings," said her father. "See, here is your uncle, who has come all the way from France to visit us!"

This news inspired a giggle and another stare. Sir Basil, attempting to hide his dismay, said, "I do not believe you remember me, Clarissa, for you were only four or five when I went abroad."

The child stared unblinking back at him and said nothing. Suddenly a strange gurgle erupted from behind the Baronet's chair, and he looked down to see the boy grinning up at him.

"And you must be Harry," continued the Baronet, still playing the part of the doting uncle. "Does not your sister speak?"

The children evidently found this question vastly amusing, for they both erupted into laughter and fled from the room.

"What very merry children they are," remarked Sir Basil after a moment, when he had recovered from his shock.

"Ah, yes! As merry as possible!" agreed Lord Hargate heartily.

Lady Hargate looked ready to burst into tears. "Nurse," cried she, "why cannot you make them stop? They are beyond everything! Why, they would not even speak to Sir Basil. And here is Alex, crying. Whatever am I to do?"

Lord Hargate heaved himself out of his chair and approached the smallest child, whose face was still hidden in the nurse's skirts. The little boy looked up in dismay and commenced sobbing more loudly than ever.

"Lord, I cannot bear another moment!" cried Lady Hargate. "Do take them away, Nurse, or I shall have another attack of nerves!"

The nurse shrugged and, picking up the child, went out. As soon as the door had closed behind her, Lady Hargate turned to Sir Basil with a peevish look.

"Only see what I am forced to endure! If you knew what a hardship it is to be a mother, I am sure you would take pity upon me."

"Nonsense, my dear!" came Lord Hargate's jovial retort. "You know you quite dote upon them. They are very young,

22

When he had been a young diplomat, just beginning to make his mark in the world, she had taken him up, and from the role of patroness, had grown into a close friend. Had she been fifteen years younger, Sir Basil might almost have been tempted to marry her. As it was, their association was the dearest thing on earth to him. He relied upon her wisdom nearly above his own. As the elder, Lady Cardovan claimed the right to teaze her friend, and Sir Basil received her jibes with a good humour which might have amazed his subordinates at the Embassy in Paris. For his own part, he had sometimes been able to perform those little services for her which only a man can do. Their friendship was based upon mutual esteem, and sealed by mutual assistance—it seemed to the baronet that he could not have looked for more from any relationship between a man and a woman.

It was to Lynch House, therefore, that Sir Basil Ives went as soon as he had paid his respects at Carlton House on the day following his arrival in London. Aside from the sheer joy of seeing her again, he had today a more particular reason for his visit. He wished to solicit her opinion upon his current dilemma, which had only been made more perplexing by the night passed at Hargate House.

He found Lady Cardovan at home, for it was her custom to work on her histories in the morning, a pastime which had commenced as a diversion and grown into a serious and, luckily (for her finances were not so well-ordered as they appeared from a glance about the house and grounds), a remunerative profession. Sir Basil sent up his card, and in a matter of a few minutes the two were ensconced upon the sofa as if they had been separated for several days instead of several years. Theirs was one of those rare friendships which may be broken off for any length of time and taken up again without a break, or any feeling of distance upon either side.

"Oh la!" cried Lady Diana, putting back her head and laughing at one of Sir Basil's tales of British diplomacy in the Tuileries. "It sounds a very rag-headed assemblage! And do they indeed make you stand for six hours before you are awarded your honours, and then force you to eat in the second dining room, as Lady Hardwicke would have us believe? A very ill-mannered lot, they sound, these Bourbons!"

"They have not changed a whit in five hundred years, Diana, and I suppose it is too much to expect they shall do so now, for no more cause than a Napoleon."

"Still, it is some compensation," responded the lady with a

smile, "to inhabit Pauline's Palace, I expect. And a pretty penny Wellington persuaded us to pay for it. Tell me—for you must see by now that I am no better than an eager, gaping *curioso*—did she really appear at one of your balls? I am told she came in upon the Duke's arm, and was stared into extinction at once. I wonder she had the audacity to show her face, with her brother finally stanched."

Sir Basil regarded his friend with a smile. No one could have been less vulgar than this lady, with her tall erect figure, her proud carriage, and luminous, intelligent brown eyes. She was all refinement, so much so that she could afford to inquire thus eagerly into the goings-on at the British Embassy without ever seeming vulgar. What a world of difference lay between her charming self-mockery and the vapid curiosity of his sister-in-law!

"No, my dear Diana," he assured her with just a trace of sardonic drawl—for it was his privilege also to tease *her*, upon occasion—"you may be sure that you have not missed the famous Pauline. I believe she is safely reconciled with her husband, Prince Borghese, now that her funds have been cut off by Napoleon. I think the instance you speak of was at the second ball of my tenure, when a very similar-appearing lady was present, whom everyone thought at first to be Pauline but who in truth was the American Miss Patterson, now married to Napoleon's cousin."

"I do believe," said Lady Diana after a moment's pause, with a playful twinkle in her eye, "that I am in danger of growing envious. How I should adore to see it all myself!"

"Why do not you come, then?" demanded Sir Basil, rising and going to a window which looked out upon the eastern gardens, now russet and ocher under a pale sun. "Why do not you come? I should be delighted to have you at the Embassy, which I am sure you are longing to explore from cellar to attic in search of any remains of Pauline's dubious past. There are more Englishmen in Paris at the moment almost than Frenchmen—it is quite the going thing. In truth, I am quite perplexed why you have not seen fit to pay us a visit before this!"

"I should love to, you know," murmured Lady Diana, almost wistfully, "but even if I could afford the time away from my writing table, I could not raise the funds. My faithful retinue of friends must be the sole source of my information. Perhaps next year—but, in truth, I ought not even to think of it."

Sir Basil looked sharply back from the view he had been perusing. "Why, are you really embarrassed for money, Diana? To look about, I cannot imagine it is true."

"And yet I am afraid it is," said Lady Diana, rising and walking to the bell cord, which she tugged, then taking her place beside the Baronet and staring out over the acres of carefully tended gardens.

"What you see is deceptive, I fear. Between them, Cardovan and my father's legacy are adequate for the maintenance of house and grounds, but above that, I have barely a penny to spare. And then, you know, I am such a poor spoilt creature. I will have my dinners, and my little balls, and cannot abide mediocre wine. No, no—my books are sufficient to live upon comfortably at home, so long as I do not indulge in any great extravagance; but to go abroad—I hardly think so!"

"And yet," insisted the Baronet, "if you were to close down only this portion of the gardens, Diana—only this one portion of all the park and gardens—I am sure it would cover your expenses to Paris. Why, what can your expenses be? Only your passage, and perhaps some little items of luxury once you are there. For the rest, I should provide everything you need."

Lady Cardovan seemed torn for a moment and almost appeared to give in, but with a sudden movement she raised her hand, as if to brush away her friend's absurdity, and went back to take her place upon the sofa.

"My dear, generous friend!" she murmured, patting the place beside her with a beringed hand, "do be still. I shall not listen to any more today. Perhaps another time—well, we shall see. But now you are here, and you are the only sight I should really be traveling for, if I *was* to come. Do let us *now* only be grateful for that. So," she continued, briskly changing the subject, for she saw by her friend's look that he was prepared to be stubborn, "you are here. But for how long? And you have not even told me what has brought you back. I suppose," with a mocking, pettish look, "it is some great matter of state which you cannot share with me?"

"On the contrary," replied the Ambassador, suddenly remembering his most pressing business and coming to sit down again beside his hostess, "it is of a rather more personal nature than that, and I have every intention of telling you about it. Or rather, asking you about it, for it is a matter which demands the counsel of a clever woman."

"Oh, la! Now we are very impetuous! Sir Basil Ives, determined and eternal misogynist, in need of a *woman's* advice!"

"Don't tease me, Diana," he reproached her, "for I really am at my wits' end."

Lady Diana knew how to tease, but she knew equally well how to be serious. She saw by her friend's look that he was distressed, and in an instant, with the most minute change of her expression and her posture, she became the artful listener so much depended upon by her admirers. This pose lasted for a mere second, however, for suddenly a look of vast dismay came over her face and she cried out, "Why, Basil! You have not compromised some poor French girl or other, have you?"

"*Do* be still, Diana!" exclaimed the Baronet irritably. "I have really a most awful problem, and wish you would tell me what to do."

Sir Basil paused, glanced suspiciously at Lady Diana, who had resumed her solemn and demure look, and at last proceeded, "I appear to be encumbered by a child."

"Good God! This is worse than I thought!"

"A child, however, who is not my own, and hardly any relation at all."

"Dear me, was there a basket deposited upon the steps of the Borghese Palace?"

Sir Basil pretended not to have heard.

"I had a letter from my solicitor not two weeks ago in which he informed me that I have just been named guardian to one Nicole Lessington, a child of nine. How I came to be thought of as a suitable guardian for a little girl, I have not the remotest idea. Be that as it may, her father, who was a distant relation of my mother's, saw fit to do so, and I appear to have been made a father overnight."

Lady Diana did not know what to say. She was too surprised and too curious to say anything, in fact, and simply nodded her head impatiently.

"The fact is, I am in a devil of a quandary, Diana."

"So it would seem, Basil. But go on, go on—tell us the details. Where is the child now, and who was Mr. Lessington?"

"The child is in Lincolnshire at present, but arrangements have been made to transport her to London as soon as I have determined where she will stay. Which, in all honesty, I cannot say I shall ever do at this rate. I had hoped she might go to my brother and Lady Hargate, but after spending an evening beneath their roof, it seems to me there could not be a less suitable home for any child, much less one who is not used to battling for her food and air. My sister-in-law appears not to have advanced much since she saw sixteen herself, and how she manages her own children is a question I would not dare to answer."

Lady Diana hid her smiles.

"Our dear Louisa, I'm afraid, is somewhat perplexed about life."

Sir Basil gave her a meaningful look. "That is a charitable way of putting it, Diana. I never saw a more feather-brained creature in my life! She seems to think there is no greater subject for debate than the superiority of muslin to silk. But then. . . ."

Sir Basil did not continue. Lady Diana, however, saw his look of momentary embarrassment and finished for him.

"But then, she is only a woman? Your opinion of my poor sex is not much improved since last I saw you, Basil."

"Oh, well!" replied he with a smile, "what should that bother you, as I have always considered *you* as so much better than the rest, that you might almost be a different race."

"Almost a man, do you mean?" Lady Diana smiled. "If that is meant to be a compliment, my dear friend, you may take it back. I have no desire to be a man, and am so unlike your account of me, that I am almost proud of being a female! Only imagine that! But here, we are veering entirely away from the subject. You and I shall never agree upon this point, I am afraid. I had once hoped to persuade you to my side, but in ten years you have not budged so much as an inch in your opinion." Lady Cardovan paused and, smiling, drew a breath. "As to the child, however, I am quite agreed in your opinion that your brother and his wife ought not to be encumbered with another. I have heard Louisa complain often enough about her own offspring to be convinced of that. In any case, she was awarded to your custody. Mr. Lessington, I suppose, might have given over his daughter to Hargate himself, had he wished. Why do you suppose he did not? Your brother, after all, is the elder, has a family of his own, and is in every outward wise a more suitable guardian to a child."

"That," said Sir Basil, rising again and walking to the fireplace, "is a point I have given some thought since I received the letter. Upon due consideration, it appears to me that Mr. Lessington—at least from what I have been able to ascertain—must have meant his daughter to live in Paris. Perhaps he was eager for her to escape the confines of his own life, or wished her to acquire the refinements which are sometimes thought to be only available in France. I do not—and indeed, I cannot—surmise otherwise."

"What sort of a man was he?" demanded Lady Diana, more and more intrigued with this puzzle.

"A lawyer, as it happens," replied Sir Basil with a wry smile, "and clever enough, it appears, to have written his wishes in such a way that I am incapable of reinterpreting them. A man, according to my own solicitor, well-respected in his profession and of comfortable, though modest, means. I believe he was the chief legal counselor in the region, and very well liked, for he seldom exacted his fee. Hence his daughter's present poverty, which I am afraid is extreme."

"Poor child!" cried Lady Diana, for she had a very feeling heart. "And where is she now?"

"At an establishment in Lincolnshire."

Lady Diana sat quietly for a moment, thinking. After several moments, she looked up with the shadow of a smile about her mouth. "I suppose you have not considered actually *doing* as you were asked—undertaking her care yourself?"

Sir Basil had been fiddling with a small ornament upon the mantle. His fiddling ceased abruptly and he looked up, shocked.

"My dearest lady! Only think what you are saying! I should not have the fir inkling of how to raise a little girl!"

"Yes, you are perfectly right," replied Lady Cardovan, complacently. "You should be the last person *I* should have wanted as a guardian when I was nine."

Sir Basil stared back in silence, his lips pressed together.

"Thank you very much, your ladyship. Whatever your opinion of me—and it appears to be excessively low—I must remain steadfast in my decision. Even were I amiable enough to fulfill your ideas of what a guardian ought to be, I should be practically incapable of the task. What, indeed, would I know of schoolrooms and tantrums, of crinolines and music lessons?"

"Nothing, I suppose," replied Lady Diana calmly. "Although you need know next to nothing about crinolines, as they have been out of fashion above twenty years."

Lady Diana's words had been spoken lightly, but still she stared at him, and Sir Basil, feeling her eyes upon him, grew more uncomfortable every moment. His expression was sullen, however. He saw exactly what his friend was about, and would not let her have her will of him. At length, however, as neither of them spoke, he burst out a little more irritably than he would have wished:

"I see what you are thinking, Diana, and I can tell you that it is absolutely impossible! Aside from the inconvenience it would cause me, and the compromises it would certainly entail in my work, it would be the least beneficial thing on earth for the child. Imagine growing up in a bachelor's house, without any other children to play with, no woman to care for her, none of the amenities of a family ready made! No, no, it would be absolutely unkind."

"As to the effect it would have upon the child, Basil," retorted Lady Diana, "I am almost in complete agreement with you, though not wholly so. Miss Lessington might actually derive as much benefit from such an existence as she would discomfort. Indeed, it was certainly what her father counted upon. But as to the effects it might have on *you*, I think they would all be advantageous."

Sir Basil stared, disbelieving his ears. Could this really be his dear friend speaking, the champion of his reputation, the friend of his youth?

Lady Diana, unperturbed, continued after a moment. "Yes, indeed. The more I think upon it, the more favourable the whole idea appears. I cannot fathom a better education for *you*, who have been so utterly indulged by your own company these many years, than to be encumbered by another being—a being young enough to be a nuisance, and no doubt sensitive enough to demand your kindness and encouragement. A being, what's more, old enough to challenge your complacency."

"My *complacency!*" No words could describe the look of ill-usage upon Sir Basil's face upon hearing this estimation of himself. His cheeks were drained of colour, the tips of his ears turned crimson, and his nostrils, which were extremely elegant and fine, were quivering slightly. Lady Diana could barely suppress the urge to laugh.

"My complacency, Diana!" repeated Sir Basil, with a wounded look. "Is this you? The same friend who has professed to admire my conduct these many years? I hope you are not forgetting, in your present mood, that my career had been marked precisely by proof of my willingness to compromise, to sacrifice, to give place in any matter for the greater benefit of my country and my King!"

Lady Diana was occupied in twiddling a ribbon on her shawl. A shadow falling across her cheek hid her smile.

"I make no doubt of it, Basil," replied she softly. "But do such compromises as you speak of take any real toll of your life? When you have just done giving up some piece of land in favour of a more lenient policy between Britain and France, does the sacrifice follow you to bed? Are your days and nights affected by the work? Are you forced to regard the happiness and health of the French Foreign Minister as dearer than your own? Do you worry if he grows aguish or takes a chill? Are his joys your joys and his sorrows your sorrows?"

Sir Basil stared back, disbelieving his ears. "Don't be foolish, Diana. Of course not."

For some reason the Ambassador could not make out, Lady Cardovan looked triumphant at this admission.

"Aha!" cried she. "But it is these very things which you should be forced to concern yourself about, had you the custody of a child. You are beginning, my dear friend—if I may speak frankly—to grow into a perpetual bachelor. You are five and thirty, and I suppose shall never marry, since you seem to regard all women as superfluous creations of the Lord. Take care, my friend, that you don't lose your humanity whilst you are governing the destiny of the human race."

Lady Diana had spoken softly, but with force. Her words, if they had been strong, had come from the bottom of her heart and from a real desire to see this man, whom she had always admired, remain admirable. She watched him now, standing before the mantle, determined to avoid her eyes, and immersed in a perusal of a little painted bird. The room was quiet save for the distant ticking of the clock at the other end of the room. That quiet, the thin stream of sunshine lying across the Turkish carpet, the inaudible rustling of the trees and shrubberies beyond the French windows, began to have an insufferable effect upon the Baronet. It was one of those moments—very rare in Sir Basil's life—when he felt the world had suddenly changed without his noticing. All at once his customary confidence in his actions and beliefs was disturbed. Could it be that Lady Cardovan was right? Could it be that he had really grown stiff and rigid in the past few years? She was condemning him every moment with those glowing, intelligent eyes, which seemed to look quite through him in a damnably intimate and knowing way, quite unlike the gaze of any man. He felt an odd prickling sensation run up his spine, and felt suddenly clumsy. The little bird in his hand nearly escaped his fingers. In vain did he attempt to summon up the arguments which had just been on the tip of his tongue. She was only a woman—superior, it is true, to any other of his acquaintance—yet still, only a woman. What right had she to upbraid him thus? Did not the everyday actions of his life affect the course of the whole civilized world? Did not he accomplish his aims in a way both universally admired and morally (according to his own and HRH's lights) in accordance with the high standards of British foreign policy? Ought he, a celebrated diplomatist, to be put in a state of schoolboy panic by these accusations?

"Oh, Lord," he murmured at last, "I was so sure this would be such an easy matter to dispatch!"

Lady Diana smiled. "*Dear* Basil!"

"Well, then, how ought we to begin? You shall help me?" There was a look of mingled resignation and terror on the Baronet's face.

Lady Diana rose and, stretching out her hand, went toward him. "Of course I shall. You ought first to have a governess. I shall undertake to procure one."

Sir Basil looked shocked. "Good God! I suppose you are right! Thank you, Diana," he said humbly. "Is there—I mean to say, is there anything else I ought to do?"

"It wouldn't," she said thoughtfully, "do any harm if you could stay in England for a month or two. I suppose that is quite out of the question?"

Sir Basil felt the reins slowly slipping out of his hands. In a resigned voice, he replied, "It might be possible. This is as good a time as any to be away. The King won't budge on the question of abolishing the slave trade. It might actually persuade him a little to our side if I were to remove myself for a short time, and give him a jolt."

"Perfect!" Lady Diana was now all bustling business. "Well then, I think you should take a house for the Season—or in any case a month or two," she corrected herself, upon seeing him beginning to look stubborn. "A month or two should suffice to make our little Nicole feel at ease with her new papa. You ought to get accustomed to the idea *sometime*, you know. In the meantime, I shall begin at once to find you the best governess in England, who shall not feel incommoded by changing her residence, and who shall, if we have any luck at all, be fluent in eight or nine tongues so that you may move from Embassy to Embassy as you please."

"It all sounds," said Sir Basil, in a rather dubious voice, "quite delightful and easy."

Lady Diana only smiled brightly and said nothing.

Chapter IV

The business of procuring a governess proved more difficult than Lady Cardovan had imagined. A week after her interview with Sir Basil, she was so much depressed by the stream of Miss Browns and Miss Smiths who had stood in line at her door nearly the instant her advertisement was sent in to the *Courier*, that she began to think it was impossible to find a decent governess. They were all admirably fitted up with recommendations, which struck her as nearly as much alike as their faces, manners, and clothing. Not a cheerful face was amongst them—they were a gaggle of dour old shrews, and endowed, besides, with an overwhelming snobbery, cultivated at the various Schools for Young Ladies which they had all attended. Was not there a fresh young person to be found, a governess who would neither frighten off a little girl nor teach her to hate life and learning with an equal passion? Lady Cardovan had herself been taught by a wonderful young woman, sensible, kind, and herself exhilarated by knowledge: It was just such a young lady whom she now sought, but like a barrel of apples that has sat too long in the hot sun, she thought there was not a fresh one among them.

Sir Basil, besides, was daily calling upon her with urgency. Where was the promised governess? He had taken a house in Regent's Terrace, admirably fitted up with a schoolroom and every other amenity. Miss Lessington was still in the custody of the orphanage and must be brought to London at once. Exasperated, Lady Cardovan tried to put him off, but with little success. And just when she had herself begun to give up all hope, a young woman appeared at her door who seemed to fit every qualification. On the tenth day following the beginning of her search, a Miss Anne Calder took her place on the little sofa where Lady Cardovan was used to interviewing the prospective governesses. Though seeming to answer none of the usual qualifications of her trade, she was modest, intelligent, and amiable. Lady Diana might have said she was much more than that, might indeed have called her charming: but whatever the case, she took an instant liking to the young woman. It may be said that Miss Calder was equally enthusiastic in her reactions to the Countess.

The interview commenced like all the others. Experience, place of birth, family, and references were inquired into. Miss Calder replied with a delightful ingenuity, seemingly unaware of how different she was from the rank and file of her kind. Her father was a clergyman in Devonshire, she was the second eldest of nine children, four of whom she had tutored until they were sent away to school. Her family had resided for some time in Devonshire, and were a very respectable kind of people—by which Lady Cardovan understood, genteel but rather short of pocket. And no wonder, with nine children, four of them daughters! Miss Calder hinted, without saying it out loud, that she was much depended upon to find a favourable situation.

"But you have never been a governess before?" inquired Lady Diana.

Miss Calder looked nervous. She was a very handsome girl, tall without being strapping, with a natural elegance about her features and carriage. Her manner was as unlike that of a governess as her clothes—she was dressed in a pretty muslin frock and had a coloured ribbon in her auburn waves. She seemed unaware that the general demeanor of a governess was meant to be self-effacing and prudish. Her own manner was direct, her gaze frank, and a hint of humour in her voice and eyes appealed at once to her interviewer.

"No," she replied, evidently ashamed of the fact, "I have not. But I believe I have had so much experience with children. Your Ladyship——"

"Yes, yes—don't bother to explain. You are certainly better qualified than some women who have spent all their lives tutoring children. You are fond of little girls?"

"Very. And of little boys. So long as they behave themselves and work hard. I believe learning ought to be fun, don't you?"

"Absolutely!" Lady Cardovan was delighted.

"I am a great reader, your ladyship, and what I cannot do

myself, I am still capable of teaching. Music and drawing are not my own forte, but I know enough to say when something is well done, and when it is not, and to teach the basic principles, even if I cannot apply them with much expertise."

What a difference there was here from the women who had filled Lady Diana's ears with their accomplishments!

"And what *is* your forte?" demanded she.

Miss Calder seemed to flush. "Literature, Your Ladyship. Also history and geography."

"Do you read much history?" demanded Her Ladyship keenly.

"Do you mean, have I read your books? Yes, I am a great admirer of yours, but hesitated to say so at once——"

"Never mind, my dear! Save your praise, I beg of you. You need not say you like them."

"Oh, but I do!" exclaimed Miss Calder very warmly. "I like them immensely! They are so very much alive, and quite unlike any other histories I have read, which are often dry, factual, and unadorned by even the slightest attempt at a lively style!"

Lady Cardovan could scarcely help responding to such warmth and ingenuous enthusiasm. She smiled.

"I am very flattered, Miss Calder. What else do you read?"

"Well," Miss Calder thought a moment, "I have been reading since I was a child. In general, I have read everything I could get hold of, indiscriminately. I probably should not admit it—but how is one to know what is good and what is not, if one has not some knowledge of *both?*"

Lady Cardovan, smiling, expressed her agreement. A further interrogation rendered up the knowledge that Miss Calder had certain strong opinions. One of these, it appeared, was a hearty dislike of romances. Another was (or seemed to be) a disdain for marriage.

The idea had first crossed Lady Cardovan's mind when she glimpsed Miss Calder, that she would have been far better off well married than well employed: so much easy grace, beauty, and education might have been much prized by any gentleman. But a delicate inquiry into the matter, for Miss Calder had given her age as seven and twenty, brought forth the following:

"Oh! I hope you are not going to tell me I had better find a husband, Your Ladyship! Am I so undesirable as a governess?"

"Not at all! I only thought you might be even more desirable as a wife!"

Miss Calder flushed, but only for an instant. Then she looked her companion directly in the eye, and said, "I have had some opportunities to marry, Your Ladyship. But I had rather not."

"Even if it means taking up a post which is hardly better than a servant's?"

"I have observed wives who are hardly better than servants."

Lady Cardovan could not suppress her smiles. How keen was this young woman!

"Nevertheless, you shall have to answer to someone at all times. A gentleman, I might add, so little used to dealing with females that he is often perfectly impossible."

"The gentleman you mean is Sir Basil Ives?"

"Yes, our Ambassador to France. He has just been relegated the guardianship of a child."

Miss Calder inquired into the situation, and was soon in possession of as many facts as Lady Cardovan was herself, besides a smattering of hints:

"I should tell you before you agree to take the post, Miss Calder, that Sir Basil may not be the easiest employer to deal with. He has been a bachelor all his life—is what one might almost call a *determined* bachelor: and determined, likewise, to dislike women upon principle. He has made an exception of *me*—sometimes I do not know whether to take it as a compliment or an insult. However that may be, he is still one of our kingdom's most distinguished subjects, a gentleman in every meaning of the word, and if sometimes a trifle overriding in his convictions, must be respected and admired for what he has done for England. He is, besides, a very dear friend of mine.

"But you shall be expected, I am afraid, to do more than be a governess. Miss Lessington, coming as she has from so different an environment, will no doubt need guidance of a more personal kind. She shall have to be taught to be a lady, and to take up her role as Sir Basil's ward. That may prove no more difficult a task than teaching Sir Basil to take up *his* role as a guardian."

Miss Calder raised a curious eyebrow, and Lady Cardovan explained herself:

"You see, besides being a bachelor of long standing, unused to deal with our sex save in the most superficial kind of

38

way, Sir Basil is the product of an entirely male family, his mother having died in his youth. From then on, Lord Hargate,—his father—ran his family much like a gentlemen's club. So long as the rules of chivalry were kept to, so long as no one interfered with anyone else, life was pleasant. The results of that upbringing, I am afraid, have been that the Ambassador thinks us all foolish, whining creatures, and cannot be bothered with some of the subtleties which make things run along smoothly, and which are generally the domain of women."

Miss Calder pondered all this with interest, and after a moment, said, "Well, if he does not absolutely hate me, I suppose I shall not hate him."

Lady Cardovan laughed. "I hope, on the contrary, that you shall like each other very well! Well, then, is it settled?"

"Am I engaged?"

"If you still desire the post, it is yours. As to what may happen when Sir Basil returns to France, you must decide that between yourselves. If you have no objection to the family, and do not mind going abroad for a few years, I doubt not but that you shall be invited to go."

Miss Calder had not considered that aspect of the post, but having given it a moment's thought, replied that, on the contrary, she thought the idea delightful.

It was therefore arranged between them that as soon as the young lady could arrange to pack her things and return to London, the three should go together to meet the little girl. Miss Calder was perfectly amenable, and gathered up her reticule to go.

"Oh, and there is one other thing," said Lady Cardovan as they were going out into the hall. "You may be required to serve sometimes as Sir Basil's hostess. If he entertains, which he must do rather frequently, I imagine, you may be expected to guide the servant's hands a little, and to do whatever else is required."

Lady Cardovan held out her hand. "I am delighted to have made your acquaintance, my dear. I hope we shall be good friends."

"Oh! I do hope so, Your Ladyship. And thank you—you have been wonderfully kind."

Miss Calder hesitated a moment and then fled out the door.

A moment later, Lady Cardovan sat down at her writing table to compose a note to her friend:

My dear Basil,

I have engaged a governess at last. She is a remarkable young woman, just what is called for, though not in the usual line of governesses. I believe you shall like her as much as I do. Her father is a clergyman in Devonshire, she has eight brothers and sisters, and is a charming creature. You may open up the little bedchamber on the third floor, and pray, do not forget to have the housekeeper air out the linens! These hired houses are so poorly kept up.

D. Cardovan

Chapter V

Another letter was dispatched from London some days later. On the Thursday following her first interview with Lady Cardovan, Anne Calder sat down to write the following to her eldest brother:

My dearest Ben:

"I promised you I should write at the first possible moment to tell you everything that has happened since I went away. There has been barely a moment to spare, else I should certainly have written sooner. However, I am now so full of news that I hardly know where to begin. I shall tell you everything, and you must decide what is fit to repeat to my mother and father, or what you must disguise a little. I suppose Mama is still angry with me for refusing Mr. Siddons, but I trust when I have proved what a capable governess I can be, she shall not think so ill of me. As to my father— who can ever tell what he is thinking? I half thought he would laugh outright when I told him what I proposed doing, but he managed to look so stern and forbidding a moment later that I cannot tell what his opinion of me really is. When I went away on Saturday, it seemed you were my only ally—so you must be very faithful and kind to your foolish Anne, and be the best judge of what is proper to tell them.

I told you then of my interview with Lady Diana. But I have now, if it is possible, even greater reason to be grateful to her. She is an extraordinary lady, and as beautiful as she is kind. If this adventure comes to naught else, I shall at least be thankful for having made *her* acquaintance. I hope she will not think too ill of me when she discovers that I am not *exactly* who I pretended to be! Never mind—I believe she has enough humour to laugh a little, despite everything. I am still amazed at my good fortune that it should have been she. Only imagine how astonished I was to find that my prospective employer was Lady Cardovan's closest friend! You know I have always admired her books and have only hoped that my own little scribblings might someday improve so much as not to be utterly put to shame by hers. It is my dearest wish that she will be able to guide my hand a little. That, of course, must wait a while. I dare not confess just yet.

As to Sir Basil Ives and my new charge, I must start quite at the beginning to do the tale sufficient justice. You will laugh out loud if I do it at all well. If not, only imagine it were dramatized by Mr. Sheridan, for it has the makings of a farce, or of a comedy, at the least.

I was set down in Huxsley by the post chaise, as you will remember, and was met there by a formidable equipage bearing the arms of the Earl of Hargate, who is my employer's elder brother. There was no one to meet me save a manservant who looked as if he was inclined to gossip, but could not, alas, for he was riding outpost. The female servant who rode within said not two words during all the journey to London, but sat perfectly motionless in her seat, staring straight ahead and hardly blinking. Withall, she seemed so eloquent in her silence that it was obvious she disliked me: a thin, dour, very dry looking woman about fifty, who, as it turned out, is Lord Hargate's housekeeper. From what I have seen of His Lordship's establishment, I do not wonder but she spends the better part of her time riding about the countryside thus, for Hargate House is a perfect shambles where the children are never put to bed, the mistress never leaves her own, and the chief amusement of the butler is whist with the upstairs maid. But never mind, I shall tell you more about that family another time.

Arriving in London about seven in the evening, we came straight here. "Here" is the house—and a very grand one, too—which Sir Basil has taken for the winter so that his ward may get a little acquainted with him before she is transported out of England. It is a modern building in Regent's Terrace, which you will remember as being only half finished when we came to visit two years ago. Now it is nearly complete, and much handsomer than I supposed then it would ever be. That great expanse of marble is quite astonishing to behold, and when the trees have grown up a little around it, I believe it will be splendid. Our own house (you see I am already become quite proprietary) is a grand place like its neighbours—so close, in fact, that the walls on the side adjoin, and there are no windows save in front and back. The frontispiece is made of onyx, the roof seems to be held up by immense columns, very like an ancient Greek temple, which in truth is the style of the whole building. Mr. Richard Nash, whom you have heard so much discussed, is the architect of this whole scheme: of all of Regent's Terrace, the new park around Carlton House, and St. James's Street. They all bear a distinct resemblance to those etchings of the Acropolis in Papa's study. I heard one wit the other day describe Mr. Nash's plan as "a scheme to get up England in fancy dress," which may be just, but I am much more pleased with *his* ideas of ornamentation than some of the others which are evidenced in the city. But enough for the time being. *Now* I must give you the picture of my own life, as it has been since Saturday last.

I was met in very grand and very exemplary style by the Ambassador and Lady Cardovan. Sir Basil Ives struck me at once as coming from a novel (perhaps one not yet written?!): tall, exceedingly handsome, and strikingly cold. His features are finely chiseled, his mouth very finely made but rather too set for my own taste, his eyes gray and piercing. Were it not for a rare flicker of humour around his upper lip and at the most extreme corner of those eyes, I should be inclined to think him utterly devoid of humour as well as emotion. As it is, I cannot quite make him out, but am inclined to believe he is the diplomat *par excellence*. He is perfectly charming, if charm consists only in uttering the correct thing at the correct moment, all with the most keen attention to form. To all outward appearances, this must make him amiable, but he lacks any of that warmth, or spark of feeling, which is an absolute requirement of *mine* for perfect agreeableness. He greeted me very handsomely, but with a sort of stiffness which made me think, as he was inquiring about my journey, the state of my health, whether or nor I was tired, etc., that we were statues speaking to each other across a gully. At dinner, which they had put off on my account, he exhausted himself at once of speaking to me. Thereafter, he addressed himself solely to Lady Cardovan, and she, with some little smiles, replied always to me, as though she were translating for her friend. I do not know if he is more afraid of me as a governess or as a woman—but I am inclined to

43

think a little of both. He is one of those gentlemen who has already made up his mind before he converses two minutes with a female that she has nothing of interest to say.

All this makes him seem like something less than flesh and blood. I cannot make out what makes him laugh or cry, but as you know my weakness, you may be sure that I am set upon finding some trace of humour even in *him*. Only from my first impression, that must come from circumstance rather than inbred eccentricities. I do not doubt Sir Basil has plenty of those (as who amongst us does not?), only they are of the type which must be put into relief by situation. And, Ben, for circumstances, you have not long to wait: barely twelve hours after setting foot in Regent's Terrace, we were off again to meet my little charge, Miss Lessington. From only the briefest sketch of her, you shall see instantly that *here* is a challenge even to Sir Basil's equanimity and composure.

We were to collect the little girl at the office of Sir Basil's solicitor, in Harley Street. Thither we drove, in all the elegance of Lady Cardovan's carriage, Sir Basil staring straight ahead of him with a perfectly pained expression upon his face, as if he was driving to his own funeral. Her ladyship, meanwhile, attempted to enliven the journey by giving me an account of every building we passed, and now and then recounting some humorous anecdote in an attempt to bring a smile to the Ambassador's face. Nothing availed, however, and although I was perfectly amused during the whole drive, the object of her solicitations remained stonily silent, whether from fright or displeasure, I do not know. The solicitor, a Mr. Hawke-Smythe (who looks amazingly like the first part of his name), we found sitting behind his desk, well littered with documents, in an office so dark and musty that for a while I thought we had really entered a tomb and began to suppose Sir Basil's terror had not been unjustified. Mr. Hawke-Smythe, a cadaverous person with a great head waggling above his long and knotty throat, rose very gravely to meet us. His solemnity was all the more astounding as, after some few moments, I noticed a little girl sitting perfectly upright in a chair to one side of his desk. She had the brightest expression in the world upon her face, which was as shining and rosy as the lawyer's was gray. She was dressed in the most remarkable fashion; a tartan bonnet perched upon her black curls, a scarlet cape about her small shoulders, and a plum woolen frock beneath. She looked exactly like a cheerful little elf, or perhaps more truthfully, a wandering gypsy child. She greeted us in a high bright voice, and remained as unperturbed as you please throughout the whole business. Said Mr. Hawk-Smythe (with many apologetic rumbles), "I have just been entertained this half hour by your ward's chatter, Your Excellency." Sir Basil bowed, took the little girl's hand, and made some rather stiff comment about how pleased he was to make her acquaintance. Miss Elf smiled like a queen, made her courtsey, and replied: "Likewise, Your Excellency. I have had the happy expectation of meeting you ever since poor Papa died." This was pronounced with a combination of such nice condescension and rapt interest that it fairly took my breath away. The child looked like a gypsy and spoke like a duchess! Sir Basil seemed equally amazed, and I saw Lady Cardovan turn away to hide her smiles.

"Child, here is your new governess, Miss Calder," said His Excellency when he had recovered from his shock. The girl turned to me and held out her hand, saying with great cordiality that she was happy to make *my* acquaintance, too. For this I was heartily thankful, I can assure you—and said as much. It had begun to dawn upon me that I had contracted for a task quite beyond my abilities. The child was already so well-formed in her conduct, so candid in her manner, so condescending in her little murmurs and smiles, that the idea of teaching her at all seemed superfluous. It must have been, from my own small experience, something akin to teaching a kitten how to play. I had already a thousand questions for Lady Cardovan, but from one glance at her, I could see she was nearly as astounded as myself. From a later conversation with that lady, I gathered that she had no more information about the child than what she had imparted to me at our first meeting. Mr. Lessington was a solicitor, a respectable and respected man in his county, and Nicole had been his only child. That he had managed to be both mother and father to her during most of her life was astounding, especially considering the precocity of her mind and the maturity of her manner.

I have grown only more astonished by Miss Lessington since that day. We are on very intimate terms, for she instantly made it clear to me, upon our going home, that she intended to be as much my friend as my pupil. She commenced, the moment I had shown her her bedchamber and the schoolroom (an apartment at the top of the house, which

45

by the look of it would more properly have been used as a ballroom) to inquire into my own family and past. She did so with such a little motherly air that I was quite intimidated by her, and before I knew what I was about, had said something more than I ought. It was a moment before I caught myself up and remembered that I am as vulnerable to scrutiny here as Nicole is to tutoring. (If ever the clear light of her eye should happen upon a hint of what I really am, Heaven help me!) Though, to be absolutely just, I believe she might enjoy the charade more than she disapproved it. I am grown very fond of her, and grateful for the affection she has so instantly and openly offered me, for it is the ony human thing in the whole place.

Sir Basil, following upon this first astounding meeting, has made only the most mechanical attempts to converse with either of us. For the most part, he is away during the day, either at his club or at Carlton House. In the evening he nearly always dines away from home, and when he does not, we have dinner together. These sessions are apparently so painful to him—for he cannot think of anything to say to a governess and a nine-year-old girl—that as soon as we are done he rushes to his library to have his port, insured of privacy even more absolute than what he might have in the dining room. For my own part, I am nearly as tongue-tied with *him*, as he with me. I have ever found the greatest insurance of awkwardness to lie in conversing with a person who feels awkward himself, and so the two of us struggle for something to say, and only Nicole, unperturbed as always, chatters on. She attends to our silences quite like a seasoned hostess, knowing that even the most nonsensical stream of chatter at table is better than nothing at all.

My life here is nothing like what I had envisioned. Nothing, even, like what Lady Cardovan made me think it would be. *She* was certain I should be called upon to play hostess myself, as well as governess, but there has not been one visitor here save Lady Cardovan since I arrived. Nicole has her lessons—at which she is remarkably apt—in the morning and in the afternoon we go abroad, either to walk in Hyde Park or to look into the shops. Nicole has been properly outfitted, thanks to Sir Basil's largesse and Lady Cardovan's attentiveness, but I have had as yet barely an hour to scribble, but am toying with the idea for a new novel. As to *that*—well, I shall tell you more when it is better formed. This much I *shall* say: It is not altogether unconcerned with the life of a determined bachelor!

I have been once to my publisher, who says I may expect a check within the month—a very great sum by my reckoning! The book is ready for the printer, and shall be upon the shelves in a week's time. Only fancy that! I am as terrified and pleased as if I were about to give birth to a baby, and only pray it shall be well received, that I may give up being a governess and live instead upon my earnings. Only think of that, my dear Ben! The idea, however, is so far-fetched, and the prospect of a book which contains neither heroes nor great romantic passions being thought well of is so unlikely, that I should probably resign myself to teaching little girls music and drawing forever. They cannot all be as astonishing as Nicole, and the novelty may soon wear off.

Till I see you next, my dear, dear Ben, wrap up warm and take care with your health, if only for your devoted

Anne

Chapter VI

Anne set down her pen, sealed up her letter, and was just rising to her feet when there came a knock at the door of her bedchamber. Hastily pushing the letter beneath her blotter, she called out to know who it was. A high voice replied, and in a moment the diminutive figure of Nicole Lessington appeared in the doorway. The child was dressed rather more appropriately than she had been on the day of her arrival in Regent's Terrace, but there managed to survive, despite the neat sprigged muslin pinafore, the ruffled cap, and delicate white stockings embroidered with clocks (a gift from Lady Cardovan which had delighted the little girl so much that she could scarcely be persuaded to take them off at night) something of the air of a sprightly elf. Her curls were black and glossy and seemed always a little disordered, her cap persisted in going askew upon her head, and the great shining black eyes peering out above the red cheeks contained such an expression of candour that Anne, who was already a little flustered, grew unwittingly crimson beneath their gaze.

"Yes, Nicole?" she inquired briskly. "I supposed you would be another half hour at least with your history lesson. Have you learned it all in so short a time?"

"Nearly," responded the little girl without much conviction. She was staring interestedly about her, for she had only been once before in Miss Calder's private apartment. The chamber was a good deal smaller than her own, and not nearly so well appointed, but it seemed to her to contain mysteries and charms far exceeding those of her own handsome bedchamber, with its crimson brocade curtains, its view of Regent's Park, and the vast bedstead which seemed to swallow her up at night. She moved closer to the oddly shaped window above the desk and gazed out upon the view of treetops and roofs.

"Well, that is not quite good enough, is it?" demanded her governess, but with sufficient amusement in her voice to offset the attempt at sternness. "*Nearly* learning a history lesson is not quite so good as learning it, do you think?"

"I suppose not," responded the truant without any remorse. "But it was dreadfully dull. I thought if I was forced to read another phrase about old Greeks I should fall asleep."

"Ha!" cried Anne, barely able to suppress a laugh, "old Greeks, is it? And what do you suppose they shall call you in a thousand years' time? I suppose they shall speak of you as a modern little English girl, shall they?"

Nicole paused temporarily in her perusal of the adjacent building to ponder this interesting question.

"Do you suppose," she inquired, leaning her elbows on the windowsill with her chin in the cup of her hands, "they shall think of me at all? If I grow up to be very great, like Sir Basil, perhaps they shall write a history of *me*."

"Perhaps they shall. But I hardly think you will be fit to take up an ambassadorship if you don't apply yourself to your lessons. I don't suppose anyone would want an ambassador who knows nothing about those *dull old Greeks*."

"I suppose not," conceded Nicole with a sigh. Then, with a brighter look, she added, "But if I was only to be *married* to an ambassador, it shouldn't matter much. I could be as ignorant as I pleased, so long as I was beautiful, and danced prettily, and knew all the clever things to say at balls. *Then* they should write about me only as being the most beautiful and witty lady in the world. I think," continued the truant, still gazing raptly into space, "I should prefer that in any case. Anyone can be clever at history. But not everyone can be the most beautiful lady in the world!"

"I shall convey your opinion to Sir Basil," responded Anne, smiling despite herself, "with perhaps the suggestion that a dancing master and a portrait painter would be more appropriately employed than a governess."

"Oh!" cried Nicole, whirling around. "I hope you will not!"

Anne endeavoured to look amazed. "Why? Have you changed your mind so soon? Ambition is only good if it is steadfast, my dear little Nicole. You shall never succeed in

49

being the belle of European society if you change your mind every moment."

Nicole stared at her governess in momentary confusion, and then giggled. "You know I am only funning you, Miss Calder. I should be an idiot if I did not wish to learn everything I could. That is what Papa said I ought to do, and that is why he made Sir Basil my guardian. Only I do wish it were possible to learn everything without having to study so hard. It would be delightful if there was some method of pouring a great deal of knowledge into your ear, in only a moment's time!"

"If that were possible," said Anne, sitting upon a little settee near her desk, "then I can assure you that the whole population of Europe would be ambassadors. But it would not avail much in the end, you know. For at least half the satisfaction of accomplishment lies in the knowledge of its having been achieved solely by one's own efforts and the cost of not a little hard work."

Miss Lessington looked much interested in this idea, and with her keen black eyes fastened intently upon Anne's amused hazel ones, cried: "Why, do you know that is exactly what my Papa always used to say! I believe you should have liked each other exceedingly well, Miss Calder—if only you had known him."

Anne, noticing a rare tinge of sadness in the child's expression, replied that she was sure she would have. Nicole's little outburst hung in the air as she turned away again to the window, biting her lip. But in a moment she had turned back again, smiling brightly.

"I ought not to speak of him," she said with a little impatient shake of her head which tugged at Anne's heartstrings more than a torrent of tears could have. "He would not have liked it. Papa told me always to laugh when I was in danger of weeping. 'If you persist long enough in laughing, my girl, you shall very soon find something to laugh *about*, for there is quite as much to be amused with in this life as there is to weep over.' "

Here was a sentiment with which Anne heartily concurred, and had she not at this moment been so torn herself between a desire to comfort the little girl and a wish to preserve her brave dignity by pretending nothing was amiss, she would have rushed to fold her in her arms and tell her so. But the sight of this tiny little woman (for Nicole, despite all her mussed curls and air of a disbanded gypsy girl still possessed a maturity in her manner and in her thoughts which quite overwhelmed her governess) struggling to collect her emotions and to present a brave front made her pause. From the first moment of their meeting, Nicole had displayed such a markedly independent nature, so little tendency to exhibit any grief over her misfortunes, or even to speak about them, that Anne was loathe to be the first to break the silence. True, the word papa had not cropped up infrequently—chiefly as introduction to some little proverb or piece of wisdom which that gentleman had apparently had in no small supply. "Papa" was forever being held up as the ultimate judge of any issue, and whether it was a question of which frock to don in the morning or which fork to use for the fish course, his preferences were always invoked. But as to any real reference to him, either to his history or his character, there had been none. Indeed, so reticent had Nicole seemed upon this subject that Anne was more and more mystified. It struck her that any recently bereaved child would speak openly of her lost parent, if only in an effort to assuage her grief. It was evident from all her references to him that Nicole had nearly idolized her father. Why, then, would she not talk more freely about him? Very gently, Anne bid the child to come sit beside her, and taking one small hand in her own, she asked if Nicole would not tell her a little about him.

Nicole received these solicitations with a solemn expression, and after wrinkling up her brow for a moment, in concentration, she nodded gravely.

"Papa," she said slowly, "was the best man in all the world. He knew everything, and taught me all he could. It was the great ambition of his life that I should be a great lady, and so he was not sorry when he died, but told me it was a gift from Heaven, for I should be brought up as Sir Basil's ward, and my guardian could do a great deal more for me than he could do himself."

"But did you have no friends?" inquired Anne, rather surprised by this little speech. "Do not you miss your old home, and all your old ways of life?"

Now it was Nicole's turn to look puzzled. "Why," she replied, "I miss Papa! I miss Papa sometimes most dreadfully. *He* was my friend, and I his." And with these words, the child gave a heaving shudder and burst into a flood of tears. Without much coaxing, Anne persuaded her to be embraced, and for some minutes the little girl shook and wept as if the end of the world had come. Anne was more pleased than sorry by this display, for it struck her as more natural than never shedding a tear, with all the fright and worry and sheer unhappiness which must have been her lot in the past weeks. And so, with much stroking and murmuring, she held the child tightly against her bosom and waited for the flood to subside of itself. This did not occur for some little while, and when it did, Nicole drew herself away and, clutching her hands in her lap, gave one last sob.

"I shall not do that again," she said, almost as if in stern warning to herself.

"Why!" cried Anne, amazed, "why ever not? I am very glad you did, indeed! And very pleased you should have selected *me* to comfort you."

Nicole gave her an uncertain smile. "You are not angry with me then?"

"Angry! Why on earth should I be angry?"

"Papa always said that no one much likes people who cry."

"Nonsense," retorted Anne, beginning to be irked with this famous papa, who had so much facile wisdom at his command but seemed more and more to have been a little inhuman. "*Some* people like them very well. I do not mean it is always proper to weep, nor that one ought to weep before simply *anyone*. But there is sometimes no better medicine for grief than tears, nor any better method of making a friend. I know that gentlemen do not always agree with this point, but you will find very few ladies who *disagree*. If your mother had lived longer, she would certainly have told you exactly the same. I wish most heartily she had, for in that case I make no doubt but that you would not be so loathe to be sad, nor show by any hint of weakness that you are a little girl, and not a grown-up woman."

Nicole seemed to consider this point with some solemnity. Then, blinking a little, she offered Anne a trembling smile.

"I think," she said in a rather hoarse voice, "I shall go and learn my history lesson now."

Anne saw the child go with mixed emotions.

She could not have said, as she rose slowly to her feet and moved toward the same window before which Nicole had stood some moments before, exactly what she felt. For some while she stood motionless, gazing out over the line of crooked rooftops leading toward the tiny arch of Westminster Bridge, with its minute line of carriages and people. In the distance the waters of the Thames sparkled beneath the brilliant sun of a clear November afternoon, and across the river only a tiny spiderweb of streets and houses hinted at the vast population of London which had never set foot in Regent's Terrace or Bond Street. Anne had not ceased to be amazed at the immensity of the city, nor at the extraordinary diversity of life going on within. The mere sight of that panorama thrilled her, with all the richness of humanity it implied. To think that she might never have come, might at this very moment have been a mere Mrs. Siddons presiding over her parlour and her dining table, with no greater ambition than serving five courses to her husband's friends and possessing a wider command of the village gossip than her sisters! The idea made her laugh, and with a triumphant expression, she turned back into the room.

"My girl," she murmured out loud, "you may very well have taken on more than you can manage, as Papa warned. But oh! I should infinitely prefer to fall upon a mountain path than to climb nimbly to the top of an anthill!"

And with this optimistic note, which her mother would have called foolhardy and would have brought a doubtful smile to her father's lips, she retrieved her letter from beneath the blotting pad and, having sealed it up with wax and inscribed the address upon it, crept down the stairs and laid it in the letter tray for the servant to post. This secret little mission took no more than a minute, and when Nicole had finished studying the chapter on the old Greeks, she found her governess calmly preparing a lesson in geography.

Chapter VII

That Anne Calder had indeed undertaken to climb a mountain rather than an anthill must now be admitted. She was not, as she had confessed in her letter to Ben, "exactly what she seemed," but neither was she so *unlike* what she seemed that the reader must suspect every fact hitherto brought forth about her. Certain points, indeed, must wait to be clarified at a more auspicious moment, but the main facts of her life were as she had painted them to Lady Cardovan. Her father was certainly a clergyman in Devonshire, and her mother had borne nine children. If Anne had implied in her account of that family a certain embarrassment for money (which might well be expected, as any father of nine will readily attest), it was her only untruth. And, as it was an untruth of omission, rather than an outright lie, she may be excused, for Lady Cardovan would be the first admit that a woman is often in need of some such little deception or other in order to exist. Mrs. Calder, however, would certainly have been horrified by such an idea, for even if she was excessively fond of complaining to her husband that she had never enough funds to redecorate her house or to buy her silk from Paris, she held a dim view of propagating such news about the countryside. Indeed, it was a point of pride with her that Mr. Calder was among the most prosperous gentlemen in the county. His profession had been chosen rather from desire than penury, as is so often the case with our clergy, and as he held one of the best livings in England and had inherited a considerable sum from his father, a wealthy squire, there was more than ample provision even for nine children. Had none of his daughters married, they should still have come into ten or eleven thousand pounds a piece, and as they were all very comely girls, that likelihood was slender. Indeed, it was amazing that they had not all of them been married before, and the reason they had not was linked closely, if somewhat obscurely, to his eldest daughter's present employment as a governess. That the reader shall not continue a moment longer in suspense, we shall set forth the story exactly as it transpired, without omitting any crucial points, but as briefly as we may:

The drama, or that part of the drama which concerns us here, and which in truth is more of a comedy, commenced one bright and warm September morning. Mr. Calder was working in his library, endeavouring to write a sermon, a task made more difficult by the presence of his wife, who had been pacing up and down the room for half an hour.

"My dear, I wish you would not walk about so much," remarked that gentleman when he had been forced to toss out a third draft of his speech for the fault of its containing seven repetitions of the same idea.

"I do not know how you can be so calm," retorted his wife, only pausing in her progress across the room to cast him an accusing look.

"If you find fault with my serenity, then I shall endeavour to be as distraught as you. Shall that make you happier?"

"I wish you would not be so cynical," replied Mrs. Calder, irritably. "You have no sympathy, and no heart."

"My dear," responded the clergyman, putting down his pen with a smile, "I am incapable of pleasing you. What would you rather I did? Perhaps I should go down to the kitchens and upset the cook by rushing back and forth, wailing all the while."

Mrs. Calder did not trouble herself to reply to this sally. Her husband delighted in teasing her, and her present mood would not permit her to indulge him.

"If you will not be disturbed upon *my* account," said she after a moment's pause, "perhaps you will just allow yourself to think of your daughters."

"I see no reason to be upset, even for my daughters, my dear. They are all strong, healthy girls, and while none of them shows much wisdom, they are not any of them dim-witted. On the contrary, I believe you ought to be thanking me for giving you four such remarkable girls."

Mrs. Calder could tolerate no more. She raised her hands to Heaven, and a strange strangled sound issued from her lips. "Do you have no pity on me, Arthur? Must you torment me into the grave?" she cried, upon which Mr. Calder looked up in amazement, and would undoubtedly have made some jesting remark had not he seen by her expression that his lady had exhausted her resources of tolerance.

"Here you sit calmly, only bent on tormenting me with your awful jokes, whilst our daughters are all in danger of being spinsters."

The clergyman raised one eyebrow and wondered how this could be. "It seems to me that today of all days you have no reason to complain. Our eldest daughter, if I am not much mistaken, is at this very moment being solicited for her hand in marriage."

"Yes, that is very true. Solicited indeed! But Anne will not accept him, depend upon it!"

"I am delighted to hear you say so, Eliza, for it only upholds my opinion that Anne is not an idiot. If she did consent to become Mrs. Siddons, I am afraid I should have to think less of her."

"Oh! How can you say so!"

"Very easily: Siddons is an idiotic boor."

"He is a fine young man, and devoted to you."

"He is a young man with four thousand a year and not another stroke to recommend him. He is also, if you will pardon my saying so, less devoted to *me* than he is to the idea that he is a fine young man."

"He gave the parish a great deal of money, you said so yourself."

"So that he might look up from his pew and see his name inscribed in gold upon the wall."

"Nevertheless," returned Mrs. Calder, resisting the impulse to lose her temper, "he would make Anne a fine husband, if she were not so ill-natured and stubborn."

"If all you have said about him is true," retorted her husband, smiling, "he does not deserve an ill-natured wife. I am so heartily set against the match, my dear, that I shall make Anne a gift of a new gown if she declines him."

"If she declines him, I hope you will scold her roundly!"

The conversation was abruptly ended by the sound of a closing door, ensuing footsteps, and the murmur of voices in the passage. Mrs. Calder put a finger to her lips and endeavoured to hear what was being said, but failing this, was forced to wait till the closing of the front door told her that Mr. Siddons had gone away. She flew out into the hallway to discover the news, and Mr. Calder, who felt a great deal more curiosity about the outcome of the interview than he would admit, returned to his labours. He was not allowed time to get much past the first page of his sermon, however, before there came a knock at the door. His eldest daughter stood before him with a bowed head.

"My mother sent me to you, Sir," said she, with the air of a miscreant.

Mr. Calder regarded his daughter with a grave look. At length he said, "You have refused young Siddons, I suppose?"

A nod was all the reply she could make. "I hope you will not think ill of me, Papa," said she, "but the idea of sitting next to him at dinner is awful enough. The idea of facing him at the breakfast table, I cannot bear."

Mr. Calder suppressed his smile, and looked solemn: "This is very perplexing news for your mother, I fear."

"I hope she will forgive me at last, Sir, but I could not bring myself to marry a man for *her* sake whom I could not marry for my *own*."

"Your three sisters will take the news very hard. They are none of them free to marry until you have, your mother says, lest we give up on you completely, and declare you a spinster."

Anne contrived to look guilty. "Perhaps that is what you ought to do then, for I do not know that I shall ever meet the man I wish to marry."

"You have rejected four already, my dear," said her papa, regarding her solemnly. "Four eligible young men have crept away from your door, mortified and wounded."

"Three of them have recovered sufficiently to marry other girls," replied Anne with equal gravity. "I cannot think I am so terrible a slayer of men as not to be persuaded that Mr. Siddons shall recover with similar ease."

Now father and daughter allowed themselves to share a smile, for they had often engaged in this discussion before.

"That is all very well, Anne," said Mr. Calder at last, "and, as you know my feelings about the young Siddons, I shall not pretend that I am excessively distraught at your refusal. However, there is a graver matter of your sisters to consider. Your mothers says they shall die of misery before they die of spinsterhood, and it is not right that you should keep them from matrimony. I cannot help but sympathize with you all—with your sisters for wishing to marry, and with you for wishing *not* to; however, you cannot all be satsified. There must be some remedy."

"Is it not a very antiquated custom to prevent the younger girls from being happy, only because I prefer to remain single?" inquired Anne. "I think you ought really to release them from it, for I am sure Mary and Gwen should be married within the year if you did."

"Perhaps that is what we ought to do, after all," replied her father with a sigh. "I have been in great hopes that you should marry, I shall not deny it: for I believe that of all four of you, you are the best equipped to be a wife. And yet I cannot urge you to do so only from a sense of duty, if it will make you miserable. And I have not yet met the man I should like to see you wedded to. I may simply be a foolish and fond old father, but I have ever been of the opinion that you ought to marry a special kind of man. It is a great sadness to me that none has made your acquaintance, for I flatter myself that if such a creature exists, he would be twice blessed to have you for a wife."

Anne was flattered to hear these words, for her father was of a restrained turn of mind, and seldom expressed himself so freely to his children.

"I cannot say how deeply I feel your compliment, Sir," she replied, "though it may be prejudiced by your affection for me. I hope indeed that it is, for I cannot share your confidence in my own abilities to make another being happy. I am only sure that I am equipped to make *myself* happy, and if, by my little scribblings, I may entertain some others for an hour or two, I shall be content. That is a subject I had wished to discuss with you in any case. I ought to tell you, Sir, that I have sent a manuscript to London, to a publisher, and that I have only just learned that they will print it."

"Why! This is astonishing news, Anne!" exclaimed her father. "You are a secretive creature, to be sure! What, is it a book of poems? I know you are always scribbling, and I am sorry I have not paid you more attention."

"It is only a little novel," replied Anne, with a great deal more modesty than she felt.

"Only a novel! Well, well! I suppose it is a romance of some kind, eh? Dear me, I never thought I should have a novelist in the family!"

"It is not exactly a romance, Sir," replied his daughter, beginning to feel uncomfortable, "although, in truth, it does contain some elements of romance, and a little intrigue. But you ought to read it yourself. I hope you will."

"Why, you know I never read novels," replied her father

58

with a twinkle, "but I shall make an exception for *you*. Well, well! What a surprise this is to be sure! I hope you have got some money for your efforts?"

Anne was able to reply with some pride that the publisher had agreed to pay her one hundred pounds immediately, and more if the novel had success. Mr. Calder was quite dumbfounded by the largess of the figure, and repeated over and over that he had never dreamed a daughter of his might add to the family wealth, unless it was by marrying. Conscious of her father's amazement, and laughing inwardly at his complacent view of womankind, Anne endeavoured to reply as modestly as she could, although her pride was not a little piqued by the profundity of Mr. Calder's amazement at having raised up a daughter who could write.

"I hope," said Anne, when her father's exclamations had died down a little, "that this news might make you take a more charitable view of my state. If I am able to earn a living by my pen, and wish to do so above everything, why cannot my sisters marry before me? You may say I am a spinster if you like, and I shall take up wearing a lace cap and going about the neighbourhood with baskets."

"Your mother's pride would not allow of it, even if yours could," replied Mr. Calder humourously, "for it might be taken as a reflection on her own beauty and charm if her eldest daughter was a spinster."

Anne had already considered her mother's reaction, and having formed a scheme of her own by which nobody's pride could be offended and her own desires consummated, she now set it forth. Might not it serve everyone's wishes if she went to London? There her single state could not possibly mortify her mother, and there too she would be exposed to all manner of life, to add fuel to her literary fire. She had long considered the scheme, and the more she thought upon it, the more desirable it seemed. She had exhausted the resources of character and drama in the little village where they lived, and now longed for some greater view of humanity to write about. Yet how could she ever do so, had she not seen something of the world?

Mr. Calder was a liberal man, and entertained for his eldest daughter a deep affection and respect. Yet he was not so liberated from what he laughingly called his "ancient ways" to like the scheme. To begin with, there were practical objections: a hundred pounds was a vast sum, to be sure, but it was not sufficient to live upon above a month in the city.

He could provide her with an income from his own pocket, but was that wise? It would certainly cost more to keep her alive in London than at home, and he could not reasonably excuse giving one daughter so much more than all the others, especially if the money were to further a scheme which no one much approved. Her mother, he was sure, would raise violent objections, and where, after all, would she live?

But Anne could be as stubborn as her father, and having once set her mind to the scheme, she would not easily be opposed. Would not it serve if she found employment as a governess? She was very fond of children, and now that all her own brothers and sisters were nearly grown, she missed tutoring them. As she was not likely to have any of her own, it would satisfy her maternal instincts, and would leave time enough to scribble when she could.

Mr. Calder only chuckled upon hearing this. Had she any idea what her mother would say to this? It would cause her no end of mortification and shame. But Mr. Calder, who had not a little love of the ridiculous in him, was so amused that he grew quite soon to like the plan. He would give his consent, then, provided her mother could be persuaded to approve, and provided also that Anne found a suitable situation. In addition, he would give her outright the cost of a year's expenses at home: no more could he justify, and the offer was very gratefully received. Anne turned to leave, but was stopped by her father's voice,

"You know, my dear, that I admire your spirit. I believe—indeed, I pray—that you shall not be the cause of your own unhappiness."

"Dear Papa!" cried Anne, "I believe for the first time in my life, I am completely happy!"

Mr. Calder looked grave. "That is all very well to say *now*, my dear, but you have only laid your plans. Perhaps when you have been a month in London, you shall think differently. You shall not have a mother or father to turn to then, and you will most certainly be very lonely. If you go, I shall expect you to stay a whole year. Else you might take your own decision too lightly. But after that, if you desire to come home, you know you may."

A tear sprang into the young lady's eye despite herself, but nodding gravely, she agreed. Her former excitement returning almost instantly, however, she flew off to make her preparations and to inform her sisters. The younger Miss Calders were amazed, and second only to their mother in the intensity of wailing they set up. At first it was: why should Anne be allowed to go to London, and not they? and soon afterward, however could they lift up their heads again, when their acquaintance learned that Anne had gone to be governess?

Mrs. Calder was most preoccupied with the last idea. What would her friends think of her?

"They may think what they like," said Mr. Calder, coming into the room just then. "If their opinion is needed in order for you to form your own, then Anne has every reason to wish to leave us."

His wife and daughters were silent after that, for they held Mr. Calder in awe. But as soon as Anne had returned from London with the news that she was engaged to be governess to Sir Basil Ives' ward, they were once more torn between envy and chagrin. Mrs. Calder wished to have a new wardrobe made up for her daughter, that the Baronet should know she was not the ordinary run of governess, and that her family was well able to dress her in silk.

"I think you need not bother, Mama," said Anne. "Sir Basil will not care whether I wear silk or flannel, so long as I am neat. You had much better spend your money on my sisters, who are all longing for new gowns." And this reply was so happily received by the younger Miss Calders that it won their good graces instantly.

Of all the family, only her father and her eldest brother seemed really sorry to see her go. Her sisters were all happy to have the field cleared for themselves, and her mama content to have the one great blot on her happiness removed from her sight. But Ben, who was the eldest child, was distraught. He was a young man of nine and twenty, but owing to a childhood infirmity which still kept him weak, had not grown to the great height and strength of his father and younger brothers. Of all her family, Anne was most loathe to part with him. They shared a special affection for each other, and were both addicted to reading books. In their childhood they had invented a world peopled by imaginary beings, half human and half elfin. For hours upon end they had told each other stories, and had laughed until tears ran down their cheeks. There existed between them a silent understanding which ran like a river beneath their conversation. Anne went last of all to bid him farewell, and found him upon a couch, for he was very seldom able to stay up all day. The sight of his poor with d frame, wrapped up in a cocoon of blankets, bearly tore her heart, and more so still when she met the smiling gaze of his eyes, which, large by any standard, seemed like two great orbs set in the midst of his emaciated features.

"So Anne," said he in his usual cheerful style, "I suppose you are off to do great things. Will you remember your Ben when you are at last a famous authoress?"

"Oh, Ben!" cried Anne, hurrying over to him and falling down upon her knees next to his couch, "how can you be so idiotic? There is not the least chance I shall be famous, and if I was, it should be half owing to your encouragement, for you know I should never have finished my novel without you."

"Tush," remonstrated the young man, but with a pleased look. He took one of her hands in his own and stroked it whilst they talked. "You know it was no such thing. It is your genius that wrote it, and if I helped at all, it was only in so far as I was able to make you cut out one or two of the more gushing phrases."

"And to set in one or two of your own," responded Anne, laughing.

"Well! What of it? I have none of your typical masculine pride about such things. When it comes to gushing, say I, I hope I am as good as anyone! Ah, well—it was fun, wasn't it? And now you shall be a published authoress, and I shall be pleased to tell everyone that you are my sister, and to visit about the neighbourhood giving away copies with my signature within."

Anne laughed and said nothing for a moment. There was no need to, in truth, for the two possessed such a thorough knowledge of each other's thoughts that conversation, when it came, was more like an intricate exercise for the fingers than a gesture which, once made, is the sum total of an idea.

"You must only promise me one thing, however," continued the young man after a moment, "that you shall set down everything exactly as it happens, only changing it insofar as it is dull, and without any merit of humour."

"And you shall not be angry if, in creating a comedy, the drama is obscured?"

"Think nothing of it! replied the young man with a magnanimous wave of his hand, "Only remember our old creed: If it is superfluous to the plot, or if it lacks all trace of human foible, it must go."

"Surely you are very hard!" protested Anne. "Even in my letters must I be so confined? Am I to be allowed no leisurely rambling passages, wherein I may express the great ideas of the moment, or survey the scenery with elegiac prose?"

"You may do so," responded her brother, pulling one of her curls, "at your peril. Only give me an idea of what is being said about London, and in one or two passages you may describe to me your surroundings—but pray leave off the elegiac prose. I shall read Byron if I am inclined to poetry; but for high jinks and keen satire, give me Anne Calder every time!"

Their mood grew more solemn for a while after this, and having irritated her brother most awfully by bidding him keep warm and safe at least three times, Anne rose reluctantly to go. As she was passing through the doorway, however, she hesitated and looked back:

"What should the plot of my letters be?" inquired she softly.

"Why!" exclaimed Ben, "have you not guessed? It is the best plot of all. The only plot, in fact, for you."

Anne looked perplexed, and smiled uncertainly.

"The story," responded Ben, "of the story's authoress." He paused for an instant and, smiling, commanded: "And let it be engrossing, if you please!"

Chapter VIII

"Miss Calder," said Sir Basil Ives that evening as they were finishing their dinner, "I would be happy if you would join me for a glass of wine, if you have not some other plan."

Anne looked up in astonishment from her pear, and replied that she was of course at her employer's disposal. So taken aback was she by the invitation that she thought she must have replied too abruptly, for the Baronet looked down instantly into his plate and would not afterward raise his eyes again save to bid his ward good night. Even the child seemed taken aback; for her usual stream of chatter suddenly ceased, and she gazed back and forth between the two grown-ups in awe. Nicole's amazement can well be understood, for in the several days since they had been a family, Sir Basil had hardly said one word at dinner. When Sir Basil joined them, he seemed to do so chiefly from a sense of duty, to judge by his long silence and the infrequency of his smiles. Whether he was simply arrogant, as Anne had thought at first, or encumbered by his own shyness, she could not tell. But she had laughed inwardly at the perplexity upon his face when he had first heard Nicole discourse upon her days' lessons, and a walk they had taken in the park. Nicole was an unusual child by any standard; her conversation was so odd a mixture of precocious wisdom, childish delight, and disjointed narrative, that she could not much blame him for his confusion. And yet Anne did blame him, if not for his perplexity, then for making so little effort to understand the child. At first he had endeavoured to correct her when she had made some mistake. But Nicole, who would not take offense at anything, merely stared back with great solemnity, nodded, and went

64

on as before. She could not be persuaded that her perceptions were not a subject of consuming interest to everyone, and Anne, after suggesting once that she ought to listen more and say less, had been dampened by the following argument:

"Why, I really think you are wrong, Miss Calder. For Papa said there ought never to be any silence at table, and if it were not for me, there should be silence always. For you and Sir Basil never converse, and Papa always said it is infinitely better when you are at table to say anything at all than nothing. Of course it is just the reverse at other times. At other times, Papa said, one ought always to be silent, unless one has something terribly clever to say. But you know," finished the child with a grave little smile, "I am only a child, and have not always clever things to say!"

There could be no arguing with this, nor with the perfectly ingenuous fashion in which it was pronounced. Indeed, it seemed to Anne after observing both Nicole and her guardian for several days that the child possessed far more of that quality which may be called graciousness than her guardian. For while Nicole exhausted herself in the effort to amuse everyone, Sir Basil had not only no notion of how to talk to children, but no intention of learning. And this, as well as some other little incidents which had made her begin to dislike him for her own sake, had made her form an unfavourable opinion of the gentleman even before she had conversed with him above five times.

It must be stated that while Anne possessed few of those vanities which are generally associated with womankind, such as a desire to be thought beautiful, or to be seated above every other lady at table, she was not altogether without vanity. All her life she had been treated as an intelligent being, her wit admired and her opinion sought. She knew she was handsome enough, and had never valued her own looks sufficiently to be proud of them. As to station—how could she have chosen the post of governess had she not sufficient humour to see the joke, not only upon others, but upon herself? She did not mind being "little better than a servant," as Lady Cardovan had put it, but to be considered unfit for conversation, to be consigned to the intellectual as well as the physical confines of her post, enraged her. From the first, Sir Basil had treated her as if she were little better than a dimwit. When he had spoken to her, which he had done barely half a dozen times, it had always been with the condescension of a fine mind speaking to a dull one. When she had sought his advice in the matter of texts to be used in the tutoring of her pupil, he had shrugged:

"Use your own judgment, Miss Calder," said he. "I do not suppose it matters much in the case of a girl. To be frank, I never supposed females had need of textbooks in any case. Indeed, it was my impression the only tools necessary for their education were a sewing basket and a drawing pad. But if you must have texts, pray do not bother me about it."

And this was how he perceived the female brain! Anne went away laughing to herself, but having endeavoured twice more to bring up the subject and having been twice more rebuffed in a similar style, she gave up. So long as she could be autonomous, she did not mind. And with a little inner toss of her head, she determined to prove just how fine Nicole's education could be under her tutelage. If it was as much for her own pride as for the child's betterment that she did so, it made little difference. Nicole would benefit for it, having as she did a keen curiosity and an amazing willingness to learn. Already this evening, Anne had felt a little thrill of triumph upon hearing her pupil narrate, in mind-boggling detail, some of the events of the Roman Conquest of Egypt. Sir Basil had looked in astonishment between the child and her governess, who only smiled calmly and corrected an error in the narration. She had been disappointed when the Baronet made no remark, and her first instinct now was to think he meant to congratulate her. "But," said Anne to herself a moment later, "you had better not expect it. Such kind of men are incapable of admitting their own errors. I believe Sir Basil, for all his reputation of sagacity in diplomatic affairs, has very little sense of diplomacy with his underlings. Indeed, he ought to have, for everyone knows that people work harder when they are commended for their efforts."

And so it was already with a negative sentiment in her heart that Anne took Nicole up to her bed and, leaving her with the promise that she should be up again directly herself, followed Sir Basil into the library.

She found the Ambassador standing by the fire with one arm upon the mantel. He was apparently so lost in thought that he did not notice her until she had stood in the doorway several moments together.

"Ah!" said he at last, with a start, "pray come in, Miss Calder. Here is a sofa by the fire, if you wish to be warm. I do not know if you are one of those females who condemns heat

66

upon their faces, but if you are, here is a fire screen. I have asked the servant to bring in a bottle of port. Do you drink port?" Sir Basil, altogether, seemed so unsure of how he ought to behave under the circumstances that Anne could not help smiling to herself.

Surely, she thought, he would not behave so nervously if I was not a governess. I suppose he believe there are two races of women: one very fine, used to drinking port, and abhorring heat upon their flesh, and another, quite rough and hu ble, made tipsy by a sip of wine, and able to tolerate any an nt of warmth." But aloud she said, with a mischievious de re to contradict his prejudices: "I am one of those females, Sir, who cares very little where she sits so long as I do not freeze to death. As to port, I am very fond of it, so you must not offer me too much."

Obviously taken aback by this sally, Sir Basil blanched slightly. "Perhaps he thinks I shall down the whole bottle at one gulp!" laughed Anne to herself.

But the Baronet had soon composed himself again, and if he from time to time cast a nervous glance in the direction of her glass, he concealed his interest as well as may be expected of a gentleman who is not used to dealing with governesses at all, much less tipsy ones. His chief preoccupation, in any case, was soon made evident.

"I am afraid I have not been of much help to you thus far, Miss Calder," said he when the wine had been brought in and poured. "I have left you pretty well to your own devices with my ward, and it may seem to you that I have not offered you as much assistance as I should have done. The reasons for this are two-fold: First, I have some obligations to the Foreign Office, which have taken up a great deal of my time. But even setting this aside, there is another reason. As you know, I am a bachelor, and unaccustomed to children. My ignorance is so vast in this area that it seemed to me I had better leave the chief business of Nicole's education to you. Indeed, my experience with little girls and what their education ought to be has been confined to what I have seen of my brother's daughter, and I must tell you that what I have witnessed of *her* has not made me complacent on the subject."

Anne could well understand this: her one encounter with Miss Hargate, on the occasion when she had been brought downstairs to meet her new cousin, had not inspired her with admiration. The Hargates were noisy, dirty, abominably spoiled children, and from meeting them once, Anne was relieved of any desire of ever seeing them again. Indeed, this was an impression she had taken away of the whole family. In half an hour they had impressed her as vulgar and rude, treating herself with contempt and her pupil with indifference. But she could not very well tell this to Sir Basil, and so she only smiled.

"But all little girls are not the same," she ventured. "Indeed, they are as unlike as grown men and women. You ought not to form an impression of Nicole until you have grown to know her better. From what *I* have seen of her, she is as delightful a little person as ever I knew: full of curiosity, and exceedingly eager to please everyone—especially you, if I may say so, Sir."

"I am very glad to hear you speak so well of her, Miss Calder," replied the Baronet stiffly. "Lady Cardovan told me that I could rely upon your judgment, and so I am doubly pleased that you approve of your pupil's habits."

"Oh!" exclaimed Anne, laughing, "I did not say I approved her habits! I only said that she is a delightful child, and if she is guided properly, will no doubt make a delightful woman."

Sir Basil seemed unsure of his ground. He looked doubtfully at Anne, whose eyes he had avoided throughout their conversation, and said with some hesitation, "I am afraid I do not quite understand you."

"I only mean," continued Anne, smiling despite herself at Sir Basil's stiff manner, "that Nicole needs a great deal of guidance. Her mind is so quick and her desire to please so thorough, that if she has *that* she cannot fail to be a fine young woman. But she has evidently received a great many peculiar notions from her father, and to unravel *those* may be more difficult than anything else."

"What do you mean, precisely?" inquired the gentleman, seeming almost to relax a little.

"To begin with, I believe she thinks that the highest aspiration possible for a woman is to be a *femme fatale*."

"And is she not correct?" inquired Sir Basil with a sardonic smile. "Is that not what every woman longs to be? Surely they must begin at an early age, if they wish to succeed."

"I suppose you are right. A great many of my sex must think so. And yet it is ironic that those who generally succeed are those who strive least for it. Lady Cardovan, for example—if you will excuse my saying so—is a very great lady, and must certainly have been a sort of *femme fatale* in her youth. And yet I have not observed that she is fond of bathing in milk, nor of any of the other vanities which my pupil associates with that state. Miss Lessington devours her history lessons in order to discover just such secrets. She has got it firmly in her mind in order to please her father's memory, she must turn herself as quickly as possible into a *grande dame.*"

"That is a most remarkable theory," observed Sir Basil. "It appears that I am destined to be as much educated by this process as my ward. But pray go on, Miss Calder—what on earth could have persuaded my cousin that his daughter ought to become such a creature?"

"I suppose it is every father's wish that his daughter will be the finest lady in the world," replied Anne (thinking of what her father's disappointment must have been upon finding that he had sired a novelist and three very ordinary marriage-minded girls). "And I believe your cousin was not much mistaken in the thinking that *his* daughter was up to the task. Indeed, Nicole has all the raw elements of one. It is my own opinion, however, that she ought to be all the more carefully guided, just for that reason. Were she a dull, plain, stupid girl, I should not worry much about teaching her to think. I should simply give her, as you suggested, a sewing box and a drawing pad, and hope she would grow passably accomplished."

"Instead of which, you suggest that she be force-fed history and Greek?" Sir Basil inquired with a cynical smile. "Will that help her to find a husband any quicker?"

Now it was Anne's turn to be sardonic. "If you suppose the whole aim of womankind is to find a husband, then I suppose not. However, if you will allow that a woman has as much duty to cultivate her mind and tastes as a man, and that such cultivation will only help her to be a better, and a happier, person—whether she marry or no—then there can be no greater benefit to a young female than to be 'force-fed' as much of history, Greek, and geography, and a knowledge of fine music and painting, as she can bear."

Anne had spoken very forcefully, and now, conscious that her outbrust had amused Sir Basil, she felt a rush of heat in her cheeks.

"I suppose you find my convictions amusing," she murmured, feeling more rage than mortification.

"On the contrary," protested Sir Basil, but still with that smile which, more even than his condescension, annoyed her. "I find them perfectly admirable. It is only astonishing to hear them voiced with so much passion. I am not used to hearing ladies vent much energy upon any greater subject than bonnets or balls.

"Then you are certainly not used to listening to them very often," Anne could not help retorting.

Now an elegant eyebrow mounted almost imperceptibly above an amused gray eye. "Certainly I am not in the habit of being scolded by them," said he softly.

Anne saw that she had gone too far. For the first time, she felt the confines of her station. Hitherto, she had been more amused by it than suffocated, conscious as she was of playing a trick upon the world. But all at once she longed for the freedom of her true social station, if only that she might contradict this insufferable man as soundly as she would have any other.

"Oh, that I might once have met him at a dinner party and heard such insults cast upon my sex! Were I not employed by him as a governess, I should let him know what I think of him!" she cried inwardly. The idea delighted her, but with the greatest effort in the world, she reminded herself that she had made her own bed, and now she must lie in it. The benefits, in the long run, must outweigh the wounds to her pride, and only this thought prevented her from speaking her mind. Instead, she bit her lip, and murmured:

"I beg your pardon, Sir. The passion of the moment made me foolish. It is only that you seem to take so dim a view of my sex, and I believed I might persuade you otherwise."

Sir Basil was regarding her in astonishment, and had Anne's gaze not been directed at her hands, she might have noticed a very different kind of smile come over his face. But it vanished as quickly as it had appeared, and when the young lady looked up again, the Baronet was wearing his old, stiff expression. He coughed once, looked embarrassed, and muttered, "Never mind, never mind. In any case, we have veered away from the subject. It was, I believe, Miss Lessington's education. I see that Lady Cardovan was not mistaken in calling you unusual. Indeed, I do not know much about other governesses, but I suppose they cannot all be like you."

"If you had rather I did not teach Nicole history, Sir——" exclaimed Anne, colouring. But she was cut off.

"No! No! I did not mean to criticize your methods. You must be the expert in this case. I suppose, as you say, I do not know much about females. Well, well! What I really wished to know was——" and now Sir Basil, who could not

70

possibly have looked more uncomfortable, cleared his throat and gave her a pleading look— "what sort of role I ought to take in all of this? Lady Cardovan has hinted to me that I ought to do more; but in truth, I am quite perplexed about it. What, Miss Calder, do you suggest?"

Anne very nearly took pity upon the man now, seeing him look as helpless and innocent as a baby. She could not help softening a little from her former rage, and looked down to hide a smile.

"That you behave as kindly as possible to Nicole," said she at last. "The poor child must be exceedingly lonely, and more unhappy than her pride will let her admit. She has been asked to do what many adults would find difficult—to go from her old home, and a way of life she understood, to something quite different. If she is sometimes a little absurd in her idea of what is required of her, she must be excused, and her only guide till now has been a father who cannot have known how much he asked of her. I cannot help but condemn Mr. Lessington in my heart for having laid such great plans for his daughter, but I suppose he meant well. Our own greatest help to her must be to let her see that she is loved, exactly as she is." Anne looked up to see what Sir Basil's reaction was and seeing only an intent, curious look upon his face, rushed on, "Sir Basil, I hope you will not think I am too bold, but what Nicole needs most of all is a father! I believe she misses her own papa more than she will admit, and longs for the same kind of affection she had from him. You could not do better than to try, as much as you can, to let her see that you like her."

"Why! I do not *dis*like her, Miss Calder!" responded Sir Basil, amazed. "To be sure, she has got some rather peculiar notions, but she is a perfectly amiable little girl. I do not know sometimes what to make of her rambling little speeches, and to be perfectly truthful, I have already taken a keen dislike to her papa. I never heard so many smug pronouncements in all my life. But as to Miss Lessington, why, I suppose she is as well as most little girls."

"A great deal more so," replied Anne earnestly. "Believe me, Sir Basil, she is a little jewel, and if you will only show her that you are fond of her, you will see her sparkle."

Sir Basil turned away to fill his glass. His voice, when he spoke, was muffled.

"Do you suppose she really cares much?" he inquired. "She seems such an independent little thing."

"Cares! Why, she cares more what *you* think about her than anything in the world!"

"Indeed?" Sir Basil looked incredulous, but rather pleased. "Well, then, Miss Calder, I am very glad that we had this little chat. Well, well. Do you suppose she would enjoy visiting Carlton House?" he inquired suddenly.

"More than anything!"

"Ah! Well then, suppose we visit Prinney one day next week? His Highness is a great admirer of children. In point of fact, he expressed a desire to see Miss Lessington the moment he heard about her."

"I shall tell Nicole at once, Sir Basil. I think she will be even more delighted than I am."

Anne had risen from her place on the sofa and, setting down her glass, now moved to the door. She stood there for a moment, waiting for a dismissal. Sir Basil seemed to hesitate, but having opened his mouth as if to say something, merely nodded.

"Thank you, Miss Calder," said he, and with a stiff bow turned away. There was nothing left for Anne to do but make her curtsey and quit the room.

Chapter IX

Anne went away from this interview very well pleased with herself. If she could not conceive of ever actually liking Sir Basil herself, at least she now had the satisfaction of seeing that she might influence his conduct toward his ward. She had been quick to understand, as soon as she had met him, that Lady Cardovan had not exaggerated her description of him. A rigid and determined bachelor he certainly was, and lacking any of that softness or flexibility of manner which is generally acquired in a man through marriage and fatherhood. In the Ambassador's case, it had struck her instantly, this rigidity was made more profound by his natural temperament. He was certainly not one of your amiable and easy-going fellows: His inbred stiffness had been increased, no doubt, by long years of being accustomed to subservience in all around him. It was not unnatural that such a man should find it difficult to change all at once so late in life. Sir Basil could not be above five or six and thirty, and yet he seemed much older, if only because he so distinctly lacked any of that trace of humour or capacity to be astounded which are the marks of youth at any age. To be sure, she had dearly wished to laugh out loud at his awkwardness! How taken aback he had been by her arguments! Well, she had learned her lesson upon that head: She could see they would never agree upon any subject, for the Baronet was so thoroughly entrenched in his ideas, and so fond of his own prejudices, that he would never be capable of changing them. But, if she could persuade him at least to be a little more kind to his ward, she should have done all she wished. What cared she what his opinion was of *her*, so long as he did not make

73

the child's life miserable? Already she was sorry she had gone as far as she had done with her own opinions. She must remember in the future to confine her exchanges with him to the subject of their one mutual interest—Nicole—for Sir Basil must always regard her as no more than a governess, little better than a servant, and expert in nothing save the tutoring of a child. She had seen at once how odd he thought her ideas.

"He must think I am some sort of eccentric spinster who must justify my state by perverse arguments," she said to herself with a laugh. "Well, and perhaps I am! Most certainly I am! But not for all the world would I exchange my situation for that of one of those females he scorns so thoroughly. Lord, what an idea! Only fancy thinking we are all of us bent on nothing but marrying, and are reduced to misery if we do not! I wonder how he thinks we get along in life?"

And Anne could only laugh to herself at his opinions, for it was certainly better than being angry. She saw she would have to draw upon all her resources of humour if she was not to be mortified by this experience. "I must keep it firmly in mind that my present situation is only temporary: a sort of bitter interlude, to pay for my later freedom. And whenever I am in danger of weakening, I shall just remember that I might, at this moment, be a Mrs. Siddons, mortified perpetually, and with no hope of an escape."

The idea was perfectly sobering. Even as she climbed the stairs to Nicole's chamber, she could not help but admit that Sir Basil had been more lenient than he might have been, considering the freedom with which she had expressed her ideas. It was certainly fortunate that he had no greater experience of what a governess ought to be than she did herself! She could well imagine how the task before her might then have been complicated! But as it was, she thought she could go along perfectly well if only she was careful and avoided any further confrontations with the Baronet. This did not seem like an impossible plan, for she doubted very much that he would seek out her company again, unless it were absolutely necessary.

"Altogether, my girl," she said to herself, "you have been very fortunate: You have got just the situation from which to observe the Great World, and all the people in it, and with not much of hardship attached. You would be wise to balk at nothing, but rather take advantage of every opportunity to observe the order of a universe much greater than the one you are accustomed to. In truth, I am tempted to believe I was sent to Sir Basil by a stroke of fate, for I am already inclined toward making him a hero of a novel!"

And this idea, the seed of which had been planted at the first moment of her clapping eyes upon the Baronet, had grown steadily in her mind since then. The more she thought upon it, the more she liked it, for it combined just those elements of high comedy, satire, and human fallibility which had characterized her first endeavour, and which was admirably suited to her style of writing. Who would have thought she would find in His Excellency, the Ambassador to France, a comic hero? And yet, as she had often observed to Ben, it was just such kind of surprises which made the real world more interesting than the common run of romance would lead one to believe. In novels, heroes were generally portrayed as handsome, dashing, and incapable of awkwardness. Their love affairs were carried off without a hitch, and their tragedies were profound. Nowhere had she seen a pair of lips that looked like rose petals, although in novels heroines were forever portrayed as possessing them. She had seen beautiful women with lips the colour of brick, and it had not dimmed their beauty one whit. Why, therefore, should a *hero* always be infallible? It seemed to Anne that, on the contrary, she would be far more amused by a perfectly fallible one, a Baronet, let us say, with a lofty position in the world, whose confidence was shattered by the thought of speaking to a governess, or conversing with a child of nine. A determined bachelor would do very nicely, for he would of course be the envy of every mama in the *ton*, and his tranquility would be put to the test at every turn by the exertions of their daughters. There ought certainly to be a love story in it, thought Anne, which certainly presented a problem, for the mere idea of Sir Basil Ives mooning over some poor young lady made her laugh. She would certainly have to observe him very closely, to see how he fended off the advances of his admirers. He must have them: she doubted not, but that so eligible a man as the Baronet must have caused havoc amongst the unmarried ladies of London and their mamas when he had returned from France, still single and without any intention of being otherwise. Certainly he disliked women, and considered them all, with the exception of Lady Cardovan, foolish and dull. However little his manner might appeal to *her*, and however much he might lack in every other appealing quality, Anne could well imagine that there were some females less scrupulous than herself. In every outward wise, he would make an exceptionally eligible husband: rich, handsome, respected, and well-connected. *Some* ladies might not blink at the idea of swallowing his coldness, so long as they could be mistress of an embassy. No doubt he had been much harrassed by them, and no doubt he thought every woman in the world must think exactly as they did. How she should love to be privy to an encounter between a strong-minded flirt and the Baronet! She could well imagine his distraction, his cold pauses, his ironic replies, whilst the lady—no doubt thinking herself much admired—pursued the Ambassador from dinner to cards and back again. And laughing all the way, Anne climbed the stairs to her pupil's room, elated beyond everything to have found the subject for her second novel so easily, and the chief character so conveniently near to hand.

But the business of being a governess requiring her immediate attention, Anne was prevented from pursuing her idea any further. She wished to impart the news of the proposed visit to Carlton House without delay, for she knew it would amaze and delight the little girl. She went directly, therefore, to Nicole's bedchamber, where she found her pupil staring at a picture book. The sound of the door opening, however, made the child look up with a frightened expression which amazed her governess.

"Why, child, what are you doing?" inquired Anne, going up to her and glancing at the volume, which was full of ornate plates of Parisian monuments.

"I was only trying to discover what France is like," responded the child. "But I can find nothing here about children, or what games are played in Paris, or what it will be like."

"I am sure it will be quite delightful," replied Anne, sitting down on the arm of the chair and putting her arm around the little girl. "Although not in any way you can foretell. It is always tempting to make up one's mind about things before they happen, but one is nearly always wrong."

"I know—for nothing *here* is like anything I expected," returned Nicole, and with such a grave little voice that Anne was astonished.

"Why, what is wrong? Where is the cheerful little girl I know? Pray don't tell me she has gone to bed and left this unhappy child in her place! I hope not indeed, for I have grown very fond of her, and should miss her dreadfully."

"Would you indeed, Miss Calder?" inquired the child doubtfully. "But if you should, you should be the only one who *would* miss me,"

"Why, whatever are you talking of?" demanded Anne in amazement.

Nicole looked down into her lap and pressed her lips together.

"I—I do not suppose Sir Basil would miss me very much. He does not like me, does he? I suppose I am a great deal of trouble, and that is why he wished to speak to you."

"A great deal of trouble! Heavens! Whatever made you think so? Foolish girl—I suppose that is why he wishes to take you to Carlton House next week to meet the Prince!"

No words could describe the look of amazement which now came over Nicole's features. But there was still disbelief in her voice when she said, "To meet the Prince! Why, what does he want to meet *me* for?"

"I suppose he wishes to see if you are as remarkable as everyone says," retorted Anne with a smile. "In any case, Sir Basil thinks you will not disappoint him, and so you may be sure he likes you very well indeed! I am sure he should not have thought of it if he did not."

"Oh, I am very glad of that!" exclaimed the child with such an earnest look that Anne could not help but smile. "For I was really afraid that he had asked to speak to you to say he did not want me for his ward anymore. I don't know what I should have done, in that case, for I have nowhere *else* to go."

"Hush, child—no one wishes you to go away, and least of all, Sir Basil. What on earth can have put such an idea into your head?"

Nicole gave a trembling smile. "Why, because he never speaks to me without that funny look—when he speaks to me at all. I know he is a very grand sort of man, for Papa told me so. Papa said Sir Basil was one of the most admired men in the whole kingdom, and that I was exceedingly lucky to be going to him. But I do not think," she finished with a confidential look, "that he likes children very well."

Anne could not but smile at the perception of this child, although she was very sorry for it, since it caused her pain. She was more than ever determined to contradict any such impression, and at the risk of fabricating a little, she replied warmly:

"Why, that is the most nonsensical thing I ever heard! On

the contrary, he wished most especially to tell me that he liked you better than any other little girl he ever saw. But you must understand, Nicole, that Sir Basil has a great many things to think about. And I do not suppose he has had much opportunity in his life to converse with children, so you must not mind it if he seems a little awkward at first. You must help him, you know—we must both help him, for I think he is actually frightened of us both!"

The idea that Sir Basil might be frightened of her made a great impression upon the child. She looked up in disbelief, and then, with a giggle, wondered if it could be true?

"Most certainly it is! Is not it very odd? But people often *are* rather odd. And thank heaven for it, too—else we should be an exceedingly dull lot."

Nicole digested this idea for a moment, and then, with a confidential tone, inquired if *she* was odd, as well?

Anne could not help laughing at the sight of the grave little face gazing up at her.

"My dear girl, *you* are original, and that is the best thing in the world to be. It is very easy to be like everyone else, but to be yourself—purely and simply yourself—is the best possible thing in the world. So if anyone ever says that you are odd—and someone inevitably will, sometime—you must just tell them so."

"Are *you* an original, Miss Calder? But, I suppose you must be. You are not like anyone I ever knew. Of course, you are not like Sir Basil, but different in another kind of way. Much prettier, anyway."

"Well! That is very good of you, I'm sure. I suppose I *am* rather different, in my own way. And I should not like to change places with anyone. Certainly not with Sir Basil, for all his eminence."

"Nor with Lady Cardovan? *She* is very pretty, and very *nice* too."

"Yes, she certainly is. But I do not think I should like to be exactly like her, either. No, to be frank, I do not think I should like to be like anyone, save myself. Now, it is very late, and you must go to sleep else you shan't be able to learn anything in the morning. I have a great dislike of sleepy little girls when they ought to be bright and wide awake."

And with these words, Anne persuaded Nicole to get up from her chair, and having helped her change from her frock into a nightgown, tucked her into bed. The child seemed content enough to do as she was bid, and having been tucked in, sank wearily into her pillows. But just as Anne was about to quit the room and had blown out the candle, she heard a small, high voice call her name.

"Miss Calder? Do you think even the *Prince* is odd?"

Anne laughed. "The Prince? Why, I suppose he is, in his own way. But you shall see for yourself soon enough, shan't you?"

Chapter X

Nicole had not long to wait. Only two days later Sir Basil returned from his daily outing and, calling for his ward and Miss Calder, announced that he had been that morning with the Prince.

"His Highness has expressed a desire to see you, Nicole," said he when the ladies had come into his library. "He is very fond of children, and little girls in particular. He has a daughter of his own, and I doubt not but that he shall have a great deal to say to you."

Nicole stood very still, nearly on tiptoe with anticipation. She had not ceased talking and speculating about the Prince since her conversation with her governess.

"Well, what do you say, eh? Do you think you shall enjoy meeting His Highness? You must have a new frock for the occasion, I suppose, and Miss Calder must practice curtseying with you. Right down to the ground for royalty, if you please, Miss Calder."

Miss Calder was doubtful of her own knowledge of the subject of curtseying before princes, but promised to do the best she could. She was in any case so well pleased with the Baronet for this proof of his desire to be kind to the little girl, that she was every moment in danger of laughing out loud. But Sir Basil, perhaps because he was unsure of how to go, grew drier every moment.

"Well, then, you had better solicit Lady Cardovan's advice. *She* will know what is best. And perhaps you had better get her to select a frock for Miss Lessington as well. You must make haste, however, for His Highness expects us to tea on

Tuesday. There shan't be time for any nonsense about ordering frills and furbelows."

The ladies were summarily dismissed, almost before they had got their breaths back, and from that moment on all thought of lessons was abandoned in favour of the more pressing business of preparing for the great visit. Lady Cardovan was called in to advise them—or rather, they called upon her in search of further wisdom, and were soon dazzled by the quantities of information they had to digest. There seemed to be endless numbers of fine points attending any visit to the royal family, beginning with the sorts of conversation it was advisable to embark upon. Fortunately, Lady Cardovan was nearly as delighted as the little girl to hear the news, and seemed perfectly expert in all the required modes of conduct. "She," as Nicole confided later to her governess, "must have seen the Prince lots of times!"

"I hope the child shan't be disappointed," said Lady Cardovan to Anne that same day, as they waited for Nicole to be measured for a new frock by her ladyship's own dressmaker. "Poor Prinney has got so desperately fat, he looks more like a dumpling than a Prince!"

Anne was a little amazed to hear this great lady speak so lightly of the Regent. But she was quickly learning that subjects which she had been brought up to consider sacrosanct, were often treated in a flippant style by the *ton*. In any case, nothing Lady Cardovan did could be wrong. She was Anne's idea of the perfect lady, combining all the merits of an elegant mind with the amiability of a warm heart. In her mouth, such a comment was less a condemnation of the Prince than an affectionate aside.

Smiling, Anne inquired what he was like. Lady Cardovan looked up thoughtfully from her cup of tea.

"Why, I hardly know what to say," she replied. "It has been so long since I conversed with anyone who did not already have his own opinion of him that I am quite at a loss. Very fat, certainly, and as vain as a peacock. He used to be exceedingly handsome, but that, I am afraid, has gone the way of all flesh. I have heard some people call him nothing more than a vain old billygoat, and others who are convinced he is the spiritual successor of Charles the Second. I am inclined to think he is a little of both. Don't look so shocked, my dear—you cannot remain above a week in London without hearing HRH spoken of thus lightly. Besides, it is only a sign of our affection for him that we speculate so freely, and criticize him so keenly. No other nation has a political system intended to check the power of the king, and that, I am positive, is what makes Britain the greatest nation upon earth. Our power derives exactly from that freedom, which is felt quite as strongly amongst the residents of London as amongst its lawmakers. We all join forces in defending Him when He is attacked, but when we are amongst ourselves, we see no reason to bite our tongues. Had the French such freedom, I make no doubt but that they should never have overthrown their Louis."

Anne listened with great interest, conscious that she was privileged to be hearing the opinions of one of the most brilliant figures of the time, a woman whose histories of Greece, Spain, and the Norman Conquest were admired both for their keen insight and their ingenious mingling of fact and speculation.

"And what is *your* opinion of him, your ladyship?" she inquired.

"I should be a traitor if I declared him anything less than what a monarch ought to be," replied her ladyship, smiling. "But between ourselves, I shall just admit that there are many sorts of monarchs. In truth, I am perfectly devoted to His Highness as a character: but if he is better company than his father, if he gives more interesting dinners, and does not cease to delight us all with his whims, he might yet benefit a little from poor King George's example. A monarch ought to possess a little self-control in his public life, even if he cannot show it in private. By that I mean to say, that Prinney might be held in greater general esteem if he did not indulge his temper and his passion so freely. Any more I cannot say without seeming to be disloyal. In truth, I am very loyal to our Prince, and sorry for him."

Anne looked curious upon hearing this, and seeing her expression, Lady Cardovan smiled.

"You are a most persuasive young woman, Miss Calder. I believe you could make a stone talk, if you set your mind to it. But I shall not say any more until you have seen him yourself. *Then* we shall have two views of the subject, and conversation will be more interesting. I should like to hear what your first impression of him is. I doubt not but that your keen eyes shall see through the gossamer of his station as clearly as my own, after all these years."

Anne could not help but feel flattered by this oblique compliment. She only laughed, however, and replied:

"Well! I do not know whether to be pleased or not, but I shall have to wait a little longer to prove my perception to you."

"What! Do not you go with Nicole on Tuesday?" inquired a surprised Lady Cardovan.

"Oh, no! Why should *I* go? I believe His Highness only wishes to see my pupil. He cannot have any interest in *me!*"

"You underestimate yourself, my dear," retorted her ladyship with a sly look. "His Highness is *always* interested in pretty young women, especially if they be amusing and clever into the bargain." But then, with a perplexed look, her ladyship added, "But in truth, I am amazed that you will not be in the party. These teas are a regular thing with his Highness. He likes to gather a great many children around him and feed them all the sweets they can devour. But I always supposed they came in the company of their mamas, or at least with some kind of chaperone."

"Well, then—I suppose Sir Basil shall go," remarked Anne, but conscious, even as she said it, of the ridiculous image of the Baronet, so proud and formal, making up a party of children and their mamas, all devouring sweets.

Lady Cardovan must have had the same mental image, for she laughed out loud.

"Good lord! The idea is almost too much to bear! I cannot fathom poor Basil surrounded by toddlers and gossiping females for above five minutes without going out of his head!"

Anne only smiled in reply. She could not agree as vociferously as she would have liked, remembering, just in the nick of time, that her employer was also this lady's most intimate friend. What can be allowed by an intimate, as a sort of affectionate rebuke, will be looked upon as an outright insult in another's mouth. And the more so, as she reminded herself, if the other party is a mere governess. She was forced to remind herself of her station more and more frequently. Lady Cardovan had spoken to her quite as an equal, which had only made her ladyship seem more superior than ever in the eyes of the young lady. Lady Cardovan did not seem to think it necessary to remind her, as Sir Basil did with every glance and gesture, that she was hardly better than a servant. *She* did not assume that simply because Anne was a governess, she could neither think nor reason. Anne could not imagine the Baronet speaking to her as openly as Lady Cardovan had just done, as if there were no more difference between them than their ages. No: Lady Cardovan must be admired more every moment, for on top of everything, she possessed that subtlety of judgment which may allow a countess to converse with a governess without making the difference in their stations an impediment. She was all grace and elegance, the more so as she had spoken of the Regent with a combination of candour and decorum. Had she said either more or less, she should have been in error: in the first case for speaking too freely about their mutual Prince, in the second, for disguising her true feelings.

Lady Cardovan was watching her intently, but pretending to fiddle with her spoon.

"You have not told me how you managed to engineer this visit to Carlton House, my dear," said she with a tiny smile.

Anne was amazed. "Engineer it! But I most certainly did not, your ladyship!"

"You need not be modest with *me*, my dear Miss Calder—" with a sly look— "I have known Basil these fifteen years. I cannot fathom his inventing such a scheme all on his own. Besides, he told me himself you had given him a stern scolding."

Anne met the lady's amused eyes with a sudden feeling of confusion.

"Why, I hope he did not! For I did nothing of the kind. I only suggested that Nicole might benefit greatly from his attention and kindness. He asked me himself, you know, what he ought to do!" Anne found herself more defensive than she had meant to be, and was torn between mortification and relief when her companion only smiled the more. Oh! that Lady Diana had not learned of her little lecture!

"So he told me. He told me likewise that he had received a stern rebuke for voicing his opinion of our sex."

"Did he?" inquired Anne in a faint voice.

"Yes, and he said he had never been more rebuffed in all his life."

Anne's heart sank. She dreaded to think how Lady Cardovan must view her now! *What an insolent girl she must think me, after having been kind enough to take me on faith, without the smallest proof that I should serve.* But alarmed, she inquired softly:

"Was—was he very angry?"

Lady Cardovan did not reply at once, but stared into the air in an abstracted fashion. Every passing second made Anne's heart pound louder, till she thought the Countess would hear it.

"More astonished than angry," came the eventual reply. "No, in point of fact, when he got over his amazement, I believe he was perfectly amused at the idea. He is not accustomed to be called down, you know—especially by ladies. Oh, I do so myself—it is a great game of mine to pull his leg. But that is rather different. *I* might be his mother, or at least his elder sister. But our Sir Basil is inclined to be very complacent sometimes. I do not believe a young and comely female has ever criticized him."

Anne was almost as amazed at hearing herself described as "young and comely" as she was relieved to hear that Lady Cardovan did not think less of her. Certainly she did not suppose Sir Basil thought so well of her, and she said as much to Lady Cardovan:

"*He* must only consider me a very rude and very offensive governess!"

Lady Cardovan gazed at her in amusement. "You must never underestimate yourself, my dear. On the contrary, you ought to be your own most enthusiastic supporter."

But just what you intended by this peculiar comment, was destined to remain a mystery, for just at that moment Nicole appeared, having been measured from head to toe, looking impatient with the business of being a *grande dame*.

"Well, my pet!" Lady Cardovan greeted her. "Are you quite through?"

The little girl's eyes widened as she nodded and moved toward them.

"And thoroughly full of pins, too! I never knew ladies had to be stuck so full of pins in order to have a new frock!"

"That is the way of it, child—all great beauty must be suffered for, and suffered keenly. But have a piece of cake, it will make you feel better."

This remedy proving not only very effective but very welcome, another piece was forced upon the willing victim, and after that had been devoured, a bowl of raspberries and cream offered and accepted. Having made short work of this modest repast, Miss Lessington took her place upon the sofa with Lady Cardovan and commenced prying her with questions about the Regent.

"Why," she inquired in a prim voice, "must I curtsey right down to the ground for him, if he is only a Prince? Oughtn't I to save that for His Majesty?"

"You must curtsey as low as possible to both of them, my dear, whenever you see them," responded Lady Cardovan indulgently, "for they are both sovereigns, and deserving of our deepest respect."

Nicole digested this advice with gravity, and then demanded to know if the King would be having tea as well?

"I think not, child," laughed the Countess. "The King is ill, and takes tea by himself."

Whereupon Nicole wished to know what ailed him, and there followed a thorough, if somewhat contracted, history of the Georgian reign. The child's eyes grew wide upon hearing that King George was ill in his head, rather than his body, and seemed to meditate upon this point during all the rest of their visit. As they were driving home in Sir Basil's town carriage, however, she inquired if the King behaved like a certain Mr. Rumple in Lincolnshire. Mr. Rumple had been a most ridiculous fellow, and her Papa had told her that he too was sick in the head.

"But I do hope not," she exclaimed earnestly, "for it would be perfectly awful if His Majesty liked to turn cartwheels in the street, and grinned at everyone going past!"

"Oh, I don't believe the King is like that!" replied Anne, laughing, "or we should all know about it. In any case, kings do not go about alone, but have always a huge retinue attending them. They are dignified and awesome, even when they are ill."

Nicole seemed mollified by this and took up her usual line of chatter, observing everything and everyone they passed, remarking upon the buildings and the citizens with equal delight. A great fat gentleman with a proud bearing drawing up beside them on his horse as they were stopped at the junction of Curzon and St. James's streets, fell under her scrutiny. He happened to glance at the carriage, and was evidently taken aback by the pair of beady black eyes assessing him as if he were a statue, for he instantly whipped his horse about and made off through the tangle of vehicles and street vendors which customarily interrupts the smooth flow of traffic at that crossing.

Anne observed the little scene, and could not help smiling to herself. What was it about a child's eyes that had the power to disconcern the most self-possessed of mortals? Men in particular seemed to fall beneath their inquiring gaze; or perhaps it was simply that men detested being looked at like mere mortals. They seemed, at least most of those gentlemen whom Anne had been acquainted with in her lifetime, to need to be thought of as so vastly superior to everyone else, that only a blushing, bashful glance could make them easy. The idea made her conjure up the picture of Sir Basil as he had stood before the mantel during their one real exchange. Certainly *he* had not been able to meet her gaze directly, but was always occupied in fiddling with some trinket, or pacing about, or staring off into thin air. He had barely met her eyes once, and then with that dreadful ironic smile, which made her think he was actually looking past her at some other person. But then, *he* was not a fair example of his sex. Sir Basil must always be thought so far above the rest of the human race as not to have any equals upon earth. Anne smiled at the idea.

"I do wish we had not to go to my cousins' this evening," Nicole was saying, in an uncharacteristically whining tone. "I should do *anything* if we could stay at home."

Anne glanced up, still smiling at her own thought.

"Oh, dear, I had quite forgot!"

"I do not think they are very nice children," Nicole said in a prim voice. "They are dreadfully mussy and rude, and do not like me in any case."

"Nonsense! It is only that they do not know you very well." But even as she said this, Anne secretly agreed with her charge. There could not have been three less appealing young people in London. However little Anne was disposed to condemn children, she could not help but do so. Or perhaps it was her own reaction to their parents which coloured her view of them. Lord and Lady Hargate had spared no pains, at their first meeting, to make her feel uncomfortable and unwanted. She had sat in the corner for an hour whilst the others conversed, and not one word was addressed to herself. Tea had been passed around, and only by a stroke of fate had she received a cup. Sir Basil must be credited with this, for he had brought it to her himself, with a little apologetic look, which, however, had instantly given way to his usual haughty expression. Altogether, she could not imagine a more disagreeable manner of spending an evening than at Hargate House. Only the consciousness that she must do whatever lay in her power to dispel Nicole's dislike of them, prevented her joining in the child's complaints.

"You ought to make an effort to play with them, my dear. They are only shy and awkward, and do not know how to let you know they like you."

"I do not know why *I* should go to any trouble," sniffed

the little girl. "Besides, I am quite sure Sir Basil detests them, too."

"Why! What can make you think so?"

"I saw how he wrinkled up his nose when they came into the room, laughing and hooting, and he would not give Clara his cheek to kiss, but pretended not to see her."

"Oh, I do not think that is the case," responded Anne, conscious of the verity of Nicole's words. "Sir Basil must be fond of his little niece and nephews, even if he does not like them quite so well as he likes *you*."

Nicole gave her governess a piercing look, which declared, more clearly than any words, that she knew she was being told an untruth. Helpless against so keen a pair of eyes, Anne could only look into her lap and smile. The sight of their own house, however, just now coming into view, saved her from any further dissimulation.

Chapter XI

If Anne had foreseen a dull and painful evening, she was at
least mistaken in what form that dullness, and that pain,
would take.

The party commenced amicably enough in Regent's Terrace, and for that blessing Anne was forced to be grateful,
for very little else in the evening's entertainment pleased her.
But Sir Basil's spirits seemed inordinately good when they
met downstairs to await the carriage together. By this, it is
meant that he actually bestowed a smile upon the two ladies
as they came in, and seemed desirous of making conversation
with them rather than staring off into space in his usual abstracted manner. True, his sallies were a little forced, com-
mencing with an inquiry into the ladies excursion to Grove
House as if he were inquiring about a funeral they had attended instead of a fitting. He looked very sober when Nicole
replied that she had been "stuck full of pins" and had consumed a quantity of cake.

"I hope you did not, Nicole, indeed! For you shall have
the stomach ache for your efforts, as well as several pin-
pricks!"

Anne did not know whether he meant to be funny or no,
but having considered the matter a moment, determined he
was incapable of humour, unless it were sardonic or lofty.
Still, he behaved genially to both ladies, and even went so far
as to compliment Anne upon her gown, an old lavender silk
she had had for several seasons and which her mother had
wished to give to a servant girl, for being too drab. Anne did
not for a moment believe he liked the gown any better than
Mrs. Calder, nor that he took any interest whatsoever in her

appearance, but she could hardly hate him for complimenting her, and very soon she found herself feeling almost cordial toward him.

"Foolish girl!" she laughed to herself as the Baronet handed her into the barouche. "Vain creature, for changing your opinion of him so suddenly, only because he has professed himself fond of your frock, which of course is an outright untruth!"

But Sir Basil persisted in being so amiable all during the drive to Grosvenor Square that she could not help softening toward him. She could not recollect his ever speaking so many words upon one occasion. He seemed, indeed, to be incapable of silence, recounting here an amusing incident at court, and pointing out there a famous monument, with a history of it for his ward. Nicole's eyes were all lit with delight: Anne could hardly help liking the Ambassador for making so concerted an effort to be amusing, if only because it had so brilliant an effect upon the child.

"Do you know," said he musingly as they were going past St. James's Cathedral, "that when I was a child—about your age, Nicole—I used to be taken by my father to that cathedral every Sunday morning for matins. There was a bishop at that time, a great fat fellow, immensely tall and overbearing, who was very fond of plums. At least, I suppose he was fond of plums, for I used to see him devouring them by the basketful directly after the sermon, while the oration was being spoke. Imagine, eating plums in his own cathedral!"

And Sir Basil chortled to himself, in a way which made Anne doubt for the first time her conviction that he had never been a little boy himself. Indeed, the laugh was utterly devoid of selfconsciousness, a quality which marked every gesture and glance of the Baronet. For that one instant his cold, piercing eyes were lively and amused. She almost fancied she could see the child of twelve, tall and lean for his years, perhaps awkward in his movements, gaping up at the bishop and knowing he was a secret devourer of plums.

"How many did he eat?" demanded Nicole with her usual practicality.

"Oh, a great many, I suppose—to grow so fat."

"Is he still there?"

"Why, I do not know! What do you suppose? But in any case, we shall see for ourselves tomorrow, for it is Sunday, and we shall go together to find out."

Nicole had no time to inquire any more deeply into the

90

matter, for they were just drawing up before Hargate House and instantly his manner changed. From the bright, almost youthful amusement which had been in his face (and which, as Anne was quick to note, distinctly improved his visage), Sir Basil's features gathered themselves into his more customary gravity. The carriage door swung open, the party descended, and there ended the most enjoyable part of the evening.

In a moment they were within the mansion—or rather, in several moments, for the butler seemed to have disturbed his nap to let them in—and in due course they were ushered in to the family drawing room. This apartment was the same in which they had been entertained before and, as Anne had noticed then, by far the least formal one in all the house. But if it was informal—if it seemed to have been overlooked in Lady Hargate's most recent decorating endeavours, lacking all those campaign desks and gaudy incidental furnishings which speckled the rest of the place—it was no more comfortable. The furniture was a haphazard collection—chiefly gilt—with about two dozen straight-backed chairs that would have more befitted a ballroom than a sitting room. The sofa was likewise covered in a cloth of red and gold brocade, and the only two comfortable-looking chairs in the whole place were pushed back into a corner, nearly screened from view by a gigantic moth-eaten fern. Everything was covered with dust and let out a dank smell, as if the room had not been aired out in half a dozen years.

The scene which greeted their eyes on coming into the room, however, was more notable for its activity than its furnishings. The phlegmatic nurse was sprawled in a chair, and barely glanced up as they came in. Her eyes were focused somewhere in the air; she seemed to take no interest in the game which occupied her charges. This was loud and rowdy, and appeared to be centered upon a doll which, lacking head and limbs, was being tossed back and forth like a ball amid piercing squeals and yells.

Anne glanced once at the Baronet and could not help smiling upon seeing his expression—so vivid a combination of horror and contempt that no words could have illucidated his feelings more clearly. Nicole only looked woebegone, and clung more firmly than ever to her governess's hand.

As no one seemed capable of uttering a word, and their presence continued to be ignored by the room's inhabitants, Anne took it upon herself to open her mouth. Her cough was not audible above the din, however, and so she fairly yelled out:

"Nurse!" Is not your mistress at home?"

The woman looked up indifferently, shrugged her plump shoulders, and then, seeing she was expected to do something, reluctantly rose to her feet.

"Shall go and see," muttered she, traipsing off.

The sound of a strangled giggle made Anne look down to see her own pupil quite crimson in the face and looking as if she might burst apart from holding her breath. Sir Basil heard it too and, glancing down, made an extraordinary gesture. The wink was so fleeting it was almost imperceptible, but Anne saw it—else she could not have believed her eyes—and Nicole saw it, too. The effect upon the child was to lose all interest in anything else save her guardian. Loosing her grip on Anne's hand, which she had held tightly since coming into the mansion, she made a timorous essay at that of Sir Basil. His long slender fingers wrapped themselves awkwardly about the little paw, as if unused to the action. So engrossed was she in watching this little scene, that Anne barely noticed that the other children had stopped playing and were gaping at the group in the doorway.

"Ah!" exclaimed Sir Basil after a moment, evidently at a loss for what else to say. "Ah! Little Harry, is not your mama at home?"

The little girl, who had edged up close beside her brother, seemed to find this question vastly amusing, for she nudged Harry and burst into a fit of giggles.

"Tsh!" said Harry to his sister, nudging her back. "Hush, Clara—it is Uncle Basil."

"I know that, stupid!" replied the little girl, and giggled again.

This was the extent of the conversation for some moments. Sir Basil seemed to be arranging his ideas, or perhaps he was hoping that some other adult would appear to rescue him. His prayers were answered, for eventually a step was heard in the corridor and Lady Hargate materialized, as if from nowhere.

The Countess was dressed in a billowy gown of pale pink lace, with half a dozen ribbons in her pale curls. She looked, as Anne noted later in her journal, "exactly like a debutante, one of those frilly, foolish girls who used to appear always at the Assemblies at home, and were transformed overnight, as soon as they were wed, into sour old women. Save that Lady

Hargate has not taken note of the change in her situation and continues as if she is eighteen, nodding and bobbing and throwing about her hands in the most flirtatious manner. She could not leave off glancing up from beneath her eyelashes at Sir Basil, as if she were trying to make him dance with her. Sir Basil, as may be imagined, seemed to find the whole charade shocking, and as little as I saw of him all evening, he seemed always to be hiding from her eyes, and endeavouring to stop her high-pitched laughter from reaching his ears."

"Oh la!" cried she, immediately she had glimpsed them. "Lord, Basil, I did not expect you so soon! Dear me, and have you been subjected very long to these noisy children—" with a coquettish glance at her offspring— "dear me, I am sure I do not know what to say!"

"Say nothing then, Louisa," replied Sir Basil in an undertone, which luckily she did not catch. "We have only been here this five minutes. But did not you say five o'clock? And it is now half past the hour if I am not mistaken."

"Oh, la! Is it, indeed? Why! I am sure I said six, so that the children could dine first. Ah, well. I am such a muddle-brained creature, to be sure—" with yet another coquettish upward glance from beneath her eyelashes— "But you must forgive me, my dearest Basil. But! Why on earth have you been shown in *here*? I am sure I left instruction that *you* should be shown into the Green Saloon. The young lady and her charge may stay here if they like, but I am sure *you* ought to be settled better!"

"Why, I am quite all right here, Louisa." Sir Basil glanced apologetically at "the young lady," who was only smiling demurely and noting everything. "I thought it was to be only a family supper, in any case."

"Oh! To be sure!" cried Lady Hargate, "a mere nothing! Only six courses, and in the small dining room, you know. Still, Brother—" taking his arm in an intimate manner— "I cannot allow His Excellency, the Ambassador, to be entertained in such a kind of way. It is only a family supper, to be sure, but I have asked one or two great friends to come as well. The Princess Lieven, you know, and the Russian Ambassador, and of course, my sister. You do remember my sister, do you not?"

Anne thought, from catching a glimpse of his expression as he bowed and said that of course he remembered her, that his memory was not all delightful. But Sir Basil, if he could be accused of many things, could never have been faulted for his manners. If they were not as easy and happy as some might have wished, they were at any rate, impeccable. Impeccably cold, in this case, Anne could not help observing. Yet he managed to bow and smile as often as was required, and seeing that he was destined to be taken into the Green Saloon, followed his sister-in-law out of the room with only a tiny backward glance at Nicole and the nurse.

"And Miss Lessington?" he inquired before he was escorted away.

"Oh, *she* shall be perfectly well! Lord! The three of them shall be so amused, they shall not want for anything, and Nurse shall see to them."

"And Miss Calder?"

"Miss Calder?" Lady Hargate did not quite remember who *she* was. "Oh! To be sure, Miss Calder! Why, she may dine below stairs with Nurse and the housekeeper, if she don't wish to dine with my little babies."

Anne was forced to look down to hide her smile upon hearing *this*, and so she did not meet the eyes which searched out her own, full of apologies and mortification, and were then called back again to attend to the vanities of the Countess.

The remainder of the evening, as may well be imagined, was not, at least for our heroine, memorable for anything save mortification and boredom. Had she known what kind of an effect the whole entertainment had upon the Baronet, however, she might have been more grateful for her plate of cold mutton and brussels sprouts, taken, in the end, upon her lap on a tray in the same room, whilst Nicole watched her cousins in silence, and they stared back with smirks and grins. Nicole, little lady that she was, would not condescend to their level of play, but sat instead thumbing over a great book of coloured plates, and whenever she was unnoticed, crept over to her governess to be comforted. The Earls' children soon grew bored with her and ran upstairs to pursue their own more boisterous forms of play, whilst the nurse slept throughout the whole in her chair with an occasional snore issuing from her lips to attest to the depth of her slumbers.

But if Nicole and her governess were prevented from eavesdropping upon the more lively scene in another part of the house, we are not obliged to keep them company, but may pass through the great walls with as much ease as if they had been made of gauze, rather than two feet of stone and plaster. In truth, the scene in the Green Saloon may have been more lively, but it was not much more pleasant, at least for some of the company. The echoes of laughter and conversation which filtered through to Anne's ears, and which filled her with more envy than she would admit, were deceptive. They issued chiefly from the lips of Lady Hargate and her sister, who, if it was possible, was even more gushing than her sister, though with a darker complexion and a more purposeful set of eyes. Of the four ladies in the room, the Princess Lieven was the only real beauty, being very dark and small, with striking eyes and a darting, birdlike way of moving. *She* spoke hardly at all, save in an undertone to Sir Basil, whom she had come to see in spite of her loathing for his brother and sister-in-law. Her husband, the Russian Ambassador, was a small square man with a diffident expression, and an air about him of giving way in every matter of importance to his wife. He wore Hessians, in the manner of the Russians, although it was an evening party, and a white military coat encrusted with gold ornaments. Having exchanged a few words with his colleague, he sat out the rest of the evening stiffly in his chair without a word. Lord Hargate endeavoured to make him talkative, but was repelled for his efforts, and at last departed for the more amiable environment of Lord and Lady Applegate, who possessed one of the most magnificent country seats amongst the peerage, and not another stroke to recommend them, save their great wealth, their lofty titles, and faces as bland and passive as peasants.

Sir Basil, meanwhile, was caught between his sister-in-law and Miss Newsome, who, having engaged him in conversation, would not leave him alone. She was a handsome enough young woman, who had somehow escaped matrimony in her eight seasons in Town. Lady Hargate was determined to make her a wife now, and from that young woman's expression, and the forward way in which she addressed Sir Basil, it was evident that she had no great objection to the scheme.

Lady Hargate had had two motives for her little dinner party—the first was to marry off her sister to her husband's brother, and the second was to parade Sir Basil before the Princess Lieven. If she meant to discommode her friend, however, she had little success. The Princess enjoyed the well-deserved reputation of being the prettiest, wittiest lady in London, and was so sure of her own stature in the *ton* that she had not hesitated to be the first to dance the brazen new waltz when it had first been introduced in London. That she received the attentions of two royal dukes was an ill-kept secret—that is to say, secret only from those who could not profit from the intelligence—and she had been upon bantering, if not intimate, terms with Sir Basil for some years. She was therefore not at all put out by her hostess's blatant attempts to make her envious and, on the contrary, only a little more bored than she was amused by the charade.

"Why, is it not a delightful thing to have Basil amongst us once again?" inquired her hostess in a simpering tone when she saw that Sir Basil's attentions were thoroughly taken up by her sister. "Lord, I can hardly believe how we have amused ourselves since he went away! How dreary it has been, to be sure! Every ball has lacked brilliance, every dinner has been without animation!"

"And yet I have not observed *you* staying away, Your Ladyship," returned the Princess, who would not condescend to call Lady Hargate by her first name, though she had been urged to do so half a dozen times.

"Oh! It is all so dreadfully boring!" sighed Lady Hargate. "What is one to do? Why, I believe I ought really to stay at home more often with my dear little children. I am sure they are far more amusing than all the assembled personages at Almack's!"

This sally, which had been meant as a jest, was a mistake, as Lady Hargate quickly saw. The Princess Lieven raised one eyebrow, and smiled.

"I did not realize we made such a dull collection," she murmured dryly.

"Oh! In truth, you know I was not serious. It is only the *ennui* of winter that I feel coming on. I do so adore bright weather, do not you, Princess?"

The Princess seldom saw enough of daylight to care if the weather was bright or dark, but she smiled in reply.

Mais oui, Madame, c'est vraiment domage quand les temps ne font beaux."

"*Oui, oui, c'est horrible,*" murmured Lady Hargate in reply, eager to prove that her French did not consist merely of one or two fashionable phrases.

But the Princess Lieven had turned away, as bored with her hostess as Lady Hargate professed to be with the assemblies at Almack's. Lady Hargate was forced to turn her attention back to her sister's progress with Sir Basil, and overheard the following dialogue:

"And now, I suppose, you must return to Paris instantly?" inquired Miss Newsome, having satisfied herself upon every point of the Baronet's house in Regent's Terrace, his appointments with the Prince, and his health.

"Why, no. I shall stay yet a while."

"Ah!" One dark eyebrow arched up. What had been a decidedly petulant look, changed suddenly to one of bright hope. "Ah! How fortunate we are! Louisa, did not you say Sir Basil had only come to London for a fortnight? I am sure you did, and I am most put out by it, too, for had I known we should be able to count him amongst the company at Almack's, I should have ordered that lavender satin gown after all. My old dresses are quite good enough for everyone else, but for Sir Basil, I should have gone the extra length."

"Tut, child," returned her sister, "your blue lace and your daffodil silk are perfectly charming. I am sure you are the prettiest woman in the company in either of them. Sir Basil will be delighted with you in any case, shall you not, my dear Basil?"

"My dear Basil," indifferent to lavender satin and daffodil silk alike, replied that he was sure he would be, if he had any ambitions of dancing at Almack's, which alas he did not.

"What! Not dance at Almack's!" cried the sisters in unison. Why, whatever could he mean by that?

"But, of course, Louisa," remarked the younger of the two, whose understanding was a little keener than her sister's, "Sir Basil means only that he prefers to play at cards. But I am sure he will allow us to coax him up from his table from time to time to join in the dancing."

"Were I any more addicted to gaming than to dancing, Miss Newsome, I could certainly be coaxed. But cards hold no fascination for me."

Here was a conundrum indeed. Miss Newsome had never encountered a man who hated *both* dancing and cards, unless he were one of your avid outdoorsmen, who could never enjoy a diversion which required him to stay within above an hour at a clap. But Sir Basil did not in the slightest resemble such a man—his whiskers were cut too close, his coat was cut too fine, and his whole person, though it was very handsome and well-formed, did not conform to that broad-shouldered and muscular type. Miss Newsome, indeed, had been careful to ask him straight away whether or not he liked fox hunting, lest she place herself at once at a disadvantage by confessing too quickly to either an aversion or a love for the sport. Sir

Basil had replied that he did not mind it, but that he tended always to side more with the fox than its hunters: a response which perplexed his inquisitor more than it satisfied her.

"But surely we shall have the pleasure of seeing you on Thursdays?" demanded the young woman, quite at a loss for which tack to pursue.

"If you mean, do I intend going to Almack's every Thursday evening and gaping at the company whilst they enjoy themselves, then no. There is nothing I like less than watching others be diverted whilst I am bored."

Miss Newsome did not know how to respond. The several subjects of conversation in her repertoire were now exhausted. In truth, she did not know what could be said about a man who hated dancing and cards, disliked Almack's, and preferred the fox to the fox hunters. Had Sir Basil been nothing more than a gentleman at a ball, she should have now turned away and given up any further attempt at conversation. Indeed, his manner was such that it was impossible to think *he* longed to keep it up. Even Miss Newsome could not help but see this. And yet she was determined to pursue the exchange. She was now in her twenty-eighth year, and had no other prospect of marriage. Her sister had informed her barely a week before that she was as good as wed to Sir Basil, whom, as Lady Hargate would have it, "is come home on purpose to find a wife. Think how delightful it will be! I shall come to visit you in Paris, and we shall have our gowns made up together, and be the envy of everyone!" Miss Newsome had had no previous ambition to live in Paris, or to be an ambassadress, or to give endless balls to foreigners, but in a week her ideas had changed so much that she was absolutely set upon becoming Lady Ives. If Sir Basil had any suspicion of the plan, he gave no sign of it. Indeed, he would have been astounded to discover that the scheme was already so far advanced that Lady Hargate and her sister had practically laid out his future life down to the minutest detail. The young woman sitting opposite him, whom he had met perhaps three times, and never spoken to above five minutes, was so sure of her success that, far from neglecting the lavender satin, she had ordered it and twenty gowns besides, with the idea that they should serve her during her engagement, even if they were not adequate for married life. With a renewed energy, therefore she persisted:

"I can well imagine that Almack's must appear very dull to you, after the brilliance of French society. But surely you will not deny your friends the pleasure of seeing you? I, for one, shall think you perfectly cruel if you do not attend at least one cotillion, if only so that we may learn, from seeing you dance, how we may improve our own performance."

"I assure you, Miss Newsome, that no one could benefit from such a spectacle," replied the Baronet gravely, growing increasingly impatient with this flirtation. "On the contrary, it could only injure your sensibilities to watch me. I am so awkward in the execution of the steps, and so heartily dislike being laughed at, that I make it a point *never* to dance. As to seeing my friends, there are innumerable ways that I may do so without being subjected to the indignities of a ball."

"To be sure you are jesting!" cried Lady Hargate upon hearing this. "He is only jesting, my dear! Fancy saying that he cannot dance! Why, I am sure he dances every night in Paris! My dear, your leg is being pulled."

The Princess Lieven, who had attended to this conversation with keen amusement, now felt it encumbent upon herself to rescue the Baronet:

"He is not jesting, Lady Hargate, I assure you. I cannot remember the time when Sir Basil could dance. As a matter of fact, if I am not much mistaken, he ruined my best slippers when last I had the misfortune to see him. Did not you, Basil?"

Sir Basil, much relieved, replied that it was true.

"But tell me," continued the Princess, "what is this I hear about your having acquired a ward? Can it be true?"

"A child of nine, the daughter of a distant cousin," concurred the Baronet, happy to embark upon another subject.

The Princess put back her head and chortled in delight.

"A child of nine! A little girl! Did you hear that, Nastasy? Sir Basil has acquired a daughter! How delicious it is! But my dear Basil, what on earth do you mean to do with her?"

"The usual things, I suppose," returned the Baronet, not nearly so amused as the Princess. "Feed her, clothe her, educate her as best I can. Lady Cardovan has managed to secure a governess for her, a most remarkable young woman."

"Ah, yes—the wonderful Lady Cardovan," murmured the Princess with a significant smile. "How is the wonderful Lady Cardovan? I have not seen her for an age. But of course, she has become so dreadfully busy, with all her books. Is she as beautiful as ever?"

"As beautiful as ever," returned Sir Basil shortly.

"And the child?" persisted Princess Lieven, seeing that her

curiosity about this particular friendship was not to be satisfied, "where is she?"

"At the moment, she is with her governess and her cousins in another part of the house."

"Ah!" The Princess clapped her hands in delight. "Then I shall be able to see her! Do send for her, my dear Basil. I *must* have a look at this child, who is succeeding in what every other woman in London has failed to do—" with another significant smile at Miss Newsome— "that is, you know, to domesticate you!"

"I am afraid you shall have to wait until after dinner," interjected Lady Hargate, barely concealing her scowl. "I see that we are being summoned to table."

The Princess was forced to defer her request until later, but only upon the absolute assurance that she should be granted a glimpse of the little girl. The line was formed, and a short dispute between the ladies ended in Lord Hargate's escorting the Princess, whilst Sir Basil walked in with Miss Newsome. Seated between them, the Baronet passed an hour and a half of misery. Anne would certainly have been entertained, if only she had been privy to the scene, for the Princess was tireless in her witty jabs, and Miss Newsome, persistent in her flirtations.

It is indeed a great pity that Anne could *not* observe her employer under these circumstances, growing uneasy from the piercing questions of the one and squirming beneath the admiring gaze of the other. As it was, she ate her plate of cold mutton in a much happier frame of mind than the Ambassador, though it was cold, and her only companions were children, whilst Sir Basil saw six courses pass before him, and sat beside the wittiest lady in England.

The Princess persisted in her desire to see the little girl Nicole, and when the ladies had risen from the table, she asked a footman where the children could be found. Slipping away by herself (for she did not wish to be encumbered by her hostess) she sought out the apartment where Anne and her charge had been ensconced all evening. The little Hargates having long since run upstairs to seek their own amusements, there was no one else in the room save the sleeping nurse. The Princess found governess and child bent over a book and, putting on her most charming smile—for the Princess could be as charming as any woman on earth when she chose—she introduced herself.

"I have come to meet the little girl about whom I have heard so much," said she, approaching them.

Nicole blushed and made a pretty curtsey, whilst Anne stood by smiling.

"What a pretty child you are! And not a bit like your guardian! Ah yes—there is just a little resemblance about the eyes, else I should not able to tell you were related."

"They are only related very distantly, Your Highness," put in Anne, quite taken with the lady's charming manner, her beauty, and the elegance of her dress and bearing. "Miss Lessington is the daughter of Sir Basil's second cousin."

The Princess smiled disarmingly. "Oh, but of course! One ought not to look for resemblances. But I am very fond of doing so. In Russia, we always say that a family has certain traits which carry down the line, and that no matter how distant two cousins may be, there is always a faint resemblance between them. Have not you noticed that it is nearly always true?"

Anne had not noticed anything of the kind, but nodded nevertheless.

"In this case," continued the Princess, taking Nicole's chin in her hand, "I think there is more than a *faint* resemblance. One would not see it unless one looked, of course—but it is there, certainly it is there. Why! I do believe you have got exactly the same eyes as your cousin, my dear! Yes, yes, and quite the same expression in them—fiery and stubborn, to be sure. Well, well! I should watch out, Miss—what is your name?"

"Calder," replied Anne.

"Miss Calder, yes—a very pretty name. Sir Basil has spoken very highly of you."

Anne doubted that, but smiled all the same, and bowed her head.

"Lady Cardovan—ah, found you, did she not?"

Again, Anne nodded and smiled, laughing to herself at the continual difficulty encountered over her station.

"Lady Cardovan is a most wonderful woman."

"Yes, Princess—she is indeed."

The Princess let go of Nicole's chin and patted her head.

"A most wonderful, excellent woman. And extremely beautiful, too. Sir Basil regards her very highly, I believe."

"They are great friends, ma'am."

"Yes, yes—*great* friends. I am astonished by it, actually. Sir Basil has always had the reputation of disliking women. I believe he finds us—ah, well! Who can explain the human heart? Well, well. And what is your name, child? Nicole, is it not? A very pretty name. I have always been fond of French names. Where do you come from?"

"From Lincolnshire, ma'am," whispered Nicole, who was evidently in awe of the Princess.

"Lincolnshire! A favourite county of mine! It is the only good hunting county in England. Else one must go to Scotland. How do you suppose you came to have a French name?"

Nicole's eyes grew round. She shook her head. "I don't know, Ma'am. Save that Papa always said it was a name he liked."

"And quite right, too—it is a lovely name. Tell me, Miss Calder—you will come to me if you need any help, will you not? I know that bachelors are often at a loss for how to deal with little girls. If there is anything you need, you must not hesitate to call upon me."

"How kind of you!" exclaimed Anne warmly, "but Lady Cardovan has been most generous with us."

"I am sure she has. Still, if there is any little service you require, please feel free to let me know."

Anne thanked her warmly, and said that she would do so.

"That is a very pretty dress, Nicole. Did Lady Cardovan pick it out?"

"She had it made at her own dressmaker's," replied the child proudly.

"Really?" The Princess raised an eyebrow. "That was a most generous present! Well, well—Lady Carodvan is a wonderful woman."

And smiling very broadly, the Princess patted the child's head and went away.

Chapter XII

If Anne had thought it a little odd that the Princess Lieven should take such keen interest in herself and in her charge, if she had noticed that the Princess had smiled very broadly at certain things which did not deserve such broad smiles and gazed more intently into the little girl's face than was perhaps warranted by the interest of a friend, she was not given time to think about it. After a very short time Sir Basil came in to collect them with an irritable expression on his face, and in the next days there were more pressing things to occupy her mind than the smiles of Russian princesses. The greatest consideration of all, at least to Nicole, was the impending visit to Carlton House. But for Anne, there were still other matters to consider.

There was, for instance, the question of her writing, which had been sorely neglected since she had come to London. When she had been at home, it had been her custom to work each morning for several hours together. This, which had been all she could manage between the demands of her mother and the teasing of her sisters, had sufficed to finish the one book which was the whole proof of her trade. And yet she knew that if she was to make a mark as an authoress, she must be diligent. She had not found, since coming to London, more than an hour altogether to write, and this she had spent on scribbling in her journal whatever of quick sketches and impression she could manage. Her publisher was already clamoring for another book, and said that he would print it as soon as one was ready. But Anne had no second novel and only a vague idea for a plot. This much at least she had decided: that her second book should be a satire of city life, just as her first had been a satire about the country. That the hero should be a determined bachelor, very much like Sir Basil in character, she had settled in her own mind, and that much of his circumstances, as well as his character could be drawn from life. But more than that she did not know. Her imagination was such that she was continually embroidering upon the plain fabric of reality in her mind, and already she had envisioned several scenes and sketches which might be useful. But she had not had the time to play with them, to toss them about and rearrange them upon paper, and she was impatient to do so. It was, therefore, her plan to spend the following morning, when Sir Basil and Nicole had gone to church, at work upon them. Accordingly, she declined the Baronet's invitation to join them and, as soon as they had quit the house, sat down at her writing table. Several hours were passed thus, and very enjoyable hours they were, too. One idea led to another, and another, and Anne's hand seemed to fly across the paper in the effort to keep up with her racing thoughts. Between concentration and delight at the ease with which the words seemed to flow, she remained immersed in her work until the great clock in the hall struck one. Startled, she stood up. Why, where had the time gone? Surely Sir Basil and Nicole must have long since returned from church! But a quick search about the house did not reveal the little girl, and the butler informed her that neither his master nor the young mistress had returned. Puzzled, she climbed the stairs back to her own apartment. The service had commenced at eleven o'clock and could not have lasted above an hour. Surely Sir Basil and his ward ought to have returned.

"Well, what of it?" thought Anne. "I shall have a little more time to myself. Perhaps they have gone to see Lady Cardovan, or Sir Basil has met one of his acquaintances. They may even have gone to the park to take the air."

But a glance out of the window above her writing table discouraged this line of thinking. What had begun as a clear, bright winter morning had grown suddenly overcast. The sky was a heavy leaden gray, and the fog had begun rolling into the city streets in great clouds. Determined, however, to make use of her few solitary hours, Anne sat down again to write. The scene she had been working upon, in which the hero of the novel was introduced, had delighted her at first. She read through the pages she had written now, expecting to be pleased with them, but instead a frown came into her eyes after only a few paragraphs.

"Why, that is not right at all," she said aloud, frowning.

"It is far too much a caricature. No one can be expected to recognize such a paper hero. Even Sir Basil is not quite so bad as that."

And so the first paragraphs were scratched out, and written anew. The same process was repeated, until Anne, bewildered and angry with herself, could stand no more. Jumping up, she walked over to the hearth and kicked the glowing embers of the dying fire. Sparks flew, but the wood refused to be ignited. Leaning down, she tugged and pushed the logs about, with little more success.

"Perhaps that is what has happened to me," thought she with a rueful smile. "I had one great burst of flame, and now I shall never again catch fire. It is perfectly plain: My skills are limited to the description of what I know. For me to describe a man of Sir Basil's worldliness is even more presumptuous than asking a child to do a man's work. I shall never be able to satirize this world until I know it as well as I know my own. Till then, my descriptions will all ring hollow, my conversations will lack any trace of life, my command of the action will be worse than a little boy playing with tin soldiers. I had better face it and be done: I have no future in this kind of work."

It was unlike Anne to admit defeat so early. For two years she had laboured to bring forth a slim volume of papers. Through crossings out and tossings into the fire she had kept her determination, and nothing had brought her up until the work was done. But neither was she one to presume to a wisdom she did not possess. All at once, in a rush of elucidation such as everyone knows at moments in their lives, the truth came home to her: her work *then* had been founded upon real knowledge, thorough familiarity with a place and its inhabitants, an absolute intimacy with its manners, morals, and attitudes. How easy it had been to transform the curate's sermons or her own mother's speech into high comedy! How easy to turn a familiar landscape into a setting, or the village near her own home into a backdrop for the action of her novel. *Now* she must draw upon a world with which she had only the most passing acquaintance, a world not her own, and never likely to be her own. Had all her grand ideas been for nought? Had she come to London with expectations far surpassing what was possible, much less probable? She had come to "see the great world." But how much of that world could a governess glimpse? So far, she had not seen much more than the street upon which they lived, the row of shops on St. James's Street, and the carriages driving in Hyde Park. She did not delude herself that things would be much different in the future.

"I shall always be condemned to sit in the second parlour, whilst everyone else converses in the drawing room. Even should I be asked to go to Paris with Nicole—which is doubtful in any case—I shall see hardly any more there! Oh! A thorough acquaintance with the nurseries and kitchens I shall gain, I expect—but more than that? Foolish girl! At least, had you been a Mrs. Siddons, you should have had your own kitchens and half a dozen maids to wait upon you. And the children in your nurseries should have been your own!"

Anne bit her lip at this, and murmured an apology to the absent Nicole. She had made her own bed. Very well, then— she should lie in it. It would be months, perhaps years, before she knew enough of the "great world" to write about it, much less satirize it. And in the meantime? For the year at least, she was forced to remain as she was. If Sir Basil would not take her to France, she must find another situation. And what if she could not delude anyone else as thoroughly as she had deluded the Baronet? It was unlikely that she would find anyone else as thoroughly ignorant of the requirements of her trade as he was, much less a friend as indulgent as Lady Cardovan.

This black mood must needs have some end, but it was some time before Anne had the heart, or the desire, to look up from her unhappy musings. The fire had by then long since died out, and the clock struck three.

Starting up, Anne went out into the corridor. Not a sound was to be heard. Puzzled, she descended the stairs to go in search of the butler. But the man was not at his usual station in the upstairs pantry, and the entrance hall was deserted. What on earth could have befallen Nicole and the Ambassador?

Just then the sound of laughter reached her ears, coming, as it seemed, from beyond the door. In a moment, the crash of the great knocker came, and Anne, who had been just on the point of ascending the steps once more, went forward to answer it.

The sight which greeted her eyes upon throwing back the door was the last one in all the world she had anticipated. There were the two figures of Sir Basil and Nicole, dressed as they had been before; the gentleman in his walking cape and top hat, the child's flushed faced barely visible between the rim of her bonnet and the fur of her collar: nothing astounding in that. The faces, however, and the expressions upon those faces were so changed from what they had been in all the time Anne had known them that she was for a moment incapable of speech. Nicole's features, more given to merriment than her guardian's, were lit up in an absolute spectacle of mirth and happiness. Her small cheeks were bright as apples from the cold, her large black eyes were dancing. But Sir Basil—what on earth could have happened to him? wondered Anne, drawing back a pace or two to let them in. Sir Basil had undergone as complete a transformation as the young lady had ever seen. Where his gaze had always been keen, intelligent, and critical, now it was softened by an expression of—could it be?—perfect enjoyment. Anne would not have believed it possible, had she not seen it with her own eyes, that any set of features could be so radically changed in the space of several hours. Taken aback as she was, she was yet lucid enough to perceive that the transformation was all flattering. Whatever of thinness, dryness, and sarcasm had lurked in that nose, those eyes and lips, and those cheeks, was now all gone, and in their place was as much human kindness as she had ever witnessed.

"Oh, Miss Calder!" cried the child, running into the hall and flinging back her cape, "we have had the most wonderful adventure!"

"I hope you have not been worried," put in the Baronet, stepping into the hall himself and closing the door behind him. "We hoped you would not be. In truth, we did not mean to be away so long."

"Uncle Basil has shown me all over London, and all the places he used to go when he was little!"

"*Uncle* Basil?" repeated Anne, wonderingly.

"Yes!" cried the child, skipping about the room. "Uncle Basil knows everything about London! We have been to Westminster Bridge, and the Tower, and of course St. James's, and driven through the Prince's Park, and up Bond Street, and past all the shops. And I saw White's, and Boodle's, and—and—"

"That is quite enough, Nicole," warned the Ambassador, resuming a more natural dignity of demeanor. "You shall exhaust Miss Calder if you go on. I believe she is inclined to send us both upstairs without any dinner as it is."

"Oh, dear!" cried the child, pausing in her progress about

the hall with a most horrified look, "you shan't do that, shall you, Miss Calder?"

Miss Calder was far too astonished to do anything of the kind. It was all she could do to muster a few words.

"Dear me. Dear me. No—no, I shan't send you to bed! I *have* been worried, but, that is—"

"Perhaps," suggested Sir Basil helpfully, "we had better adjourn to the library and have some tea. I, for one, am famished. I do not recollect being so hungry in all my life. Do you suppose you could persuade them to give us a very hearty tea, Miss Calder? If so, I shall promise to do anything you like. I believe I shall be open to any kind of punishment you have in mind, so long as I am fed."

"I don't think Miss Calder is really very angry," confided Nicole to her guardian, when Anne, dumbfounded, had gone in search of a maid.

"Do you not?" Sir Basil seemed reassured. "Then she is rather different from every other governess I have known. But never mind—I shan't let her beat you."

"Thank you very much," replied Nicole, grinning widely. It had taken her some time to understand her guardian's odd sense of humour, but after an hour or two of driving about London, she had come to see that the Baronet was fond of making outrageous statements and that he was far more pleased if one laughed at them than if one did not.

"I hope she shan't beat *you*," she added, tugging at his sleeve. The Baronet was gazing into space and did not react at once.

"What? Oh—oh, yes. I hope not, too."

But Nicole saw that her guardian was not attending to her. He was still gazing into space in a kind of peculiar, rapt way, and seemed lost in his own thoughts. He hardly replied to her suggestion that he remove his cape and hat, and when the butler appeared to repeat the suggestion, Sir Basil only gave him a blank stare.

Tea was soon ready, and the little party adjourned to the library, where Anne begged to be informed of the particulars of the morning's adventure. Sir Basil had now regained most of his usual sobriety, as Anne was a little sorry to note. To her question whether they had ascertained if the bishop was still fond of plums, he replied only with a confused look.

"The bishop," repeated she, "is he still fond of plums? You mentioned yesterday that when you were a little boy—"

"Bishops ought not to be made fun of, Miss Calder," responded he gravely. "They are our loftiest clergymen. We had do better to heed their sermons and pay less attention to their eccentricities."

"It is a different bishop," interjected Nicole. "This one is quite thin and important-looking."

Anne looked interested. "And did he have anything of great import to say?"

"He said a great deal about serving one's country and one's king," reported Nicole, her mouth full of cake. "It was from Revelation, Uncle Basil says."

"The passage was from Revelation, not the sermon," the Baronnet corrected her. He gave Miss Calder a keen look.

"Your father is a clergyman, is he not, Miss Calder? I suppose you know a great deal about sermons and the like."

"Only what everyone else knows," replied Anne, bewildered by this sudden change in the Baronet, and feeling her usual urge to goad his pomposity, despite all the promises she had made to herself.

"And what is that?" Sir Basil wore a thin little smile, quite a sardonic smile, thought Anne. It was a pity she had not kept on with the sketch she had been writing.

"That sermons are never better than the man who delivers them, and often worse: for a great man may not speak so well as his inferiors in virtue, and a petty, selfish man will sometimes move you to tears with his words, though his actions do not correspond to his ideas."

"An interesting theory," was all Sir Basil gave in the way of a response, but his look, more than his words, spoke volumes. Anne saw at a glance how he despised her, and the knowledge made her wish more than ever to bait him.

"Perhaps your experience has been different from my own," said she. "I have been acquainted with a great many clergymen besides my father, whom I believe to be an admirable man even despite my own prejudice, and not one of them has suited that idea of charity and universal love which is thought generally the nature of the profession. There are as many weak, vain, and selfish men in the clergy as in any other walk of life. Perhaps more: for some are drawn to the Church precisely for the easiness of the work."

"Do you take so dim a view of all mankind?"

Anne regarded him a moment with a faint smile. How she would have liked to take up his challenge! But a sudden idea warned her to keep her peace. I am sure he would be delighted to be given so easy an excuse to criticize me, thought she, and aloud she said:

"No, I do not. But I have observed that there are more of us who are inclined to sloth than to hard work, to leisure and pleasure than self-sacrifice."

"Ah! Then you include yourself?"

"Most assuredly. I am not superior to other mortals, but on the contrary, certainly more foolish and lazy than most."

Sir Basil smiled upon hearing this, which served as further proof to Anne, had she needed any, that he could not have agreed more heartily. But he said nothing for a moment, only staring off into thin air. After a moment, he inquired if she did not sometimes resent the fate which life had dealt her?

Anne glanced uneasily at Nicole, who, though seemingly immersed in the consumption of an immense piece of cake, was obviously attending to every word. This seemed a most peculiar topic of conversation to pursue before a child.

"Resent it, no! But then, I chose it of my own free will."

Sir Basil had seen her glance toward the child, and evidently thinking better of it himself, remarked that it was a most interesting subject, which should be pursued further in the future.

"In the meantime, Nicole," said he, coughing, "I suppose you have consumed sufficient cake to keep you happy for an hour or two. Mind you do not give yourself a belly ache, else we shall not be able to go to Carlton House."

This was certainly the one remonstrance capable of making the child nearly choke, and she instantly set down her plate.

"Oh, dear! I have not eaten so very much, Uncle Basil!"

Uncle Basil could not have looked, at that moment, less like a doting uncle and more like a somber Baronet. He made, however, a faint attempt to smile indulgently, an attempt which struck Anne as exceedingly strange after the natural easiness of his manner so short a time ago.

"But it is enough. Now then, ladies, I fear that I have work to do. You will excuse me?"

And rising from his chair, the Ambassador made a curt bow, and left the room.

Chapter XIII

If Anne had been twice stunned that afternoon, the first time at seeing her employer changed from his usual self into a laughing stranger, and then, as quickly, back again, she was destined to be still more amazed by the events of the next few days. Nicole could offer no explanation for her guardian's transformation, but with a child's acceptance, would not question it either. It seemed to her only that Sir Basil had come into his true self, had found the good nature which, before, had been hidden by some freak of nature or accident. She was, therefore, perplexed by her governess's questions more than by the change itself.

"Why, I suppose he has not been feeling well," she offered, with a shrug of her shoulders. "In any case, I like him much better now—and I believe he likes me a little bit, too! We did have such a lovely time, Miss Calder—if only you had been with us!"

Anne wished she had been there even more than her pupil, if only to see what had set off his good humour, for she would not believe it had happened of itself. As to the succeeding transformation, she was perfectly sure that she knew what had caused *that*—the sight of her had obviously affected him very badly. What else could explain his instantaneous change of mood, the moment he had seen her? If this was too unlikely an explanation, considering that she could not mean anything to him, she nevertheless managed to explain it to herself: "It is perfectly clear: Sir Basil detests women, and even I, a lowly governess, must represent to him the idiocy of my sex."

The explanation would not satisfy her completely, however.

Anne was too keen to judge of human nature, for so she had always believed, to think that so profound a metamorphosis could have been set off only by the sight of her. She would not give it any further thought, however: what had been once of great interest as the subject of a novel, could offer no further amusement now that she had given up the project. And well out of it I am, too, thought she. Sir Basil is beyond everything for changefulness and obscurity. Had I the time and the energy, I might devote myself to a lifetime study of his character and still remain as puzzled as I am now.

Indeed, Sir Basil was so unlike any gentleman that Anne had ever seen that he defied every preconception she had ever entertained about manhood. Even excepting his difference in station, wealth, sophistication, and education, she could not reconcile his strange ways with any idea she had ever had of human nature. When he ought to have been warm, he was cold, when another man might have been angry, perverse, or passionate, Sir Basil remained aloof and cool. Never mind: She would do her work, and have done. Only let some other theme present itself to her, and she would take up her pen again. *The Determined Bachelor* (for so she had already entitled the proposed novel) would never be written, at least by her. Let some more philosophical, some wiser and older writer undertake the chore, if there was such a creature upon the earth.

Thus Ann perceived her employer on that Sunday afternoon, and, had she been allowed the time or interest to think upon it again on Monday, she would certainly have felt the same. But Monday was taken up with so many preparations for the impending visit to Carlton House, which was to be on Tuesday, that she had not a moment for any other thought. Nicole must be clad and tutored, drilled in table etiquette, and etiquette before the Prince. She must be taught which fork to use, when and how to lift her cup, and what she might offer in response to His Highness's questions, should he address her directly. Lady Cardovan was of vast usefulness in all of this, and seemed so delighted by the whole process, taking such infinite pleasure in watching the little girl progress from ignorance to expertise, that she might have been going herself on a first visit to the Prince.

"Have you discovered who shall go to chaperone Nicole?" asked she of Anne whilst they were waiting for a servant to fetch a ribbon from the Countess's own dressing room.

"I can only assume that Sir Basil will go," replied Anne. "Nothing has been said to me to make me think otherwise."

"Lord! I wish I could be an invisible observer to see it!" laughed Her Ladyship, and Anne joined in her mirth.

"Why do not *you* go, Lady Cardovan? You have known the Prince longer than Sir Basil, and are certainly better fit to undertake the task than he."

"Oh, *do* come, Your Ladyship!" exclaimed Nicole, tugging at the lady's hand. "I should be so happy if you would—for I am sure I shall do something wrong, or say something amiss."

"Hush, child—there is nothing to be afraid of. I shall not go. I do not go about much any more. When someone wishes very much to see me, they come here."

"Even the Prince?" demanded Nicole, her eyes very wide.

"Even the Prince," responded Lady Cardovan with a nod. "He has not come very often, but he has come. I believe he likes to get away from his perpetual train of pomp from time to time, and pretend he is no different from the rest of us."

Anne smiled at hearing this. Yes, it must be true—how cumbersome it must be, sometimes, to be a monarch! And yet, she could not imagine a better chaperone for Nicole than Lady Cardovan. She dearly wished Her Ladyship could be persuaded to go, but no amount of coaxing or argument would make her change her mind. No: it was the place of Sir Basil, or Sir Basil's governess, to go. Lady Cardovan must be only a friend, and however dearly she loved the little girl, she would not usurp the proper duties of her guardian.

Anne saw the wisdom of this at last, and ceased to argue. Nicole, however, was determined, and much dismayed when Lady Cardovan gave her a final, and very firm, response. She had only recently commenced to feel at ease with Sir Basil, and may be excused for desiring a more trustworthy companion on her first visit to Carlton House. What if she should make some terrible blunder? Sir Basil, she was sure, would not excuse her so easily as Lady Cardovan or Miss Calder.

The matter was arranged in the end very differently from what anyone had envisioned. Nicole and her governess took their supper alone that evening in the schoolroom, as was their habit when Sir Basil dined away from home. With a great deal of coaxing, Nicole was persuaded at length to lie down in her bed, although she swore that she would not be able to sleep one wink all night from excitement. Anne, hoping to use her free time that evening to write a letter to Ben, went directly to her own bedchamber as soon as Nicole had been tucked in. She had only just commenced to write, however, when a knock came at the door. Thinking it was Nicole, incapable of sleep and desiring to be kept company, she rose from her chair to answer, arranging her features into a stern look. But the figure at the door belonged to a footman, who inquired very civilly if Miss Calder was too busy to speak to the Ambassador for a moment?

Amazed, Anne shook her head. A glance at the clock told her it was not yet ten o'clock—much earlier than Sir Basil was accustomed to return from an evening party.

"Sir Basil wished to say that he would not disturb you if you were occupied," declared the footman.

"No, I am perfectly at liberty to come," responded Anne, wondering what the matter could be. Seizing her shawl, she descended the stairs behind the footman, who, opening the door to the library, bowed and withdrew.

Sir Basil, still in his evening clothes, was standing before a wall of shelves filled with volumes. He did not turn around when Anne came in, but a slight movement of his head made her believe that he knew she was there. Uncertain what to do, she stood in the doorway and waited for him to notice her presence.

After a moment, Sir Basil spoke. His voice was meditative, as if he were only continuing a conversation he had been holding with himself silently.

"I have often thought," he murmured, "that if I had my life to live over again, I should have chosen to live among books rather than people."

Anne, at a loss for how to respond, said nothing. She knew not what was expected by the Ambassador, nor if he really desired a response. For a moment, she actually thought he had been speaking to himself, and feeling the embarrassment that one does experience upon stumbling upon a private conversation, had a sudden urge to turn and go, as quietly as she had come. But just then the Baronet spoke again.

"What do you think, Miss Calder? But, no: *you* do not have my difficulty. I suppose you cannot even comprehend what it is like to feel so much easier among ideas than human beings."

Now the Baronet turned and, with a quizzical smile, seemed for several moments to examine her countenance. Not knowing whether to smile or speak, and feeling uncertain of what she *could* say, even if she had any desire to do so,

Anne remained silent, only growing increasingly nervous beneath his gaze.

What did he mean? Was this the preamble to a dismissal? Had she angered him in some way which she could neither remember nor guess at? Sir Basil had already proved himself beyond her comprehension: and with every passing moment, Anne became less sure than ever of her convictions.

But if Sir Basil had some motive for this interview, he evidently did not mean to reveal it at once. Bidding her to take a chair, he remained himself upon his feet, first walking to the hearth, where he toyed for a moment with some little artifacts upon the mantel, and exclaimed:

"How I loathe rented houses! Everything in them is strange, yet oddly complete, as if some retinue of decorators and a model housekeeper had come in, simply in order to anticipate one's needs. Everything is in its place, down to the last gew-gaw. Yet nothing has any personal significance. What a mockery it makes of one!"

Hardly more sure of herself than she had been before, but sensing that she must say something, Anne murmured:

"You must be restless to be in Paris again, Sir. I can well imagine how you must miss the Embassy."

"Bah!" grunted the Baronet, setting down the miniature he had been examining with a thud. "I don't miss the Embassy one bit. It is only another temporary address, one of a long line I have occupied, Miss Calder. "I miss my *work*—it is abominable to be away. I am completely at a loss when I have nothing to occupy me."

"But surely you have a great deal to attend to here, Sir!" exclaimed Anne. I know that you are every morning with the Prince, and every afternoon at the Foreign Office."

"Where the entire scene consists of several fat old men, gossiping behind each other's backs. Don't look so shocked, my dear Miss Calder. Governments are very little different from other branches of human endeavour; they are no better than the men who make them up, and I have not found in the whole length of my life, above one or two men whom I should trust with the destiny of a village, much less of a nation."

"But the Prince, Sir—does not he regulate England's destiny?"

Now Sir Basil, who had wandered over to the bookshelves again and had been staring abstractedly at them, swung around with a brilliant, if sardonic smile:

"What innocence! The Prince! Miss Calder, do you know who has governed our destiny since the King succumbed to his—ah—malaise? A vain, fat, infantile peacock, who cares more for his cravats than for the whole human race put together. Excuse me. Try, if you will, to erase that from your memory."

Anne, her eyes as wide as her ears were stunned, mumbled, "I shall forget it, Sir Basil. Pray do not speak to me any more, for I am afraid I shall not be able to listen if you do."

Sir Basil's whole face had been frozen when he spoke, but now, watching the governess sitting in her chair, her hands pressed tightly together in her lap, her usually candid eyes large with shock and uncertainty, his own features relaxed into a smile.

"I beg your pardon, Miss Calder: I ought not to have put you in such an awkward position. You must realize that His Highness, is, to me, more than a mere sovereign—he is my employer, to whom I must justify myself every day, and upon whom I must depend to be infallible. When he is not, as most employers are not—" this with a rueful smile— "it affects not only my disposition, but in some cases, the whole population of England."

Anne, grateful for the intended, if not spoken, apology, smiled down at her hands.

"We are all of us fallible, Sir."

"Yes: but some of us ought not to be so. And when we are, we ought to be capable of accepting our errors. You yourself very justly criticized my shortcomings not long ago, and I have struggled to improve. But princes may not be so easily berated, nor are they inclined to accept advice so humbly."

Anne's smile broadened: She did not know whether this conversation was about Sir Basil or the Prince, but in either case, the word *humble* did not seem very appropriate. Sir Basil was watching her keenly.

"You think me disloyal? Or perhaps only arrogant? My effort was real, you know, even if it was not as effective as you might have wished."

"Neither, Sir—I think you neither arrogant nor disloyal. As to the Prince, I cannot say, nor could have any way of understanding your feelings. As to *you*, Sir——"

"Ah!"

"As to you, sir," continued Anne, firmly, "I would have spoken of my own accord, had I not supposed you would

116

think I was rude in doing so. It is not my place to criticize you, Sir. I only meant to speak on my pupil's behalf. And you have done much more than I asked."

Sir Basil looked pleased, almost threatened to break into a smile, but seeming to remember himself, replied formally:

"Thank you, Miss Calder. It is not such a frightening task as I thought it might be."

Now it was Anne's turn to wish to grin, and to suppress the urge.

"Children *can* be rather frightening, Sir. They always speak their minds, which is an addiction grown-ups seem to be rid of."

"*Some* grown-ups, Miss Calder."

"If you mean that I spoke out of turn, Sir Basil, I am heartily sorry for it, and should be *more* sorry still if it had been to no avail. But Nicole has improved so much since you have taken the trouble to be affectionate with her, that I can only be glad I spoke out of turn, no matter how angry it made you."

Sir Basil's expression, observed carefully by Anne, gave no indication of his feelings. He said nothing for a moment, and then, taking a chair and very deliberately turning it a little toward the young woman's, sat down.

"It did not make me angry, Miss Calder. "I very seldom lose my temper."

The Baronet's fingers drummed upon the arm of his chair. *Here is the infallible ambassador again*, thought Anne, rather sorry that the moment of honesty had passed.

"I apologize, Sir. I did not mean to imply that you did."

"You may imply what you like."

Did a trace of a smile appear at the corners of his mouth? Anne thought for an instant that one had.

"I may imply nothing, Sir: I am a governess."

"Yes, that is true. You ought to say nothing, unless you are spoken to. Certainly not as regards anything save your pupil.'

Anne bowed her head. She felt a flush creep up her cheeks, whether of mortification or anger, or a combination of both, it was impossible to tell.

"I hope you will forgive me, Sir. In the future I shall confine myself to that subject. I hope I have learned my lesson."

"I hope, indeed, that you have not!"

Anne looked up, astonished. Sir Basil looked grave.

"Sir?"

He did not meet her eyes when he spoke, but stared off into the air.

"I hope you have not learned your lesson. However unbecoming such lectures may be in a governess, *I* find them quite refreshing. I am not used to governesses, Miss Calder—and have no prejudice in favour of silent ones. I do, however, have a strong prejudice against dishonesty. I see it about me everywhere—particularly, if you will excuse me, in members of your sex. But even men are not exempt from that great weakness."

"Even men, Sir?"

Sir Basil did not appear to notice the slight inflection of sarcasm.

"Yes: it is a huge disappointment to me, to find that so many of my colleagues are more bent upon being thought well of than they are upon speaking the truth. Do you think me foolish? I ought to have grown used, after all these years, to the vanity of mankind."

Anne could not help smiling. Here was a view of the Baronet she had never glimpsed, or perhaps she had only failed to observe. The man who sat before her now, staring pensively off into space with a wry smile, was another being altogether from the one she had been growing used to.

"No, Sir," she declared earnestly, "I do not think you foolish at all. *Some* people may think it is wise to be untruthful. I do not, nor could I condemn anyone for feeling as you do."

Sir Basil turned toward her slowly, with the first really ingenuous smile he had ever bestowed upon her. There was nothing of irony in it, nor of formality. It was the smile, interested and a little eager, of a friend.

"I hoped you would say so!"

Now Anne smiled, and looked down into her lap. Something prevented her from meeting those eyes after that first, brief contact. She coughed, and there followed an awkward silence. Anne continued staring into her lap, and after a moment, Sir Basil took his eyes away from her and the old formality came back into his voice.

"I suppose you think it very odd that I should speak to you like this, Miss Calder."

Anne did not know what to say, and said nothing. Evidently interpreting her silence as a reproof, Sir Basil went on:

"I am aware of how odd you must think me."

"I do not think you odd, Sir Basil."

It was evident, however, from the Baronet's expression,

that he regretted having spoken so openly. In truth, he did not know what had made him do so. He had been irritable and impatient since coming back to London, and his own behaviour in the last days had amazed himself more than anyone. Lady Cardovan had remarked it upon two separate occasions, and he had dismissed the charge. But what in the name of heaven had come over him? This evening, for instance, he had gone straight from the Foreign Office to the Duchess of Lisleford's, where a party of pompous fools had been gathered together. He had been instantly attacked for interfering with the good of the nation by endeavouring to stop the French slave trade, an action which had been introduced by the English some years before. Sir Basil was too seasoned a diplomat to mind the ranting of boors, and on any other evening, he would have smiled calmly and ignored them. But this evening he had done what he prided himself upon never doing: He had lost his temper, and, rising in the midst of dinner, had made his excuses and left the party. And now, here he was baring his breast to a young woman he had known for scarcely a fortnight, and a governess besides. What could Miss Calder know or care about his troubles? What on earth had possessed him to send for her in the first place? He remembered having some vague idea of inquiring into his ward's progress. He was aware that even that had been simply an excuse to seek Miss Calder's approval of his conduct with the child. Bah! What an idiot he must seem to her! And she was a most appealing young woman—irritatingly argumentative, to be sure, but refreshingly devoid of any ulterior motives, a thing with which every *other* female upon earth seemed heavily encumbered. Perhaps that was why he enjoyed her company. In truth, it was not nearly so bad as he had envisioned to have a female in the house. He had come rather to look forward to his evenings with Miss Calder and the child. The afternoon, when he and Nicole had come from church and gone off on that spontaneous tour of the city, he had been more light-hearted than he remembered feeling since his own youth. It had even crossed his mind that fatherhood was not such an awful state as it had always struck him, but rather a reincarnation of sorts. A great many things were beginning to make sense to him which had always been mysteries before. Perhaps Diana had been right: clever woman! And he supposed she was delighted at seeing him so knocked about now, after teasing him so cruelly about his self-complacency. Miss Calder, however, need not be burdened with any of this. He might at least spare *her* the embarrassment of his own uncertainties.

Rising from his chair abruptly, the Baronet walked to the fireplace again—he was devilish restless.

"You need not say so, Miss Calder. In truth, I do not know *myself*, of late. I suppose it is a great shock to find myself suddenly responsible for the welfare of another human being. You must forgive my behaving so strangely. And please excuse me for burdening you with my troubles."

"There is nothing to forgive, Sir! On the contrary, I am flattered that you should wish to speak to me."

Sir Basil grunted, and said nothing.

"All the same—it is not really fair to you. And besides, I did not call for you in order to bemoan the state of our government. In point of fact—" Sir Basil had luckily been rescued by an inspiration—"in point of fact, I sent for you to ask a favour."

"Yes, Sir Basil?"

"I had hoped—ah—rather, I have just discovered that I shall not be at liberty to take Nicole to Carlton House tomorrow."

"Oh, dear, sir! She shall be terribly disappointed! Still, I suppose, she will get over it. . . ."

"Oh, I had not meant to disappoint her! I only hoped that *you* might take my place."

"Take your place, Sir!"

"It will not be too inconvenient?" Sir Basil glanced at her nervously.

"Heavens, no! But, Sir Basil, would that be correct? Ought not Lady Cardovan to go?"

Lady Cardovan! Why, how stupid he had been—but another second reminded him that Diana never went abroad, and detested Carlton House in any case.

"No, no—she won't go, either. And I have an urgent matter to attend to with the French Ambassador. So Nicole's only hope must be you, Miss Calder. It shan't be too awful: although I have heard these affairs are enjoyed more by His Highness than anyone else. Still, Nicole shall have the benefit of a glimpse of the Prince, and even *you* ought to approve of that."

"I think," said Anne, endeavouring to hide her smile, "that I shall bear up perfectly well. And it *is* a sort of educational experience, is it not?"

"Absolutely! Well put, Miss Calder! And I shall expect a detailed report from you upon the child's conduct."

"I think you are more likely to get a detailed report of the Prince's conduct from the child, Sir Basil."

The Baronet smiled.

"Then so be it, Miss Calder."

Chapter XIV

The visit to Carlton House elicted so many different reports, in fact, and from so many different sources, that it was for some weeks the subject of debate in drawing rooms from Devonshire to London. Let us simply record now, however, that so many of the Prince's guests were destined in the space of three hours to be stunned, enlightened, and disappointed by the events of the afternoon, that it may in truth be said to have changed the courses of several lives. The Prince himself was moved to remark to Lady Jersey at the end of the festivities that Sir Basil Ives' ward was the belle of the whole party.

"I never saw a more dazzling child in all my life. Do you know what she asked of me? She inquired whether my papa was feeling better! Heh, heh! You never saw so many faces fall at once!

"*I* thought she was a horrid little thing," snapped Lady Jersey. "She ought to be taught to hold her tongue. Fancy being allowed to say anything of the kind!"

"I make no doubt she did not ask permission first, my dear," responded His Highness. "That is what I adore about children. They say everything they oughtn't, and never anything they ought. It is mightily refreshing."

Lady Jersey was in a shrewish mood, and having been reminded often enough herself to hold her tongue, would not deign to reply. She did, however, impart a piece of gossip she had heard which made the Prince's eyes grow round, and brought forth a chortle.

"Ha! Ha! Sir Basil Ives! I don't believe you!"

Lady Jersey smirked and said that it was true.

"Ha! Ha! I never would have dreamt it of him! I thought he hated women, ha ha!"

"Still waters, don't you know," murmured Lady Jersey, pursing her lips.

"Lady Cardovan, I suppose?"

My Lady Jersey would not venture this far out loud, although she was secretly convinced of it. She liked to keep up her own appearance of being above such things, and only sniffed.

"Well, Your Highness—I suppose she is not *quite* so saintly as she would have us believe."

"Well, well! One never knows, does one?"

And the Prince glanced grinning at his mistress, who certainly looked like the most virtuous woman in England.

Nicole herself gave a very different account to her guardian, when he inquired into the events of the afternoon that same evening at supper. The little girl would seem to have aged almost overnight, and from the wide-eyed child who had been led trembling by the hand down the royal pathway to the royal teahouse, she had been transformed suddenly into a composed young woman, conscious of her social success, and full of new perceptions.

"How did you like the Prince, Nicole?" asked Sir Basil, as soon as they were seated at the dinner table.

Nicole, extraordinarily, paused for a moment to arrange her ideas.

"He was very nice," she said finally.

One eyebrow shot up. "Very nice, eh? I dare say, yes."

"But I did not know he was so fat," added the child. "Anyhow, he didn't look anything like what I expected."

"No, how so?"

"He was not nearly so handsome as I thought he would be. I mean, he did not look at all like a prince, except that he was all dressed up in crimson and gold. But he did not wear a crown!"

"I expect he saves it for state occasions," smiled Sir Basil. "But what did he say to you?"

"He pinched my cheek very hard, and would not let go for ever so long. I think he must have forgotten about it, for he began talking to his friend, and I thought he would never stop."

"Princes are sometimes forgetful," ventured the Baronet. "Who was his friend?"

123

Miss Calder intervened, "My Lady Jersey was with him, Sir."

"And what did you think of her, Nicole?"

The child's brow puckered up. "She was exceedingly ugly, Uncle Basil. She looked just like a prune—and she was not nearly so nice as the Prince. When I asked if the King was feeling better, she gave me a great scowl and walked away."

Sir Basil's features lit up with delight.

"You asked if the King was feeling better?"

Anne coughed and stared at her hands.

"Is this true, Miss Calder?"

"I'm afraid so, Sir."

"And what did he reply?"

"He said it was kind of me to ask, but alas his papa was not much improved. And when I inquired if he would come to have tea with us, everyone tittered."

"And was that the extent of your conversation?"

Nicole thought a moment, and replied:

"No, Uncle Basil. After we all had our tea, and before the games commenced, he called me over to his side and made me sit upon his lap."

"Fortunate young woman!" breathed Sir Basil. "And what did he say then?"

"He wished to know where you had found me, and where he could get a daughter just like me! It was very odd, Sir— for his own daughter was there, and he did not speak to *her* half so much as to me. And then he wished to know if I had any idea of when you were going back to Paris, and if I would come to visit him from time to time."

"And what did you say then?"

"That I thought we were going to Paris after Michaelmas—I thought so, at any rate, for you mentioned it the other day—and that I would be glad to visit him. Actually," added the child in a confidential tone, "I do not really want to, but I thought it would be rude to say so."

"And very right, too." Sir Basil congratulated her. "You are a most dreadfully politic young lady, Nicole. I fear you shall usurp my own post, if I do not have a care. But are you sure you had rather not stay at Carlton House than go with me to Paris?"

Nicole looked very dismayed. "If you would like me to," she murmured.

"Dear me, no! I only thought a mere embassy would be dreadfully dull after a palace. To be frank, I did not at first

124

think the Embassy could hold both of us—but now I am so completely of another mind that I would dread going back without you."

Nicole, misinterpreting his remark, exclaimed eagerly:

"Oh, if there is not enough room for me, Uncle Basil, I shall be quite happy to sleep in the hall. I don't mind where I sleep, actually. Only *do* please let Miss Calder come! She may have *my* bed, and I shall just curl up in a chair, or whatever is easiest."

Now Anne could not control her mirth. A small gurgle escaped her lips, pressed tightly together for some few minutes.

"I do not think Sir Basil was referring to a shortage of bedchambers, Nicole."

"Miss Calder is quite right," interjected the Baronet with a solemn look. "There is space enough for both of you, that is—" with an inquiring glance at Anne "—if Miss Calder will consent to come."

"Oh, *do* come, Miss Calder!"

And Miss Calder, more pleased than she would admit by the enthusiasm of the child and the civility of the gentleman, admitted that she could hardly refuse such an invitation.

Anne's own impressions of the Prince, and of Carlton House, went something further than her pupil's, and as these were recorded with great faithfulness in her next letter to Ben, we shall simply set it down exactly as it was:

December 1, 1819

My dearest Ben:

I have been, since my last letter, to see the Prince. I can imagine what you must be thinking—"from governess to visits with royalty in one fell swoop!" But it was precisely my position which enabled me to go, and you must say so to my mother if she is still upset with me. You must omit telling her, however, that I had not time to have a new frock made up, and was at the mercy of my best resources to make my old gray silk as dashing as possible, with only the benefit of one or two ribbons and the cameo she gave me last year. She would never forgive me *that*: never mind that I had barely twelve hours' notice.

The occasion was a tea party, held on Tuesday at the Prince's teahouse, only for the benefit of children. I am told His Highness dotes upon little children, and having a passion for amusing himself on a not much more elevated level than that which appeals to little girls and boys, has made a regular thing of entertaining them. In truth, the whole event was vastly entertaining from my own standpoint: I doubt not but that I was much better diverted than Nicole, who was too awe-struck to be much amused.

We went in the best carriage, with Sir Basil's family arms emblazoned upon the doors, and were set down a little distance from the gatehouse (an edifice about three times the size of our own house). From there we proceeded on foot, more or less in a parade of children and their mama's, nurses, governesses, and friends, through a variety of exotic gardens and pathways, over a tiny Chinese lacquer bridge which led over a lily pond, and through a maze of waterfalls, pavilions, gazebos, and hothouses. Wandering unrestrained throughout was the largest collection of wildlife I have ever seen gathered in one place—species, in fact, which I have never glimpsed even in pictures, and which were said to have been brought from the far reaches of the earth. Birds, some of them as tall as men, waded in ponds and fed upon the branches of trees. It was uncommonly warm for the time of year, but on cold days, I was informed, the birds and other beasts are rounded up and put into buildings where they are kept warm by innumerable fireplaces—quite like people! There is even a whole staff of servants only to oversee their happiness, which made me think that some clever poor family might do better to masquerade as wild animals and appeal to the mercy of the Prince in *that* disguise than in their natural one.

At length we came to the teahouse, which is said to be a tiny replica of the Regent's pavilion at Brighton. The Prince is said to have a passion for oriental artifacts, which dominated the whole decor of the place. The walls were hung with Chinese tapestries, the floors covered entirely in the most splendid carpets I have ever glimpsed. The roof is even made up of minarets, as are said to crown the palaces of Turkey and India. Only these are so small—to suit the size of the whole edifice—that at first it looked quite like a toy house. In point of fact, everything is on just such a miniature scale, as if an entire palace had been cut down to suit the proportions of children. The dining table at which the little guests took their tea was long enough to seat seventy children, and yet of a smaller dimension than that which would suit grown-ups.

Their chairs were small and close to the ground, but ornamented in the most extravagant detail, with as much gold and silver as must have been used in the construction of the originals. A tiny music room, complete with a stage, is used for theatrical entertainments, and after tea was served we all sat down to watch a performer playing extraordinary tricks. He made a covey of doves appear from nowhere, much to my own and Nicole's delight, poured water out of the hat which had been upon his head, and tugged gently at his sleeve, out of which there proceeded to fall about a mile of silk handkerchiefs, all knotted together.

But the best performance of all came about half an hour after we had arrived. In the meantime, we had stood about haphazardly, talking amongst ourselves, and Nicole, who would not leave my side, had been inquiring every instant where His Highness was. Well, my dear Ben—he came at last, and in such procession as you cannot imagine. First a trumpet sounded, evidently to warn us to be silent, and about five minutes later there began to arrive a stream of secondary Personages. Princess Caroline, whom I had hoped to see, was said to be aguish and had stayed at Carlton House, but all of her ladies in waiting came. The Princess Lieven, whom I had met once before—the Russian Ambassador's wife, and a famous beauty—was with them. About fifty footmen in livery next appeared, and formed a double column between which the Prince's own retinue would pass. Meanwhile, another dozen footmen bade us form ourselves into a line, the children standing in front of their respective chaperones. Those who were familiar with the ritual commenced yawning and smiling between themselves—I soon saw why. But I was myself eager to catch every detail of the spectacle, as you can imagine, and Nicole was on tiptoes all the time.

Another trumpet sounded, and now the parade commenced in earnest. First came a servant in crimson livery, bearing a large golden chair—a sort of portable throne, I suppose, for the Prince would not sit down in the tiny chairs with which the rest of us were forced to struggle, and his weight is such that I have no doubt none would have supported him in any case. This was set down at one end of the hall in which we stood—a sort of vast entrance hall, but in miniature, the walls all lined in scarlet silk, save for some spaces which were covered with mirrors. Next came a retinue of nurses, the second major domo, and two surgeons, lest any of the guests should stuff themselves too thoroughly. Another trumpet sounded, and in waddled a tall, almost grotesquely fat man, attired in the trappings of the most extreme dandy imaginable. For an instant I did not know who it was, but as my companions began to sink into a communal curtsey right down to the floor, I was soon enlightened: Here was the Prince! As soon as I could lift my head, I managed to examine his features, which must have been exceeding handsome in his youth, but which have now been so swallowed up in folds of flesh that his face is more like a pillow than a set of features. His eyes are still very fine, however—dark and shining, with that sort of fierce, soft brilliance which is the first sign of a passionate disposition. The object of that passion, at least for the moment, followed a few steps behind. Lady Jersey is said to be a royal inamorata; a more unlikely mistress you cannot imagine. She is about five years older than the Regent himself, being somewhere between five-and-forty and fifty years of age, her eyes are cold and glaring, her lips thin and gray (to match the rest of her features), and her figure is as skinny as a stick. She has, moreover, the reputation of fierce religiosity, which would certainly make my father laugh, as she is precisely that combination of outward virtue and actual immorality which seems to cause him so much delight, and which he is forever holding up to us, in his more playful moments, as the model for a politic life. From what I have gleaned of the Prince's history, from gossip and the cartoonists, her ladyship is only the fourth or fifth in a long line of mistresses. There was, of course, Mrs. Fitzherbert, whom many believe to be his real wife, but she has retired to the country and sees no one since she was replaced in the Prince's affections. Lady Jersey seems to be a kind of penance for the rest: No doubt she is a very awful one, for I cannot imagine looking to that pair of glaring, scowling eyes for affection or amiable companionship. But enough: I promise I should not philosophize, but faithfully recount to you the high points of my life.

His Highness commenced to make his way down the line of children, pinching a cheek here, and saying a word there, with Lady Jersey following close behind, scowling as hard as His Highness smiled. To the women he said hardly a word, for he seemed to think this the children's party, as indeed it was. I did not expect him to notice *me*, and was a little amazed when he inquired my name and spoke several civil phrases. The others took it very hard, for I was a mere governess whilst they were by and large mothers, aunts, or sisters, and most of them countesses at the least. Miss Newsome, in particular, scowled very hard at me—she is Lady Hargate's younger sister, and had come, as I believe, only on purpose to catch a glimpse of Sir Basil, for she could not have taken less interest in her little niece and nephews. She was most seriously annoyed when she saw *me* in his stead, and asked rather rudely where "His Excellency" was, and why he had not come.

But it was instantly evident that the Prince took a great fancy to my pupil above every other child, and that made me like him at once, for I have developed such an affection for that little girl that I am become quite as horribly prejudiced in her favour as any mama you ever saw. Having uttered barely one or two phrases to each of the others, His Highness paused before Nicole and gazed at her raptly. Then, taking her little cheek between his great fat beringed fingers, he turned away for nearly five minutes to praise her to my Lady Jersey, who only scowled, and looked as if she could not have disagreed more heartily with his remarks, though curtseying and smirking as much as possible. Nicole bore up very bravely through all of this, and when the Prince turned back, gave hardly any sign that she was in pain—which indeed she must have been. He bestowed upon her several compliments and, chucking her beneath the chin, declared she was the prettiest child in the whole place and that he wished his own daughter was as bright and comely. This I thought in rather bad taste, as the Princess (who does indeed a little resemble a young cow) was standing by all the while, looking as if she would have cut off her right hand to receive so much solicitude from her papa.

When the Prince had passed quite down the line, he moved off to the next room, where the banquet table was ready set, in solid gold plate! His chair had been set up in the middle, and there he ensconced himself, smiling, and waving for us all to take our places. I did not know which way to look at first, for there seemed no accomodation for a governess. When I saw my own charge settled—the children were all seated at one side, and their elders at the other—I whispered to a footman, who stared back as if he had not heard. But the Princess Lieven took me by the arm, for which I was most grateful, and propeled me toward a chair next to her own. I found myself between *that* elegant lady and Miss Newsome, who is certainly the most vulgar creature I ever knew. Having made one brief inquiry into Sir Basil's health, she turned away and did not address another remark to me all the while. I was saved from boredom, however, by the Princess. *She* could not say enough, whether in praise of Nicole, or my employer, or even of myself, questioning me closely in the most extraordinary fashion. I did not comprehend at first what she wished to know, but very soon guessed. I would not whisper a hint of it to any other living soul, my dear Ben, but to you I must confide everything. Can you imagine? I am perfectly certain she believes that Nicole is the natural daughter of Sir Basil. That implication—never voiced, of course—shocked me so much, and certainly enraged my loyalty to Nicole, if not to her guardian, that I scarely knew where to look. But when I had gleaned a further imputation—oh! so subtly made—that Lady Cardovan was the mother, I nearly got up from my place and ran out of the room upon the spot. How was I to reply? The idea is too ludicrous to even consider, never mind contradict. And yet here was this gentlewoman—a lady in every respect, my superior in age, station, and elegance—querying me in the most outrageous manner. I kept my seat, endeavoured to change the subject, and finally managed to subdue my outrage. At the time it was extreme, as you must imagine. But in the last day and a half, I have had time to think upon it more soberly.

Sir Basil detests women, which is universally known, and yet he nearly idolizes the great Lady C. They are such intimate friends that she alone advises him upon every subject. It was she, as you remember, who first engaged me for this post, she who governs Nicole's education more even than Sir Basil or myself, she who dresses, reprimands, and serves generally as benevolent godmother to the child. Her affection for Nicole, once more, is so extreme—far surpassing the natural warmth of a woman for a little girl who is not her own—that I am torn equally between outrage and credulity, at the Princess's implications. Most certainly I am intrigued, as you must guess. And infinitely sorry for the child, should any of this ever come to light, moreso even than for Lady Cardovan, who is the finest creature I ever met. I cannot believe it, and yet my incredulity strikes me from time to time as founded solely upon wishful thinking. All the facts point to the truth of the Princess's suspicions, and yet in my heart I cannot believe it.

What perplexes me most, as you must imagine, is not whether or not the suspicion is true, but how to deal with the rumour, should it sooner or later come to light. Lady C. must never hear of it, and yet would not it be preferable if she did, than to hear of it through some less sympathetic channel than myself? I cringe to think what might be her reaction to such a piece of news—true or false; and I would not for all the world be the bearer of it. Sir Basil ought to know, however, if only to protect his own and the lady's honour. So far I believe I am the only one who guesses, for I am sure the Princess Lieven was only endeavouring to get some proof from me the other day—with which attempt you can be sure I would not help. I only pray that before I had guessed what she was about, I did not inadvertently say anything to keep her fire ablaze, or make it grow. She had so ingratiating a manner that I could not help but speak freely to her, though saying nothing, if I recollect aright, which could by any stretch of the imagination have increased her suspicions. From having admired her as the most elegant woman I ever saw, I am now reduced to an extreme horror at her mind. Who would have thought there would be so much evil and conniving within that beautiful head?

I fear my letter must be as confused as my brain at this moment. Every day has brought such violent changes in my attitudes, every moment so increased my humility before the maze of human conduct, that whatever I once had of certainty, right-thinking, or clear-headedness is utterly lost. When I recollect the complacency with which I arrived in London only a fortnight ago, I can only smile. Sir Basil's character has so much defeated me that I am incapable of attempting a satire of him. My few inadequate pages were torn up long ago, and even my former confidence in the handling of children is gone up in smoke. I hope you will not be very ashamed of your poor Anne when she creeps home, defeated and rebuffed by her own illusions of grandeur!

My manuscript appears tomorrow in the form of a book. I am to collect two volumes from the printing house in the morning, and shall send you one direct. Only wish me success, and know that if it comes to pass, it will be our joint effort that made it so.

I remain your faithful, and much humbled,

Anne

Chapter XV

This was the content of Anne's letter, but not of her heart. It was the truth, but not all of it, for however much she trusted her brother, who was her dearest friend as well as closest ally, she did not trust her heart and all the conflicting emotions which were waging war within her. She did not, for instance, mention the new sensations which had begun to plague her whenever she was in the Ambassador's presence, for she was not herself sure of what they meant, but neither could she laugh them away with the old satiric mirth which had protected her from any vulnerability toward the male sex in the whole course of her life. Neither reason nor understanding served to make them comprehensible, for in many ways Sir Basil still seemed to her the very antithesis of what an amiable man ought to be.

But amiability, as any woman will attest, is not always the first requisite of a tender sentiment, and very often it is the exact opposite quality which first excites those instincts capable of making the feminine heart leap up. As to that, in fact, Sir Basil had already upset her first prejudice against him, which had been founded, if the truth must be known, as much upon her own vision as upon what that vision saw. He had proved himself, if not exactly disposed to warmth, at least less icy than she had first thought, and there had been moments, sometimes no more than flashes, when she thought she had detected something more. In any case, he was more in the way of a man than she had ever had to deal with: more experienced, more seasoned, more intelligent, and certainly more handsome. So many commendable qualities are seldom met with by a female without some slight emotion, and Anne, for all her stubborn intractability, was no exception. But the quality which had first touched her, had been his awkwardness in the face of his new responsibilities. That such a man, a man used to dealing with great issues without a flicker of self-doubt, should have been brought up short before the idea of fatherhood, had amused her at first, and had gradually made him what nothing else could have done in her eyes—human. From there it was a short step to liking, and for all her determination to the contrary, she had found herself touched, moved, and flattered by the humility with which he had invoked her approval that night before the visit to Carlton House. Since then, there had been more to make her stop and think, more even than the issue of Nicole's parentage, which had certainly done much to sober her.

The very night of the visit to the Prince, Sir Basil had again requested her to stay with him after the child had been put to bed, and this time his conduct had been such that she could not help liking him. The suspicion in her heart, founded upon the Princess Lieven's peculiar conversation that afternoon, however, had ruined her enjoyment of the interview, which ought to have been the cause of some elation. But all Sir Basil's geniality toward herself, all his interest in her opinions and invitations to express her ideas, had been marred by the confusion in her heart.

Sir Basil seemed to have no point in requesting the interview, and commenced it by excusing himself.

"I hope I am not keeping you from some more enjoyable occupation," said he in a rather muffled tone as soon as they had been served their coffee.

"Oh, no!" responded Anne, perhaps too quickly

"Are you sure? You need not stand upon ceremony, you know."

"I am perfectly sure, Sir Basil," replied Anne, smiling now. "I was only going to read a book. But I am so much stimulated by the day's events that I doubt I should be capable of any concentration."

"Ah! Did you enjoy yourself? I hope it was not too dull."

"Dull! No, nothing like it! I believe I was more amused than Nicole."

Astonishingly, Sir Basil put back his head and laughed.

"Sir?" inquired Anne.

"I was just thinking of what the others must have thought when she asked if the King was better."

Anne smiled uncertainly. "The Prince did not take any offense. He looked rather more amused than angry. It was only the others——"

"Ha! I can imagine. I should have done a great deal to see Lady Jersey's face."

"It *was* rather comical, Sir."

Sir Basil smiled and turned about his coffee cup upon its saucer. There was a moment's pause.

"And what did you do, whilst the little ones stuffed their mouths?" he demanded in a moment.

"I was very well looked after by the Princess Lieven, Sir. She took me under her care during the whole of tea, and asked me a great many questions."

Anne glanced uncertainly up. Sir Basil, however, was still immersed in his coffee cup, and gave no sign of any keener attention than the outward response required. For an instant she was tempted to blurt out what she suspected, but a moment's thought made her keep her peace.

"A very beautiful woman, Livvy."

"Exceedingly beautiful, Sir. And exceedingly charming."

"Makes a profession of it. She has two or three children herself, but I cannot fathom where she finds the time to see them. She is so much in demand about Town, I hardly think she glimpses her own husband above once a week."

"She was most interested in Nicole."

"Was she? How kind of her." Sir Basil smiled ironically. "I did not know she was a lover of orphans."

Now Anne was sorely tempted to divulge the matter which had been uppermost in her mind all afternoon, but again, refrained. She satisfied herself by saying, instead, "Of *some* orphans, I suppose. She spoke in glowing terms of *you*, Sir."

"Did she?" The Baronet raised an eyebrow. "Well, well. That would not be the first time Livvy ever spoke *glowingly* of anyone."

Anne hesitated. "She spoke very highly of Lady Cardovan as well."

"Ah! Well, of course. Lady Cardovan is deserving of high praise from everyone."

"Indeed, Sir." Anne felt a sudden sinking sensation, the cause of which she could not fathom. "Lady Cardovan is the greatest lady I have ever met."

"You show very good taste, then, Miss Calder," replied Sir Basil with feeling. "She is the greatest lady *I* have ever met, as well. Had it not been for her—ah, well. . . ." The Baronet's voice trailed off.

Anne had leaned forward eagerly, ready to catch whatever Sir Basil, in his instant of ingenuous confidence, would tell her. But the instant passed, the Baronet's face mirrored a change of heart, and a moment later he had struck up the conversation again on quite a different note.

"So! Now you have seen the Prince. And what do you think of him?"

Anne, rather disappointed, replied that she had been amazed by him, but that "as to her reaction she could not tell on such short acquaintance."

Sir Basil laughed, a hearty, frank laugh which brought a smile to Anne's face as well.

"You are too reserved, Miss Calder. By Jove—I never thought I should say that to you! But you must feel under no obligation to dissimulate with me. Goodness knows, I have spoken freely enough to *you*. And now you must do me the honour of responding in kind."

"Sir?"

"Tell me, Miss Calder, under pain of dismissal, your true reaction to the Regent."

"That is very strict, Your Excellency. Am I under pain of dismissal to think poorly of him, or well?"

For a moment, their eyes met. There was an expression of astonishment in those of the Baronet, one of challenge in Anne's.

"The truth, Miss Calder, I demand the truth. I believe I may count upon *you* to be honest."

Anne smiled, a trifle ironically. "Well, I am glad of *that* at least, Sir. I thought him very fat, which was no surprise, and rather jolly, which *was*. I cannot be a judge of his rule, Sir— but as a most expansive and genial host, he outdoes every expectation."

Sir Basil's eyes narrowed as he continued to stare keenly at the governess, whose cheeks grew hot beneath their gaze. His words, spoken a moment later on an expulsion of breath, however, were hardly critical.

"A most remarkable young woman."

It was spoken like an appraisal more than a compliment, and Anne, bridling with the feeling that she was being remarked upon as if she were a child, or a horse, or absent from the room, cannot be much blamed for taking offense. She could not reply, and hardly knew where to look. Therefore, she kept her gaze fastened upon her hands. Sir Basil did not seem to mind.

135

"You have family in Devonshire, do you not?"

"Yes, Sir."

"And your father is a clergyman. No doubt it is owing to that that you seem incapable of dissimulation. And yet you have not a very high opinion of the clergy, as I recall."

"Only of those clergymen who have taken up their profession to satisfy their own pockets, or vanity, or because they suppose they shall not be required to make any exertion."

"And your father, I suppose, is not one of those?"

"No, Sir, he is not. My father has always exceeded what was required of him in every way."

"Certainly in the way of children," responded Sir Basil with a little smile. "You have eight brothers and sisters?"

Anne nodded.

"Five brothers and three sisters."

"Good God! And are they all like you?"

Now Anne could not suppress her smiles. "No—at least, that is what my mother tells me. I am the only undutiful one."

Anne would have been glad to leave off the conversation here, for having so recently been praised for her honesty, she thought she might very soon be forced to lie. But Sir Basil's curiosity had only been whetted, or so it would seem.

"Undutiful!" exclaimed he. "But are you not doing your duty *now?*"

"I am doing what I must do to keep myself," replied Anne carefully, silently offering up a prayer for mercy for any untruths she might utter.

"Ah! To keep yourself. Well, well. I suppose no living would suffice to keep nine children. Are your brothers employed?"

"I have a brother in the Navy, and another who is himself studying for the ministry. The youngest is still in school, and the eldest is unwell."

"I am sorry to hear that," said the Baronet with real kindness. "I know what havoc illness can cause in a family. My own mother was unwell during most of my childhood, until she died. I do not remember much about her, of course—for I was very young—but I recollect a perpetual gloom about the house, and my father was made miserable by her suffering."

Anne was grateful for his sympathy, for indeed, Ben's illness had been a great weight upon the family happiness for several years. They were forever living in hopes that some one of the doctors called in to see him would offer up some cure, but the disease was an obscure one, and no treatment seemed to avail.

"And your sisters? Are they all like you?"

Anne could not help smiling at the idea.

"Hardly, Sir!"

Again, those keen gray eyes peered at her, as if trying to see quite into her mind.

"No—no, I suppose they are not."

Sir Basil seemed at last to have satified himself upon every point of his governess's background and family. The conversation continued a little longer, having shifted to more general subjects, and after twenty minutes, Anne rose to leave. It seemed a suitable time to go, for they had done with their coffee and Sir Basil had drunk his glass of port. She did not rise willingly, however, for it had been among the most enjoyable half hours she had known in some time, and Sir Basil's look, as she did so, mirrored his own feelings of reluctance at seeing the interview ended.

If there was some resentment in her mind that night, however, that so congenial a friendship should have been struck up between people whose stations and lives prevented it ever being advanced, that resentment was only increased the following evening.

Lady Cardovan had come to dine, as she had promised to do for some time, breaking, as she said, her general rule of never dining abroad. She was as eager as Sir Basil to discover the events of the tea party at Carlton House, and once more Nicole and Anne recited them. But now the governess had more cause for restraint than in either of her previous recitations. The intervening night and day had seen her opinion changed a dozen times upon the subject of Nicole's parentage. The little girl, oblivious to the scrutiny she had been under during her morning's lessons—to find what the Princess Lieven had called "this striking familial resemblance"—had in her own way helped to increase Annie's suspicions, and with them her fears, uneasiness, and pity. In no way did she resemble, by any outward feature, either of the supposed parents. There was, perhaps, some trace of Sir Basil about the mouth, though the eyes, contrary to the Princess's assessment, were nothing like his. But the more Anne looked, with less of disinterest than she would admit to herself, the more she thought she could detect a something of Lady Cardovan in her. It was not so easy as the shape of the nose, the colour of flesh or hair; it amounted at the most to a certain quickness, an inner animation, and above all, a kind of inbred elegance of mind. That elegance could not be ascribed, Anne thought at first, to the heritage of a country solicitor. What was known of the child's background, once more, was so slight, amounting really only to what Nicole herself had been able to impart and the summary description offered by Lady Cardovan at that first interview. Was not it altogether likely, was not it, in fact, highly probable, that the offspring of such a forbidden alliance should have been hidden away in a remote part of Lincolnshire? She would have been found the most auspicious guardian—a distant cousin, unknown about the Capital, perhaps in need of money, and willing to exchange his service as a father, and his wife's as a mother, for the guarantee of a decent living. That the surrogate father should have turned out to be so open-hearted and kind a man, must have come as a blessed surprise.

What an ironic twist this new view put upon the subject of Sir Basil's charity in taking her in! All at once, Anne was forced to view the events of the last weeks in an altogether new light, and with that improved vision, how she smiled ruefully at her own innocence! To be sure, it explained everything. Sir Basil's first awkwardness with the child, his pretended indifference to her, Lady Cardovan's extraordinary kindness, her unwillingness to be seen with Nicole in public, and finally, that extreme change which came over Sir Basil on that fateful Sunday, when his open, easy manner with Nicole had changed abruptly into icy formality upon coming into the house again, and knowing himself observed. Imagine what he must have thought of *her* when she had dared to suggest he behave more kindly to the little girl! He must have seen then how well his scheme had worked, and perhaps at the same moment understood how he might use the governess to further the dissimulation. And with that thought, Anne could scarcely control her anger and hurt. Fancy thinking, as she had begun to do, that he really depended upon her advice and sought her approval! Far from it—he must every moment have been laughing inwardly at her, for being so close to the truth and never noticing it. Anne's rage was only heightened by the thought of her own weakness in having begun to really admire him. She would not for a moment admit there was anything more than that in her opinion of him.

The evening of Lady Cardovan's visit with them, then, was the cause for extreme anguish on the part of our heroine.

The greater the amusement of the others, the happier they seemed, the more they laughed, the more miserable she grew. Lady Cardovan positively glowed, and looked more beautiful than ever. Sir Basil was as charming as Anne had ever seen him, and Nicole, encouraged by these two, bloomed beneath their combined attentions. Only Anne, suffering in silence, would not take part in the general levity. She forced herself to respond when she was directly addressed, but more than that, she would not do. If anyone noticed her silence, it must have been of little interest; or else, it was only the expected manner of a governess in the company of her betters.

Dinner was over at last—for Anne it had seemed an interminable interlude between the partridge and the hot-house grapes—and at length everyone rose from the table. Sir Basil would not take his port alone, and invited them all into the drawing room that they might take their coffee together. Lady Cardovan excused herself to go upstairs and look at Nicole's bedchamber with the child. Anne contrived, in the general commotion, to slip away unnoticed.

"Why, what is the matter?" inquired Lady Diana of her as she was beginning to mount the stairs to her own apartment. "I hope you are not going away, Miss Calder?"

"I have a headache, your ladyship. I hope you will not mind if I do not come downstairs again."

Lady Cardovan looked concerned. "Of course not, my dear. Go and lie down. I shall send a poultice up to you."

"Oh, no! I am perfectly all right. I shall be very well if only I am able to lie down."

"I hope it is not a migraine, my dear. I have been cursed with them all my life. Run along, then, and let us know if you need anything."

So easily dismissed, Anne sought the solitude of her own chamber with a feeling of relief. But half an hour passed, and the sounds of laughter wafting up from the drawing room prevented her thinking of anything else. "What are they saying now?" she wondered, and thought, ironically, that she could not be much missed. Lady Cardovan and Sir Basil must welcome the opportunity to be alone with the child— their child. A sort of secret reunion of the family, prevented by circumstance and time from being reconciled for all these years. A little while later she heard the sound of footsteps on the stairs leading to Nicole's bedchamber, and presumed, from hearing the low voice of Lady Cardovan and the high-pitched one of Nicole, that the orphan was being put to bed at last by her own mother. A moment later the door closed again, retreating footsteps sounded down the stairs, and Anne knew that the lady and gentleman were closeted alone. How seldom they must have the opportunity to meet like this! The Princess Lieven had said to her, with that significant little smile which seemed to encompass the frailties and eccentricities of all mankind, "Ah! The wonderful Lady Cardovan. Sir Basil is devoted to her. You know, her own husband deserted her years ago. I wonder why she never has remarried? In England, of course, there is nothing to prevent it. You wonderful English! You have devised so many ways to make life more enjoyable! In Russia, there is no such liberty."

Anne could not bear to let her mind run on any further. She rose from her bed and very deliberately took out paper and writing instruments from her desk. She then sat down to compose the letter to Ben we have already seen, so different in tone and subject from the real burden in her heart and mind.

Chapter XVI

For a decade, Lady Cardovan's soirees had been a regular
tradition amongst the literati of the *ton*. What the Duchess of
Devonshire's Wednesday nights had done for the cream of
London Society, Diana Cardovan's Thursdays had done for
the intelligentsia of the Capital. Through the years the membership of her little club—for if it was not one in name, it
was more exclusive than any of the gaming establishments on
St. James's Street would ever be—had been narrowed down
by default as much as taste, to about two dozen of the finest
minds in England. Some of these were very prominent, some
known only in the spheres in which they moved. Fox had
come regularly until he died, and the Regent, when he was
fed up with being a Prince, had once or twice put in his head
to listen to what he called the "snobbish prattle of the
bookey-minded." There was George Gordon, Lord Byron and
Percy Bysshe Shelly, and the bastion of the Utilitarians,
Jeremy Bentham, and Walter Scott, when he could condescend to come out of hiding, and some, like the young Disraeli, who though he was barely nineteen and a Semite to
boot, amused Her Ladyship and was therefore suffered by
the others. There was, besides, a smattering of the nobility
who either cherished the idea of being thought fashionable
amongst this odd group, or had nothing better to do. The
evenings were as famous for those who would *not* come as
for those who would: Georgina Devonshire claimed she
would not set one of her dainty feet in the place, Wellington,
who might really have enjoyed it, disliked going anywhere he
was not the only star in the heavens. Still, the soirees survived
without them, and if Lady Cardovan had rather gained the

reputation of being eccentrically disposed, preferring the wit of journalists and poets to that of earls and dukes, she was rather held in awe by those who pretended to scorn her. Amongst these, it might as well be admitted, were the Princess Lieven and her neighbour (though hardly her intimate in any other matter), Lady Hargate.

Neither of these ladies would have been tempted to visit Grove House on a Thursday even if they had been amused by the idea, for that was the evening upon which the vast doors of Almack's regularly swung open to admit the less serious-minded members of the *ton*, where champagne was drunk by the gallon, and the conversation did not stray much beyond the personages within its own hallowed walls. Never before had either of these ladies been absent from the festivities. Imagine, therefore, if you will, the astonishment of Lady Cardovan upon seeing them, together with Miss Newsome and the Earl of Hargate, appear in her drawing room on the evening following her dinner with Sir Basil.

It was evident from the first that the little party had arrived at once, their carriages having swung into the drive at exactly the same moment and, despite the exertions of the Princess Lieven to make her coachman slow down, together they had arrived beneath the portico. They came in, therefore, as a little cluster, were announced all at once, and caused a communal eyebrow to be raised by the party already assembled about the room. For a moment there was absolute silence, so intense that Bentham's laugh, having caused him to choke upon his biscuit, sounded as loud as a thunderclap. No one knew what to say or do, for the appearance of these socially incandescent figures amongst this plainly clad and distinctly intellectual assemblage was about as amazing as the appearance of a flock of geese.

Lady Cardovan recovered almost instantly from shock, rose from the sofa she had been sharing with Bentham and a celebrated essayist, and moved toward them. There were expressions, as may be imagined, on either side of welcome and nervous pleasure. The Princess had come on purpose to see Sir Basil and the lady of the house, while Lady Hargate had engineered her own family's visit in order to further what she optimistically termed the "courtship" between the Ambassador and her sister. They discovered simultaneously, and at one glance, that Sir Basil was not present, and the fallen faces of Miss Newsome and Lady Hargate were sufficient to make their hostess suppress a smile.

The Princess Lieven, however, was only half as disappointed as they, for while she had *hoped* to find the Baronet, she could perfectly well content herself with Lady Cardovan. The Ambassador's absence, moreover, only served to add fuel to her fire, for did it now show that he was consciously avoiding such public meetings with his inamorata? The Princess was, besides, far more socially versatile than the other two ladies: She was on amiable terms with half the figures in the room, though she would not, of her own accord, have sought most of them out. Pressing her cheek against that of Lady Cardovan and murmuring some meaningless phrases about having wished for "eons" to see what all the fuss was about, she moved deftly in the direction of the incandescent Byron, who was listening to a criticism of *Childe Harolde* by Shelley and the young Disraeli.

The Hargates, however, and Miss Newsome were left at a loss. The Countess cursed herself inwardly for having failed to foresee this eventuality, and uttered with wide eyes her astonishment at not finding her brother-in-law in the company.

"Sensible fellow," muttered Lord Hargate, directing his attention toward a footman who was carrying around a tray of champagne goblets.

"I thought you said Sir Basil always came when he was in London," murmured Miss Newsome crossly to her sister.

"Hush, my dear. Well! What a charming assemblage, Lady Diana! I had no idea you drew such a crowd upon these evenings. I do not believe I have met a single one of them. Who is that gentleman over there?"

Lady Cardovan glanced in the direction intended and replied that "the gentleman" was Charles Newcastle, the famed cartoonist.

"Dear me! The one who does those shocking caricatures of His Highness? Well! I never supposed he was so well-looking!" Lady Hargate paused for a moment, glancing around the crowd, which had now resumed its various conversations.

"I always believed you had a great many politicians and people of that sort," continued she, as if she were referring to some sort of curious animal. "And writers—novelists and things."

"Well, there is Sir Walter Scott," offered Lady Cardovan softly, seeing that gentleman approaching them. "I wish we had persuaded Miss Austen to join us before she died."

"Speaking of Austen, my dear Diana," said the great man,

coming up beside her and glancing curiously at the other two, "I have just read the most extraordinary book. I could swear it was an early manuscript of hers. A most extraordinary novel, to be sure. I should like you to take a look at it. My publisher gave it to me the other day to look at. Said it was the young woman's first work, but I cannot believe it. It resembles so much in tone and animation the early novels of our Jane. I told him so at once, and wondered if it could not have been a younger sister, at the least. But he said, 'no, of course it couldn't be, he should know it anywhere.' Besides, the lady's credentials were all intact, though of course she would not publish it under her own name. The usual 'By a Lady' sort of thing. Absurd notion! Why should not women write under their proper names? It makes a mockery of the rest of us!"

Lady Cardovan glanced apologetically at the sisters, who had begun looking about them impatiently. "I should love to read it, Sir."

Pshaw! I can see you are only offering me a placebo. I shall interrogate you about it next we meet."

Lady Cardovan smiled at the little man, so great in his achievements, so short and squat in his physique, and with the face, as one wit had put it, of a plum pudding.

"I shall read it at once. As soon as I can acquire it. What is it called?"

"*A Country Parson*." Sir Walter coughed. "And I have brought you my own copy. But mind you, give it back. I warrant it shall stand amongst the finest of contemporary satires. Shan't take you long to read—not a lengthy piece of work. And fraught with humour. You'll enjoy it, my dear Diana, see if you do not. I mean to give it to the Prince. You know how he adored Miss Austen's books."

And the little man waddled off, leaving behind him a slim volume, and an astonished expression upon Miss Newsome's face.

"Was that Sir Walter Scott?" exclaimed she.

Lady Cardovan nodded.

"Why! He is so small and fat!"

"His mind, however, is very large," responded her hostess with a little smile, "and has no excess flesh."

Miss Newsome did not comprehend the jest, but she understood very well the tone. With a sniff, she excused herself and went to find the tea tray. Lady Hargate stayed behind a mo-

ment, endeavouring to make conversation. She had long held
Lady Cardovan in awe, though thinking her rather queer.

"I was so positive that Basil would be here! I am sure my
sister is heart-broken over missing him. They had the most
delightful conversation the other evening."

"Did they?" Lady Cardovan smiled politely. She had heard
a rather different report from the Baronet.

"Oh, Lord, yes! You would have thought they had been
lovers forever! Basil is so quaint, you know—pretends to
despise us all. But really, it is high time he married. In point
of fact," now the Countess lowered her voice to a conspir-
atorial tone, overjoyed to be in possession of knowledge superior to Lady Cardovan's, "in point of fact, he has confided
to me that he came home on purpose to find a wife!" Lady
Hargate watched this news be digested with delight. Evidently
Lady Cardovan, with all her airs, did not know *some* things!

"Did he indeed?"

"I should not repeat it, of course. It was told me in the
strictest confidence. But then, you are so intimate a friend of
his—quite one of the family, by now! Do you not think it delightful?"

"Perfectly delightful," echoed Lady Cardovan, wondering
if she could believe her ears. "Has he settled yet upon the object of his affections?"

Lady Hargate simpered. "Perhaps 'settled' is too strong a
word. And yet I might just venture to hint that I have my
suspicions. Would not Henrietta make a delightful ambassadress?"

Here was a hint too clear to be missed. Lady Cardovan
followed her companion's gaze, which had shifted to that part
of the drawing room where the tea tray was set up. The fortunate Miss Newsome, apparently unaware of her imminent
happiness, was sulking in a corner by herself, ignoring the attempts of the young Mr. Disraeli to draw her into conversation. Lady Cardovan studied her for a moment, and then
turned back with a brilliant smile to her companion.

"Quite a charming young ambassadress," affirmed she.

"Lord! I can scarcely wait! It shall be so diverting! To
have two brothers married to two sisters! And, of course, we
shall all go to visit in Paris regularly. Henrietta and I have already settled upon *that*."

"How amusing it shall be!"

"Oh certainly! As amusing as anything upon earth! Dear

me, and I had just begun to fret from boredom. Really, there is nothing to equal this Town for dullness! Ah, well, all that shall be over soon!"

"Indeed it shall. Soon you shall be crossing the Channel as often as you are used to traversing Bond Street. And when shall we expect the happy occasion to take place?"

Now Lady Hargate was something at a loss. She had a moment of panic, thinking that perhaps she had let the cat out of the bag too soon. But as easily as Lady Hargate could find a reason to bemoan her unhappy lot, so could she find an excuse for her conduct.

"Of course it is not absolutely settled," said she primly. "But you shall be the first to hear, I am sure!"

"Thank you very much." The irony of her hostess's smile must have escaped Lady Hargate, for she only laughed and exclaimed, "Think nothing of it! I know Basil regards you as quite a sister—an elder sister, of course."

Lady Cardovan smiled again.

"Well—may I be the first to wish you joy? A secret joy for the moment, of course."

"Hah, hah! To be sure! A secret joy!"

If Lady Cardovan had been taken aback by this interview, she was soon to be astounded even more. Not long after Lady Hargate had gone off to spend the remainder of her visit whispering in a corner with her sister and scowling at Lord Hargate's attempts to drink the entire contents of their hostess's wine cellar, the Princess Lieven approached.

"*Ma chère Diana*," exclaimed she, upon finding the Countess alone at last. "I never was more diverted in all my life! *Ces gens sont si amusants!* It is really the most delightful gathering I have attended in an age! But, *chérie*, why are you looking so amused?"

Lady Cardovan smiled up at the small, dark Princess from her place on a sofa.

"Oh—I have just heard the most amusing thing," said she.

"*Vraiment*?" The Princess ensconsed herself cozily on the sofa beside her hostess. "Then recount it to me, please! There is nothing I so love as an amusing story!"

"I am afraid I cannot, Livvy. It was told me in the strictest confidence."

Princess Lieven looked crestfallen, and then petulant.

"Really, you English are so secretive! I never could comprehend it!"

"I should love to tell you, Livvy—for I believe you should think it as amusing as I do. Well, then—what do you think? I have just been informed that Basil means to marry Miss Newsome!"

"Miss Newsome!" The Princess looked horrified, "The ugly Miss Newsome? But, *chérie*, how can this be? I do not believe it! I won't believe it!" And then, with a sly glance, she murmured, "*Ma pauvre chérie!*"

"It is the most comical thing I have heard in an age," continued Lady Cardovan, unaware of her companion's pitying glance. "Imagine Basil marrying anyone, let alone Henrietta Newsome!"

"It must be a shock," murmured the Princess softly.

"A shock! Why, it is absurd. Come, Livvy—don't tell me you believe it!"

The Princess nodded slowly. "With difficulty, but yes—one never knows about these determined bachelors. Anastasy was the same. Imagine, he was almost forty when I married him! They go along, hating every female they meet, and then one day—poof!—they are smitten with love!"

"But Miss *Newsome*? My dear Livvy—I have known Basil for a great while. I cannot fathom his marrying anyone who prefers horses to conversation!"

"Yes, yes—it is the attraction of opposites. Anastasy and I have hardly anything in common. He loves to play his little political games, and *I* love to dance! And yet—we are so much in love."

Lady Cardovan strongly doubted that. At the moment, it was common knowledge that the Princess was "dancing" with the Duke of Clarence. Still, she was a charming woman, and witty to boot. Lady Diana dearly loved to hear her speak, with that small, low, chirping accent that was more like a bird than a woman.

"Do you really think so?"

"*Ah! Mais oui!*" The Princess raised her tiny hands, sparkling with jewels. "*Absolument!* Why, the other night, they could hardly take their eyes away from each other."

Lady Cardovan could scarcely believe her ears. "The other night?"

"At Lady Hargate's," explained the Princess. "They seemed to like each other very well. To be frank, I could not believe it myself—she is so like a horse, you know—so *beeg!* But, one never can tell about what gentlemen like!"

"How odd! Basil himself told me all about it! But he certainly has not hinted anything of the kind!"

"But of course, my dear, Diana," murmured the Princess softly, touching her hand, "he would not. He is far too much the *gentilhomme*. And after all—but! May I be perfectly frank?"

Lady Cardovan nodded, more bewildered every moment. Not the least cause of that bewilderment was to hear Livvy wishing to be "frank"—a quality she had in very short quantity, for all her other charms.

"You must understand, my poor Diana, that, whatever he feels for you, he must think of the child as well now. Such a delightful little girl! And really, she must have a mother. Even if not her *real* mother—" with a significant smile— "still, a mother. I believe Basil understands his duty perfectly. And you, my dear lady, must endeavour to understand as well as you can. However difficult it may be for you."

The Princess paused, gazing sympathetically at her friend. Lady Cardovan did not meet her glance, but stared at her own hands with an ironic smile, saying nothing.

"*Ma pauvre chérie!*" breathed the Princess.

This was really too much for Lady Cardovan to bear. So much pity from so unlikely a source—and for so unlikely a cause—made her wonder for a moment if she had lost her mind. Could it be true? Basil had spoken to her in the most contemptuous terms of the young Miss Newsome. He had not even lavished upon her enough attention to be suspected of protesting too much—only a snort, a sardonic commentary about her sex in general and of the young lady in question in particular. Nothing could have struck her as more improbable than that a man so adamantly disposed to scorn the whole female gender should so suddenly have lost his heart to such an unlikely representative of it. She was insulted, and more— hurt—that he should have felt it necessary to lie to her. The Princess must have seen her expression, for she commenced again, in that same soft, twittering voice:

"I comprehend how you must feel, my friend. It is never a pleasant thing. And after so many years—Basil has always admired you so much."

"Really, Livvy!" exclaimed Lady Cardovan suddenly. "I cannot believe what you are saying to me!"

"It is so difficult to believe what one wishes to ignore," concurred the Princess, with a wise nod of her elegant little head. "And especially—the child, after all, must make it doubly hard on you."

Lady Cardovan only stared back, uncomprehending.

"Oh! Nicole! Why, she is better fit to be an ambassadress, at nine than Miss Newsome will ever be!"

"Yes, yes—of course you are prejudiced. How natural! And the thought of giving her up, just when you had begun to know her! I know how you have always longed for children, my good friend."

"Yes, it's true. Nicole is as dear to me as if——"

The Princess cut her off with a quick motion of her hand.

"Tell me nothing, Diana, I beg of you! It will be easier for you in the end. These things happen, but it is better not to dwell upon them too much. If only you had been free those many years ago—"

"I do not see what good it would have done."

"Oh! Do not dissimulate with me, I beg of you! Are not we *chères amies*? My dear Diana, you must not pretend to me that you have not tender feelings in your heart for our dear Basil. Had you been free, I have no doubt but things would have been much happier for you. *C'est vraiment tragique.*"

Lady Cardovan stared at her companion, incredulous. Could she believe her own ears? Good God!

"My dear Livvy," she inquired sharply, "what are you suggesting?"

"Why! It is common knowledge, is it not? Everyone knows that Basil has always been in love with you, and you with him. In truth, it is a great relief for me to find that you have not denied yourselves *all* of the pleasures of love."

"Are you suggesting . . . ! Good Lord, Livvy!" Lady Cardovan rose abruptly to her feet, her cheeks colouring profusely. "How dare you suggest that to me! And all the while, I supposed you understood me!"

And with these words, spoken with more passion than Lady Cardovan was accustomed to exhibiting, even under the most agonizing circumstances, she brushed by her friend and moved quickly off. The Princess watched her go with a sad little smile. "*Quelle horreur!*" thought she. "I will never understand these English! So much indignation over so little! Why, one would think it was a crime against nature! When, of course, it is precisely the opposite!"

But the Princess had at least found the final proof for her little puzzle, and that, if nothing else, made her rise a moment later with a gay little smile and require the exceedingly ugly, but rather sympathetic young man called Disraeli to summon her carriage.

Chapter XVII

The next morning, at ten o'clock sharp, Sir Basil Ives entered the drawing room of Grove House, that same drawing room which, the evening before, had been the scene of so much amazement on the part of the lady of the house. Sir Basil had long ago given up standing upon ceremony when he visited Lady Cardovan and therefore did not wait to be shown in, but only sent word to her that he had come, and let himself into the drawing room. He had done so often enough before, and accustomed as he was to her ways, did not show any surprise when she did not appear at once. Lady Diana always worked upon her books in the morning, and when she was interrupted in the midst of an idea, would not leave her writing table until it had been completed upon paper.

The Baronet, therefore, was perfectly prepared to wait, and occupied himself in the meantime by walking up and down the room, staring out at the gardens, and at last, having exhausted all the diversion of watching a cold rain fall upon the lawns which had been put to rest for the winter, sat down upon a small sofa near one of the fireplaces. Glancing down, he noticed a slim volume upon the rug, and thinking it had dropped from an incidental table, picked it up. A brief glance showed him the title—*A Country Parson*—and inscribed beneath, the legend, "A Satire, by a Lady."

It was unlike his friend to leave books about like that, for of all of Lady Cardovan's loves, literature was the greatest. She prized the contents of her library as dearly as she prized her friends—indeed a good deal more dearly, Sir Basil sometimes thought. He was not himself a great reader of novels; he had always claimed they were idle amusements for idle minds. His own time was ordinarily much too crammed full of more constructive work to allow him leisure to pursue the fanciful wanderings of imaginary people. However, having nothing much better to do whilst he waited, he commenced turning over the pages, more (as he assured himself) to find out what ladies did with their afternoons than from any interest of his own.

The first page made him laugh three times, which was a wonder, for Sir Basil was rarely made to laugh at all, save by some few extraordinary minds. The first chapter was soon finished, and had excited his amusement so much that he commenced the second. In truth, it was very astounding. Where he had expected to find the incoherent ramblings of a female intoxicated by romantic antics, he found instead the brisk and lucid style of a seasoned essayist. The characters, moreover, leapt from the page, and the dialogue, consisting so far chiefly in the interchanges of an idiotic, egocentric parson and his intended, struck him as so fresh and alive that he felt he knew them better than he did most of his acquaintance. The style struck him as clear and intelligent—he was amazed it had been written by a woman at all. Indeed, after finishing the second chapter he was determined in his mind that it could not have been the work of a woman, but of a man ashamed of being accused of novel writing, or else for some reason unwilling to be identified.

Thus amused and, one might add, amazed, Sir Basil passed a very pleasant hour. It flew by so quickly that when he heard the clock strike eleven he started up in amazement. Lady Cardovan had yet to appear. Ringing for a servant, he inquired if she had been informed of his presence.

"Yes," said the footman, "My Lady has been told. But I shall go and remind her myself."

The footman reappeared a moment later with a puzzled look.

"My Lady Cardovan is unwell," reported he. "She begs you to excuse her, Your Excellency, but she has got the headache."

"Unwell!" cried Sir Basil. "Then why was I not informed before? Unwell!"

The footman shuffled his feet and looked noncommittal. "I am sorry to have inconvenienced you, Your Excellency."

"Pshaw! Well! I have wasted the whole morning! Be so kind as to give your mistress my regards, and tell her I shall wait upon her tomorrow. No—better yet, bring me paper and a pen, if you will. I shall send up a note to her."

Writing instruments were duly brought, and Sir Basil, having thought a moment, jotted down several lines. Having finished, he commenced folding it up, but in an afterthought appended his intention of borrowing the book he had commenced reading. The footman bowed, took the note, and saw the Ambassador safely into his carriage.

Sir Basil felt twice injured during his drive back to Regent's Terrace. First, because he had been made to wait above an hour, which was injustice enough; and secondly— and far more cruelly—he had been snubbed. He could not explain his friend's conduct in any other way. Why else had she condemned him to sit for an hour before he had been told she was unwell? Lady Cardovan had behaved similarly once before, and then it had been owing to her displeasure and not to any oversight of footmen or maids. No, no—Diana was in a pique, but whatever could be the cause of it? He had seen her only two days before, and *then* she had been jolly enough. Really, women were the very devil! Even Diana could be as low and petty as the rest of 'em. He supposed she was angry at him for not having turned up at her soiree, that odious conglomeration of little old men who gossiped as badly as little old women, effete poets, and narcissistic politicians. And well out of it he had been, too! Really, then! How could she be so petty?

Sir Basil had passed, in the end, a far more enjoyable evening. He had stayed at home with Nicole and Miss Calder, had dined with them, and afterward had spent a most refreshing hour with the young lady in his library, discussing the Slavery Question. Miss Calder was really a most amiable young woman, and far brighter, in the end, then almost all his male acquaintances. Certainly she possessed none of that urge to be complimented that was so obnoxious in the rest of her sex. Her remarks were always insightful—even if a trifle impulsive—and her manner was perfectly engaging. Why was not most of womankind fashioned along such sensible, and amiable, lines? She was not, he had noticed, an unhandsome creature, either. Rather to the contrary, though of course that was not really his line. A fine pair of eyes, a lovely, graceful bearing, and the glow of health made up for whatever slight lack of perfection existed in her features. Of course she was not a classic beauty, like Diana. But there was that in her smile, in the light of her eye, and in her rather peculiar, windy laugh, which was certainly most enchanting. He wondered—not for the first time—why she had not been snapped up long ago by some quick-witted young man? He himself might almost have been tempted to do so, had he been younger, and of that turn of mind. Now, of course, his ideas were too settled, his style of life too pleasantly laid out, to make such an idea plausible, Still, there had been moments when he had wondered—but! Marriage had ever appared to him an unattractive business, entered into, more often than not, in a weak moment by an unsuspecting victim, only to be regretted bitterly forever afterwards. Even those marriages most expected to succeed, where birth, station, and education suited the partners to each other admirably, were apt to become, in short order, burdens to both parties. Only look at his brother! Louisa ought to have suited him down to the ground! And who could have forseen that that pretty little thing would turn so quickly sour? No, no—it was an idea too appalling to contemplate. And yet . . .

And yet, mused Sir Basil, absently watching the passing faces and streets, Miss Calder was nothing like his sister-in-law. In every aspect save birth, she was infinitely superior to Louisa.

In looks, manner, intelligence, and breeding, Miss Calder put her to shame. Indeed, it was a pity that such a fine young woman should have been relegated by ill-fortune to her present position in the world. He supposed her father must be a gentleman, to have sired such a lady. And then, of course, there was the invalided brother—tragic, really. Sir Basil, watching with unseeing eyes the passing of the outskirts of London and then the slow progress into the center of Town, had a sudden inspiration. It had occurred to him once before, actually, but had been set aside as too impulsive an idea. But, after all, one must not pass by every chance in life simply for its being impulsive!

The Baronet smiled to himself. Who would have thought he would end up one day chiding himself for being too staid? No, no—he would prove to all those who had long accused him of it, that he could be quite as impulsive as anyone, when he chose. So saying, he jumped down from the carriage before his club and, having ordered his luncheon, proceeded to put into action his little scheme.

Chapter XVIII

"How would you like to go on an errand with me, Nicole?" demanded Miss Calder of her pupil at about the time that Sir Basil was sitting down to his partridge in St. James's Street.

"Why, I should love it!" exclaimed the child, throwing down her pen with an exasperated sigh. The lessons had gone very badly all morning. Incapable of concentration, Nicole had been for an hour upon the events of the Roman Conquest of Asia Minor without taking in one fact. Her mind, it seemed, could not be kept away from the recent, and more exciting events of her own personal life. Since the visit to the Prince's teahouse, she had been unable to talk of anything else. "The Great World" outside of her own window held far more fascination for her than that portrayed within her text.

"Where are we to go?"

But Miss Calder would not offer any concise answer. She replied simply that they were to go to a part of London where Nicole had never been.

"Have you been there yourself?" demanded the child with wide eyes.

"Only twice."

And Anne stood up to go and fetch her bonnet and a pelisse. Nicole could obtain no further information from her until they had walked several blocks down St. James's Street. Then, a fine icy rain beginning to fall—for it was now the first week of December—the people hurrying up and down the street began to seek shelter in the shops and galleries lining the street. Seeing a hackney cab letting out its passenger, Anne signaled for it.

Now Nicole was in greater suspense than ever. She had

never been in a hackney before, and declared that this was almost as exciting than going to see the Prince. Was their destination far off? How would they get back? It was not much farther, replied her governess as they stopped at the intersection of Jermyn and Cardon streets, waiting for a procession of geese to be herded across the street to a marketplace. This part of Town was different from any other Nicole had observed. The pedestrians were not so fine, and the shops were much simpler. It was a district full of the bustle of business being conducted on every corner, and within the buildings lining the streets. Few of the grand vehicles which hourly rattled past their own house were visible here; here was a working class, men of business and merchants, printing houses and law offices. Not far from here, but in a more fashionable section, they had first met at the office of Sir Basil's solicitor. How long ago that day seemed now! thought Anne, studying the profile of her little companion. Nicole's bright eyes were fastened upon the passing men and women, her little nose nearly twitching from excitement, and made pink by the cold air. She had grown to be so much a part of Anne's life that she could not fathom living without her. How she would miss that high ringing voice, that sparkling laugh, those endlessly curious, candid questions. Most of all, she would miss the child's natural point of view, her guileless reactions, and her peculair distinctions between people and events.

"In a few years' time," said Anne aloud with a trace of nostalgia already, "you shall be driving about in your own barouche, quite a lady of the world! After a year or two in France, and with the benefit of a cosmopolitan education, I don't doubt but you'll be the toast of London—and perhaps Paris, too!"

Nicole turned her wide brown eyes upon her. "Do you think so? I do hope so, Miss Calder! It would make Uncle Basil very proud, don't you think?"

"He is already as proud as he needs to be," replied Anne. "You could not be improved one whit in his eyes."

Nicole looked very pleased, too pleased even to respond, but after a moment's silence, she murmured, "I am a little afraid of going to France, Miss Calder."

"Why? Oh, my dear—you mustn't worry about anything. You shall see how easy it will be."

Well, perhaps if *you* are there it shall not be too awful,"

156

responded the child, slipping a little hand into Anne's muff. "I don't think I should be afraid of going *anywhere* with you!"

Anne did not reply. A hot prickling sensation in her eyes made her blink and turn away with a forced smile. If the truth be known, she felt the same way about Nicole—*her* company might ease the way through any dilemma. She hoped that would be true now, when she needed help the most, and in such a difficult moment. But it was far better this way. A thorough search of her own heart had assured her of that. No good could come of her remaining in London, at least not in her present situation.

The hackney cab drew up shortly before an old brick establishment, over the door of which was inscribed the legend, "Peabody & Peabody, Publishers of Books." The coachman handed down the young lady and the child, and received his payment with a nod and a little bow. Having pulled the bell, Anne and Nicole were soon admitted to a rather dark and musty hallway, smelling strongly of ink. A young man, evidently an apprentice or clerk, inquiring who they wished to see, was told, "Mr. Carlysle." And who, if he might ask, should he say was calling?

"Anne Calder," replied Anne.

The young man's eyebrows instantly shot up.

"Miss Calder?" His formerly diffident manner vanishing, he bowed and led the way straight through an outer office, where several clerks were working at their desks, and knocking at a more handsome door than the others in the place, disappeared within.

"Who was that?" demanded Nicole, her eyes large.

"A publishing assistant," came the response.

There was no time for further comment. In a moment the door opened again, and the young man bowed them in.

"Miss Calder!" exclaimed an elderly man of dignified aspect, rising from his chair behind an immense desk littered with papers. "I had expected you yesterday. Do sit down, please. And the child?"

Anne smiled at the gentleman's uncertainty.

"A young friend, Mr. Carlysle. Miss Lessington."

"Ah! Miss Lessington—well, do you please take a chair as well."

The two females were soon ensconced in chairs before the desk, and the elderly man resumed his own. Mr. Carlysle blinked and smiled—rather, as Nicole very justly remarked later, like an owl.

"I suppose you have come to collect your books?" demanded he after a moment.

Anne nodded.

"Well, well! And I have them here for you, all done up in paper and string. But I suppose you shall want to look at them?"

"If it is not too much trouble, yes."

"Very well, very well," the elderly man responded, with a rather fatherly indulgence. "Yes, yes—it is not quite the same till one sees it in print, is it? Always looks rather different."

The parcel, rather small, thought Anne, was duly taken up and a knife applied to the string. All this took a good deal of time, as Mr. Carlysle was of a quite deliberate temperament and rarely rushed along. At last, however, the string was removed, the paper unwrapped, and there, before Anne's astonished and delighted eyes, lay two slender volumes of red morocco.

"Looks pretty well, don't it?" demanded Mr. Carlysle. "We did quite a good job on it, I think."

"A lovely job!" murmured Anne, taking up a volume. It was some moments before she had recovered her breath enough to turn to the first page, and to see, after the title and the nominal legend, the first few lines transposed by the miracle of modern science into neat black type.

"A pity you won't use your name, Miss Calder. It is getting rather fashionable to do so, even with ladies. You see what a change it made when Miss Austen revealed her identity. And, of course, Mrs. Radcliffe has not suffered from it."

"Perhaps in time," murmured Anne, turning over the pages and marveling afresh every moment at the improvement which the regularity of the lettering and the weight and quality of the paper had upon her simple language.

"How long shall it be before I know if it is well received?"

"Oh, not long at all!" exclaimed Mr. Carlysle. "Why, have not you seen the *Courier*? Mr. Nash has already given it high marks. Let me see, I had it here somewhere. We always let about two or three copies to the journalists, you know."

Mr. Carlysle rummaged amongst his papers and retrieved a clipping from a news sheet.

Accepting it from his hands, Anne had the profound shock, amazement, and delight, of reading six paragraphs of glowing praise of her little work. It was termed variously "lively, truthful, and cleverly wrought: as neat a satire as Miss Austen ever gave us. As neat a piece of work, in fact, as any of our novelists has handed us upon the subject of life amongst the squirage."

"Well, well—what do you think?" inquired the publisher, peering at her from beneath his great bushy brows.

"I—hardly know what to say!"

"But it is well-deserved, my dear, so you oughtn't to feel too humble. I warrant you shall have your share of comedowns after all. One always does, you know. Pay heed neither to the praise nor to the criticism, save where you can profit from it. That is my credo. By the bye—another client of mine has expressed some pleasure with your little book. I shan't mention his name, but you ought to know he is one of our most celebrated novelists."

Anne could only nod, barely able to comprehend her good fortune.

"But, in the long shot, of course, the thing that's important is not the praise of the journalists, but of the people. I've often seen works die upon the stand which were thought great by the critics. 'Tis the general public which must decide at last upon the merit of the book."

"And—and how long shall it be before we know *their* verdict?" inquired Anne, afraid of pushing her luck too far.

"Why! Not long; not long at all. A few months, a year or two—by then one ought to know something. Don't look so crestfallen, my dear Miss Calder. You must occupy your mind with another novel, so it shall be neither a disappointment nor a false triumph. The great thing is to get on with one's work."

Now Anne had cause to feel miserable. How dare she confess her own doubts just on that point? Only a few days before she had thrown the remnants of her latest work into the fire, and since then had hardly dared put pen to paper. She heard Mr. Carlysle's next words with some dismay:

"A flash in the pan is no good, of course. You must prove yourself capable of repeating your success, else no one shall think twice about you. Especially with this sort of novel, which must draw a limited audience—since it can hardly appeal to our greatest reading public—it is necessary to write another as soon as possible. I suppose you have got something underway?"

"Only," murmured Anne, "an idea. I had thought I might do a satire of city life."

"Along the same lines?" demanded Mr. Carlysle quickly.

"Well, Sir—no, not exactly. I had thought it might be upon a broader scale, but indeed, I don't know if I'm up to it."

"Hm," said the gentleman, scratching his chin. "Don't know about that. Mustn't jump from one thing into another quite so fast. Better to keep up with the same thing. Wouldn't you like to do another country story? Something different, of course, but along the same lines—perhaps leaving the clergy out altogether. A merchant's family might do nicely."

"A merchant's family!" breathed Anne. "But I know nothing about merchant's families!"

"More than you do about life in London, I'll warrant. You said you had only taken up residence in town a few weeks ago, did you not?"

"Yes, Sir."

Mr. Carlysle regarded her with his keen, blinking eyes.

"Take my advice, Miss Calder. Go back to the country and give us another country satire. There are not many who can do them well, whereas there are a hundred novelists who can weave a yarn about the city with a flick of the pen. The key for that sort of thing is to have a solid understanding of the society. I believe you are better placed in a simpler environment. Trust me," continued he upon seeing her crestfallen look. "It takes far more skill to make a simple subject interesting, than a complicated one. Stick to your own ground."

Meekly, Anne nodded her head, feeling a great deal more defeated than she would let on. How glad she was that he had not glimpsed her unfruitful attempt at satirizing a baronet! And how right he must be, too. She ought to have seen it from the start.

But she had not much time to bemoan her situation, for in an instant Mr. Carlysle rose, as if in a sign of dismissal, and held out his hand.

"You have a fine hand, Miss Calder. I should hate to see you roughen it by attempting a subject too broad for you. Very well, then—good day. Do you speak to the clerk, and he shall make out a check for you."

Nicole, dumbfounded by everything she had seen and heard (though who can say exactly how much she comprehended of it), held out her little hand and curtsied prettily. Mr. Carlysle granted her one brief, twinkling smile. In a moment, the two were out the door.

Having been tongue-tied during all of the foregoing interview, Nicole could scarcely suppress her curiosity. As soon as they were out in the street again, she demanded urgently to know what Mr. Carlysle had meant. What were the books he had given her? Was she really an authoress, like Lady Cardovan? And why had he said she ought to go "back to the country"?

Anne steered the child across the street, through a tangle of traffic and to the other side. Her own head was so full of ideas, impressions, and bewilderment, that she could hardly reply to Nicole's inquiries. For the moment, she put her off by suggesting they go into a nearby coffee house and have a cup of chocolate, a suggestion which Nicole agreed to instantly.

Once ensconced inside at a little table with a view of the bustling dining room, Nicole repeated her questions, now with a much graver look, for she had had time to decide in her own mind that she was about to lose her dear Miss Calder.

"Are you going to be a famous authoress, Miss Calder?"

"Hardly, my dear," returned Anne, smiling. "I don't think I am much in danger of *that*. I have only written a little story, which so far hardly anyone has read. And it must remain a great secret between you and me—you are capable of keeping a secret, aren't you? Of course you are."

"If you would like me to, I shall keep it. I shan't tell anyone, not even Uncle Basil or Lady Diana. They are not to know either?"

"No one save you and me."

"And Mr. Carlysle," added the child, who had been much affected by that gentleman's manner.

"Yes, and Mr. Carlysle. But not another soul."

"Why?" asked Nicole, after a moment's hesitation, for she possessed a natural sense of delicacy which was a continual source of amazement and delight to her elders. "Why must we keep it so secret? If *I* had written a book, I should want everyone in the world to know about it at once!"

"Perhaps not, Nicole. You see, it is not so much the book which I wish to keep secret. Of course I wish everyone to read it, and to delight in it as much as I delighted in writing it. Nothing could give me more pleasure. But for the moment, I should rather that neither Sir Basil nor anyone else know about it. You see, it is not thought very proper sometimes for ladies to write novels."

Nicole pondered this idea for several seconds.

"Why not? Lady Cardovan writes books, and she is a lady.

And Mrs. Radcliffe, and that other lady Mr. Carlysle mentioned——"

"Jane Austen. Yes, but in the case of each of them, there is some reason why they may be accepted from the general rule. Lady Cardovan is—well—she is not the common run of ladies. And she is so exceptional a person that no one could find fault with her for doing anything. Besides, she does not write novels, but histories, and there is a great difference. Mrs. Radcliffe is a widow, and therefore must support herself by some means, just as I support myself by teaching *you*. In her case it is not thought very bad, for she is older than I am, and besides, does not care much what people think of her. And Miss Austen, of course, was a genius. A genius will always be excused from the general rule. And even she wrote most of her books anonymously. That means," continued Anne, seeing the puzzled look upon her pupil's face, "without using her own name, just as I have done. For a young unmarried woman, it is thought better to keep one's identity a secret."

"How queer!"

"Yes, it is, rather, isn't it? Very queer. But I do not make the rules of society, but only live by them, just as we all must."

Nicole was twiddling with her spoon, seemingly immersed in thought. After a moment, she looked up, and with a grave little face demanded what she most wished to know:

"What did he mean, Miss Calder, when he said you ought to go back to the country? You shan't go away, shall you?"

"No, no, my dear," responded Anne quickly, though this was the very question which was uppermost in her own mind and which was as yet unresolved. But there was no point in upsetting Nicole before she was even sure herself of what she ought to do.

"I shan't go away. Not for a long while, at any rate. But—what difference can it make? In a month, you shall be in France, and have so much to occupy your thoughts that there shan't be a moment left to think of me!"

"You are not coming to France, then."

It was a declaration, rather than a question, and made with such a reproving little look that Anne felt instantly penitent.

"Why, does it make so much difference to you?" she inquired softly.

But Nicole would not reply, nor meet her gaze. She stared

into her lap and shook her head with a stiff little motion which was an exact contradiction of her feelings.

"If you had rather go home, Miss Calder, than I shouldn't want you to come with me."

"My dear!" Anne reached out her hand and touched the child's wrist. "Dear little Nicole! I do believe you like me a little bit, do you not?"

Neither of them spoke. Anne saw the child making a brave effort against her tears, and would not interfere with that courageous heart. Poor child! She had lost so much within so short a time! Another loss—slight as it must be—must frighten her sadly. Anne watched her pupil gather hold of herself again and smile up into her eyes.

"I never liked anyone so well in all my life! Except Papa, of course."

"Well! I never liked anyone half so well as you, either. You shall be my dearest little friend so long as I live. But, what are we speaking of! I wish you had not made me say so much, Nicole, for I am really not at all settled in my own head. It is a rather complicated matter, and must require some time to consider."

"Please come with us!"

"Well, well—we shall see. Have you finished your chocolate? Come along, then. We had better hurry back before Sir Basil gets home, or he shall ask no end of questions—and we have got a great secret, have we not?"

Nicole nodded, eager to be included in the scheme, though it had presented possibilities she had not foreseen nor liked even to think about. But for the moment she had made up her mind to be as brave as possible, and determined only to offer up several prayers a day that her governess might stay with them. She had in her head, as well, something a little better than a prayer, or so she hoped. But grown-ups were sometimes so very peculiar that one hardly knew what they might do next. All she could do was hope, and being of a very optimistic turn of mind, she possessed a good deal of that.

Chapter XIX

Sir Basil, having partaken of a pleasant luncheon in the
soothing male environs of his club, having dispatched his
little errand of charity, and feeling altogether satisfied with
himself, returned to his house in Regent's Terrace that afternoon in a very happy frame of mind. The unpleasant
thoughts he had had in the morning about the idiosyncrasies
of the female brain had vanished with the clouds. What had
begun as a thoroughly miserable day had been transformed
between his breast of partridge under glass and the braised
pears in champagne, into a brilliant winter day. Drops of
moisture sparkled upon the cobblestones still, as he walked
(forsaking his carriage) up St. James's Street and past the
great stone steps of the Cathedral. But as he turned into
Bond Street, for the short cut to the Terrace, he noticed that
all signs of the morning precipitation had disappeared. He
had neatly avoided being glimpsed by his sister-in-law and the
awful Miss Newsome only a moment from his own door. Evidently immersed in their own gossip, they had vanished chattering into one of the shops before they had spotted him,
darting behind a lamp post. The whole world seemed to be
out in full swank. Even the dandies parading up and down in
their absurd get-ups did not bring the usual snort of contempt
to his lips. Somehow everyone and everything looked better
than usual this afternoon. Perhaps it was the beneficial effects
of knowing he had performed (or at least arranged to perform) a great service for a poor invalid. Perhaps he should
do this kind of thing more often. In any case, he was in a
splendid state of mind. He practically skipped up the steps to
his door and rat-a-tat-tatted upon the knocker very gaily.

But the occupants of the house were evidently not in a mood to match his own. The butler responded to the knock with a very dour look, and when he was asked if anyone had called, only proferred the silver salver with three cards upon it.

"What has got you in such a gloom, Squibb?" inquired Sir Basil, glancing at the names upon the cards. Lord Duff had been, to inquire yet again, no doubt, into his position upon the Slavery Question, and his sister-in-law had called (thank heaven he had not been imposed upon by *her*) and there was also a card inscribed with the Princess Lieven's name.

"The cook is indisposed, Your Excellency, and has determined to make our lives miserable."

"Why, what did she do? Poison the soup?"

"No, Sir Basil. She has been ranting and raving about the pantries all morning."

"Well, you had better speak to Miss Calder about it. Miss Calder will know how to deal with her."

"Yes, Your Excellency. But Miss Calder is not at home."

"No? Why, where has she gone?"

"I do not know, Sir. She and Miss Lessington went off together an hour or two ago. They did not say where they were going."

"Ah, well—suppose they are off on some errand or other. Wonderful creature, Miss Calder. When they return, ask her to come in and see me, will you? I shall be in my library."

"Very good, Sir."

Sir Basil proceeded forthwith into the aforementioned room, dropping the cards onto the salver as he passed. There, comfortably established in an armchair, he stretched out his legs before the fire and recommenced the little novel he had borrowed from Lady Cardovan. Such moments of leisure were very rare in his life, and he took a secret pleasure in the knowledge that the House of Lords was at that moment reconvening without him. Blessed little good it did in any case, when he *was* there! The old dotards would have their say, eulogizing endlessly the merits of a proper stance against the French trade, and all the while happily pocketing the difference between the cost of free trade articles and the slave industry across the Channel. In the long run, in any case, the matter would not be in their hands, but in his own, the Regent's, and of course the French Royal House's. Those few intermediaries, like himself, who would have any real influence in the matter, never spoke before Parliament. It was an unwritten rule that those who *did* were silent; those who didn't (or couldn't) gabbled happily away, oblivious to the fact that no one paid them any mind.

Happy in the knowledge that he was escaping the droning voices of half the peerage, therefore, Sir Basil immersed himself again in his book, and found that upon the second perusal, it had not lost its power to amuse him. Half its merit, of course, lay in the fresh and easy style, a style so down-to-earth and unbeguiled by the sway of self-consciousness that he suspected yet again it had been written by a man. He said as much to Miss Calder, when she looked into the library, following his instructions.

"Ah! Miss Calder!"

"Sir?"

She stood tentatively in the doorway, obviously uncertain whether to come in or stay where she was. Sir Basil rose and gallantly drew forth a chair for her. With a grateful look, she settled down, and the Baronet, returning to his own armchair, could not but notice the glow in her cheek, no doubt a result of walking in the fresh air. The glow belied her rather humble mien, which was unusual. Miss Calder generally marched in like a young Diana, with her head held high and her shoulders back. It was one of the things he had first remarked about her. Today, her whole countenance was softened by something—sadness, perhaps? Ah, and well he knew what the cause of it might be!

"You have been out?" he inquired, rather redundantly, considering that he had been twice informed of the fact.

"Yes, Sir. Nicole and I have been upon an errand."

"Satisfactory, I hope?"

"Yes, Sir—perfectly."

"Ah!" Sir Basil gazed at her intently, but she would not meet his eyes, seeming almost to flush. She looked very comely: very. That fine pale blue whatever-it-was became her very well, set off the high colouring of her cheeks and lips, and brought out the sparkle in her eyes. There was something about her that reminded him of a high-bred filly, a spirited and naturally elegant young animal.

"I hope you have not had some bad news from home?"

Now she looked surprised. Aha! Had he hit the nail upon the head? Her surprise, however, was quickly concealed, as he noticed and she turned her face a little away from his gaze.

"No, Sir."

Really! One could never believe a woman! He must keep in mind the one general rule to use in interpreting their remarks: reverse 'em completely.

Well, well. I have been amusing myself with a novel, Miss Calder. I highly recommend it to you. I do not go in for novels much myself, as a rule, but this one is particularly apt. You must have it when I am through. A most fresh wit, a lively tale—just the thing to distract you from your present distress."

"Sir?"

Now the poor young woman looked doubly dismayed. Well, he should not press the point, nor give any hint of what steps he had taken to remedy the situation. Let that come as a surprise. Oh, how he should love to see the look upon her face when she discovered! *Then*, perhaps she should form a higher opinion of him. The glow of anticipated gratitude made Sir Basil smile.

"Come, come, my dear Miss Calder. I hope you have learned to think of me as a friend. You may trust me, you know."

The young woman smiled, a delightful smile, artless and humourous at once. Did he detect the trace of a blush upon her cheek?

"I do, Sir," said she earnestly. "I am most grateful to you for all you have done for me, when really I deserve none of your kindness."

"Ah, well! haven't done anything much, you know. Only what any man would. And *you*, Miss Calder, have done a great deal to make my own life happier. Certainly you have been more than kind to Nicole. The child dotes upon you."

Miss Calder smiled and peered into her lap, where her fingers were twining and untwining rather nervously.

"I am very glad of that, Sir."

Now there came an awkward silence, during which Sir Basil wondered what he could say next. He supposed the book was a safe enough subject, however, and finally clearing his throat, he said:

"I highly recommend this little novel to your attention, Miss Calder. I should like to hear your opinion of it, for it is very much along your lines, I think. All about a country clergyman, you know, and his insipidity. Lively view of that spectrum of life."

He did not notice her start.

"And so well written," continued he, oblivious to her sudden change of colour, for he was lifting up the volume and weighing it in his hands thoughtfully, "that although it is said to have been written 'by a lady,' I can only believe that in point of fact it was not, but written by a man."

"Oh?" Anne looked extremely interested in this idea. "What makes you think so?"

"Well, the objectivity of it, for one thing. I do not believe females are capable of so much distance upon a subject, and the humour is almost masculine."

"What, if I may be so bold, is *masculine* humour, Sir Basil?"

"Why, I do not know, in fact," admitted the Baronet, "though I have the feeling there *is* such a thing. Perhaps it is the dryness of it. I don't know. But I have never read anything by a woman that did not portray a life romanticized beyond all recognition. To do so, in my opinion, is to deprive existence of its innate humour."

"Have you read a great many novels written by women?" inquired Anne, still with the same expression of genuine interest.

"Oh, no—to be sure, not very many. I have not time to read such stuff, you know. I have read Lady Cardovan's books, at least most of 'em, but they aren't fictional, after all. More in the line of dramatized history. I find them rather fanciful, but perfectly accurate. She is a devil for documenting every fact. Quite wears one out, her knowledge of dates, places, and battles."

"And you do not find this book fanciful? And yet you said it was a novel, a made-up story. Is that not more fanciful than the truth, whether or not it is dramatized?"

"Do you know, Miss Calder," returned Sir Basil, after a moment's thought, "you have quite puzzled me there. And yet I shall persist in my opinion: This tale, though fanciful, strikes me as a clearer mirror of reality than any of Diana's books. It shows a thorough knowledge of the idiosyncrasies of human manners and morals. Though it is a very broad comedy—its sole weakness, in my opinion, is the very breadth of it—it manages to retain the seed of truth. The gentleman must have an extraordinary eye."

"Then you are quite determined that it *was* written by a man?"

"No doubt about it. I can't fathom why he should masquerade as a woman, but! ah, well—I suppose he is waiting to see how his little book shall be received before he reveals his identity. I wonder who he is?"

"I am quite as curious as you, Sir, to find out who this clever man could be."

Did Sir Basil detect a note of sarcasm in her tone? The devil of it! She was as bad as Diana. Perhaps all these women were alike. How odd, though, to take offense at his suggestion that a realistic satire could not be written by a woman. Was there nothing they could admit doing less well than a man?

"I see you think me unduly prejudiced, Miss Calder," said he, in an attempt to smooth down her ruffled feathers.

"No, sir."

"Only excessively so?"

Now he was granted a tiny smile.

"It is not my place to say, Sir. You are my employer, I am your ward's governess. Were we equal in every way, I might tell you what I think, but as it is, I am prevented by my station."

"Forget that for a moment, Miss Calder. I am tired to death of being reminded of your station. Say what you think, please."

"I think you are less prejudiced than ignorant, Sir. Excuse me—but you asked me to tell you my honest opinion. It is clear you have not much familiarity with the working of the female brain, much less of its powers. You think we are all foolish, stupid creatures who cannot direct our thoughts to any greater issues than a bonnet or a pelisse. You think we have no view of the world around us, no opinions worth listening to, no morality beyond a superficial kind of etiquette. You dislike us so thoroughly that you will not even grant us a sense of humour! Only a man of your own vast arrogance could have lived upon the earth as long as you have done and still fail to see that half the population of the earth is not deaf, dumb, and half-witted. It is a pity you do not have any idea of how *you* are regarded by some females!"

"Yourself in particular, I suppose?" Sir Basil's voice was low and cold, his cheeks pale.

Miss Calder was shaking too violently to reply. With a seeming realization of what she had said, she looked down into her lap and coloured fiercely.

"I beg your pardon, Sir."

"No, no! Go on, I beg of you!"

"I ought not to have spoken so fiercely. You did not

deserve it. I have been worried about another matter, and am not myself."

"Perhaps you are *more* yourself, Miss Calder." Sir Basil hesitated for a moment. "Perhaps you are right. Perhaps you have not underestimated me. But I assure you, whatever my opinion of the rest of your sex, I feel very differently about you. I think you neither deaf nor dumb, and I know you are not half-witted. You are a most intelligent young woman, and I have enjoyed talking to you as much as I have ever enjoyed talking to any man. Indeed, if there were more women like you, I should have a higher opinion of your whole sex."

"Perhaps you have not known very many of us, Sir Basil. You will grant that Lady Cardovan is an exception to the general rule? And you know *her* better than any of my sex."

Now Sir Basil smiled. "Then there are *two* exceptions to the rule. And perhaps you are right, perhaps I have not made an effort to converse with ladies in any depth. But in all fairness, I must say that there are not many whose ideas I much wanted to hear."

"Do you find every man of your acquaintance worth listening to?"

"Heavens, no! Far from it!"

"Well, then."

"Miss Calder, please do not look so condescending."

"I am not looking condescending."

"You make me feel like a child."

"I doubt I am exceptional enough to do *that*, Sir," said Anne rising. "I hope you will forget my outburst. Now I must go back to Nicole."

"Here, take this book, Miss Calder, I shall not have time to read any more today. Tell me if you like it."

Anne glanced at the book and smiled. She hesitated a moment, and then reached out her hand to take it.

"Thank you, I shall enjoy looking into it."

"Tell me what you think."

"I shall try to form a fair opinion of it."

Miss Calder closed the door behind her, and for a while Sir Basil stared after her with a bemused expression. Then, sighing, he rose to his feet and went to his desk to dispatch a letter to the Paris Embassy.

Chapter XX

Mr. Calder laid down his pen in resignation. He had been attempting to compose a letter to his solicitor, but the several people in the room who had come in to disturb him would not let him continue.

"I thought a man's library was meant to be his private domain, even if his home has ceased to be his castle," remarked he.

"How *can* you be so calm?" exclaimed his wife in return. "And how can you speak about castles when your daughter's welfare is at stake?"

"I am afraid I do not catch the gist of your ideas, my dear."

"I am speaking about your daughter, Sir! Kindly do not make fun of me!"

"I should never make fun of you, Eliza," returned the minister with a reproachful look, "least of all, when you are speaking about Anne. Why, what is wrong now?"

"Why, Sir! What do you think? How can she be so selfish? To wish to come home, just when she is getting along very well! Does not she have any consideration for us?"

"That is what you wished to know when she first desired to go away."

"But then things were very different. She had not been to Carlton House, nor begun to be on intimate terms with a good kind of people. I thought she was going to make a mockery of us all."

"But now that she has met the Prince, you think she shall do us credit?"

Mrs. Calder sniffed.

"I am of Mama's opinion," put in the second Miss Calder, a handsome, strapping girl of plain speech. "Anne ought not to come home now. After all, she wished to go away, despite the mockery it made of us to have her acting as a governess. Maria is getting along very well with Mr. Siddons, and I have no doubt they shall be soon engaged to marry."

"And you, Harriet, are doing pretty well by yourself, too," added her father, with a sly look which Miss Calder chose to ignore.

"I am not speaking on my own behalf, Papa. But for Maria's sake, and my mother's, I think it is unfair for Anne to come home, just now. It is certain to ruin everything between Maria and Mr. Siddons, just when things were going along so well."

"And for the greater convenience of Mr. Siddons, I am expected to let my eldest daughter make shift as well as she can in a strange city," remarked Mr. Calder ironically.

"She has shifted perfectly well thus far, my dear," his wife pointed out. "Why, only look at her! She went to London with an hundred pounds, and has now as her circle of acquaintance two countesses, a baronet, and the Prince himself!"

Here Ben, who had risen from his couch to join in the family argument, chose to speak up. "I do not think she regards the Prince as quite her intimate acquaintance, Ma'am."

"Why, she took tea with him! And sat next to the Princess Lieven all the while!" retorted Mrs. Calder. "At least, that is what you have told us. It would have been very kind in her to write about it to her parents, rather than that brief little note!"

"That is neither here nor there, Eliza," interrupted Mr. Calder. "I am not a reader of minds, and cannot guess what has made her so unhappy. But unhappy she certainly is, or she would not give up so easily. It is not like Anne to admit defeat."

Now Ben added his agreement, and his mother, seeing herself as one against two, appealed to her daughter for support:

"Do not you think it most unkind of her, Harriet, to come home just when she was getting to the point where she might have done us all some good, rather than harm?"

"Most unkind, Mama," affirmed the young lady. "She ought to stay where she is. Why, perhaps Sir Basil will marry her!"

"I do not think so, Harriet," interjected Ben with a smile.

"From what I gather, she does not hold a very high opinion of him, and he sounds too arrogant to fall in love with his ward's governess."

"What do you think has made her so miserable, Ben?" demanded his father. "Be so good as to be silent for a moment, ladies, and let us hear Ben's opinion."

The ladies, who had both opened their mouths at once, subsided with equal discontent. Their eyes turned simultaneously upon the young man, wrapped in a blanket and sitting upon a chair.

He thought for a moment, and then replied, slowly:

"Indeed, Sir, I cannot guess. It is the first time I have ever been so completely ignorant of Anne's thoughts. Her letters, until this last one—" nodding toward the missive which lay upon a corner of Mr. Calder's desk— "have all been cheerful and full of her usual good humour. Perhaps she has been concealing things from me—I don't know. That must be the case, for she has given no hint of any misery, if indeed there is any. Save that she was discouraged with her writing, and had been unable to put anything down that she liked."

"Pooh!" exclaimed Harriet. "Why should that make anyone miserable?"

"It could not, my dear," replied her mama. "No doubt there is some other cause. I doubt not but that she has changed her mind about Mr. Siddons, and wishes to marry him after all now that he is nearly wed to Maria."

"I beg of you, ladies, to be quiet for a moment!" commanded Mr. Calder, and turning to his son, he inquired if there had been no other mention of her work?

"She did mention that her novel had come out, Sir, but said no more about it. Only that her publisher advised her to keep up in the same line rather than to change. But I have got a clipping here from the London *Courier,* Sir, which speaks very glowingly about the book."

"Why, let me see it!" Mr. Calder glanced over the sheet, and after a moment, exclaimed, "Why, this is most high praise! Fancy! I never knew we had a genius in the family!"

"A most selfish genius!" sniffed Harriet, doubly cross to see her sister defended, on the one hand, and praised for what she had always considered her idiotic scribbling, on the other. "Why, what does it say?"

Mr. Calder read them some excerpts of the column, and lifted his eyeglass to gaze at his wife.

"Now, then, Eliza—what do you have to say about your daughter?"

Mrs. Calder had several things to say, not the least of which was a condemnation of the young lady for being ashamed of her family name.

"Why should she keep it secret? Has she no pity for us? After shaming us all by going to be a governess, she might at least salvage our reputation a little by letting it be known who she is, when at last she does something we might all take pride in!"

"She did not wish to offend you and my father," put in Ben gently, "in case it was not well received. She would not make you the laughing stock of the whole neighbourhood, she said."

"Now here is something I hope you will attend to, Eliza," pronounced the lady's husband, much in the same voice he used upon the pulpit. "Here is a sentiment worthy of your respect and gratitude."

Mrs. Calder said nothing. Her nerves were faring very poorly, and she was too confused to know what to think.

"We shall welcome her home with open arms," continued Mr. Calder, "and let her know that she is well loved here, whether she choose to marry or no. The other girls have my consent to marry as they please, and you, my dear, must just accustom yourself to the idea that one of your daughters may live a solitary life. I have already written to tell her so, in any case. I dare say we shall see her any day now."

"It was you, Arthur, who made her promise to stay for a whole year," cried Mrs. Calder, "lest she take her own decision too lightly."

"Well, well—perhaps I was wrong to do so. Even *I* am occasionally mistaken. Now run along, all of you, and leave me in peace. Do you, Ben, only wait a moment, please."

Ben was very glad to stay, for he had more to say to his father than he would mention before his mother and sister, and when those ladies had left the room, he spoke up.

"Father, there is one other thing. . . ."

"Ah! I thought there might be." Mr. Calder regarded his son very keenly. "You and Anne have always been as close as two peas in a pod. I supposed you might have some further insight into the case. What can have made her miserable, when she seemed to be going along so well?"

"I believe," replied Ben slowly, "that it has got something to do with this." Whereupon he handed over the last letter, but one, he had received from Ann, in which her visit to the Prince was described. "Only read the last two pages, Sir. The rest I have already told you."

Mr. Calder did as he was bid, and after a while, looked up with a grave expression.

"I see what you mean. Such a suspicion must have made her situation very hard. Poor Anne! And she is so devoted to the child, as well as to Lady Cardovan. No doubt she has got some proof of her suspicions now. It would make her position exceedingly delicate. I suppose she thought she could not go along any more knowing what she did."

Ben nodded. "That is my assumption, Sir. To be in constant contact with the lady whom she esteems so highly, and all the while suspecting what must never be mentioned——"

"Yes, yes," nodded Mr. Calder. "It is not unheard of, for such a child, the product of a brief or illicit affair, to be brought up by strangers. That she should have come back, in this kind of guise, to her true parents must be the proof of a very skillful and secretive hand. No doubt it was arranged long ago, to look like a simple adoption. Everything points to it, does it not? Did not you say the father was only a very distant relative? Such kinds of things do happen, I am aware, in the more elevated levels of our society. What would be unheard of in a poor farmer, is quite common amongst the *ton*. Why! Look at the example our own Royal Family as set! Royal dukes think nothing of raising up a whole herd of illegitimate families! Poor child!"

"And poor Anne!"

"Indeed. Well, I am very glad you told me of it. It seems much clearer now, and I am glad Anne understands her duty so well. She could hardly stay on in that position."

"That is my own opinion, Sir."

"Yes, yes."

The young man rose to leave the room, but was detained by a word from his father.

"Ben—I am aware of what you did to help Anne with her little triumph, and do not think I don't esteem you for it."

The young man coloured. "I had nothing to do with it, Sir."

"Well, well—you have always been a modest fellow. But you are as clever as anyone, I know."

Ben was too embarrassed by this show of praise to reply. He turned and fled out of the room as soon as he could.

Mr. Calder smiled after him, shaking his head. After a

while, he resumed his letter writing. But the minister's tranquility was destined to be disturbed yet again that morning, for in an hour the post arrived, brought by his youngest daughter from the village, on her way home from a visit to a friend. Mr. Calder looked over the correspondence briefly, and was surprised to see that one of the letters was directed from Regent's Terrace, in an unfamiliar hand. He cut open the envelope, and read in amazement the following letter:

Friday, December 7

My dear Sir:

I hope you will not think me too forward in writing to you in this way, without the benefit of your acquaintance. And yet, if you do not know *me*, I feel almost that I know *you*, for I have heard much praise sung of you by your daughter, and believe you to be an exceptional kind of man.

I am writing to you unbeknownst to Miss Anne Calder, my ward's governess, and of course, as you know, a very remarkable young woman in her own right. That such an exceptional member of her sex should be reduced to the position of seeking work as a governess to support herself strikes me as a great injustice of our society. To remedy just these kinds of injustices is, in a way, my work, though naturally on a rather different level. As you may know, I am presently under appointment by His Highness, Prince George, to the Court of the Tuileries. Though unable to perform many services of a personal kind, I have made every effort throughout my career to attempt, through diplomatic means, to improve England's situation. My present obligation, therefore, seems clear, and I hope it will not strike you as odd or presumptuous, but only as the duty of a fellow Englishman, more blessed by circumstance than yourself.

Your daughter has mentioned to me that you have nine children, and that one of them is an invalid. My own mother was ill during a great deal of my childhood, and I know only too well what suffering such an illness can bring into a family. My father, Lord Hargate, was fortunate enough to provide the best medical attention for her, which must have eased some of the burden from his mind. I cannot fathom how it would have been, had he not been so well disposed, nor how much greater our own suffering would have been as a result. You, Sir, burdened with the support of so large a family, must feel doubly unfortunate. Accept, therefore, as a favour to myself, the enclosed bank draught. I have already spoken to Mr. Soames, the Regent's own physican, who has kindly agreed to supervise your son's care. When it is convenient for you, please be so kind as to let me know whether or not your son is too ill to travel. If so, Mr. Soames shall travel to your home. If not, I should be more than happy to have the young man reside with me whilst he is attended to. The accompanying draught should cover all of his expenses. Any more that is needed may be obtained through my banker, Harold Connhoughton, in Bond Street.

I know what a proud man you must be, but pray, for your son's sake, do not allow false dignity to prevent any chance of his recovery. I am,

Your faithful servant,
Basil Ives

No words could express Mr. Calder's amazement upon reading this document, nor his further astonishment when he was sufficiently recovered to glance at the enclosed check. One thousand pounds! One thousand pounds of misplaced charity! And all on account of his daughter's desire to play a trick upon the world!

"Anne, Anne," murmured the minister out loud, "what a devilish creature you are! And how am I to deal with *this*?"

Chapter XXI

"Good God, Diana!" cried Sir Basil Ives at about the same moment that Mr. Calder was scratching his chin over the Baronet's letter. "I wish you would say something! I have been trying to get a moment of your time this past week!"

Lady Cardovan, ensconced upon her own sofa in her own music room, did not see any reason to gratify the Baronet instantly. She continued stirring her tea calmly, as she had been doing for the past five minutes, and murmured, "Dear me! Has it been so long? I was sure it had only been four days."

"Four days, then! But it is quite long enough! Shall you tell me what has made you so blitheringly silly, or shall I leave?"

Lady Diana shrugged her pretty shoulders. It was a matter of very little importance to her.

"Very well, then!"

Sir Basil picked up his gloves, but made no motion to leave the room. He stared at the Countess for a long moment, and at last, in resignation, sighed.

"Oh, do be kind to me, Diana! At least do me the favour of telling me what is in your head! I never saw you act so mulish!"

"Perhaps there is something *you* have failed to tell me, Basil. Or shall I be the first to wish you joy, only on the basis of a rumour?"

"Wish me joy? What in Heaven's name d'you mean?" Sir Basil's jaw had dropped slightly.

"On your imminent engagement."

"Engagement? What engagement?"

"Your imminent engagement to Miss Newsome."

"Good God! You must be jesting!" The Baronet's whole person now dropped into a chair which was very luckily, just behind him. He could not believe his ears. Was it the whole world that had gone mad, or only himself? A slow smile crept over his features.

"You are teasing me, Diana, but I must say it is a dashed cruel jest. You mustn't suggest such an idea, even in fun."

"It is not much fun for *me*, I can assure you, Basil, to be made the laughing stock of London. I have never prized the opinion of the general public very much, but when it is directed, with a leering grin, most odiously in my own direction, even I cannot ignore it."

"Leering grin?" Sir Basil seemed incapable of making any original remark this afternoon.

"Oh, come, my friend—don't play the innocent with me, I beg of you. It is bad enough, thank you, to be informed in my own drawing room, at my own soiree, that my dearest friend has become attached to a young lady he had only the night before claimed to hold in contempt to my very face, but to have you throw it back at me with such astonishment is really too much!"

"Forgive me, Diana," said the Baronet after a moment's consideration, "if I do not absolutely understand you. Perhaps you will repeat yourself. You say that someone told you I was to be engaged to Miss Newsome?"

Lady Cardovan nodded.

"Well! I wish you would tell me who it was! I never knew I had such an extravagant enemy!"

"It was Livvy, Basil, and please do not play the outraged hero with me."

"Livvy!" cried the Baronet. "The Princess Lieven! What on earth could have put such an idea into her head?"

"I am afraid I put it there, Basil, by bringing up the subject. Your sister-in-law had just finished informing me of the happy news, which I was foolish enough to think a great joke, and I happened to mention it to her."

"And she did not laugh?"

Now the Countess granted him the look Sir Basil had been deprived of for some moments. It was sufficient, however, to turn his blood cold.

"No. She did not laugh. On the contrary, she said she had suspected it the evening you all dined together at Hargate House. She said you could not keep your eyes away from the delightful Miss Newsome."

"Really, Diana!" cried the Ambassador. "How could you believe such rubbish? Why, I recounted to you everything that went on, and I hope you have a higher opinion of me than to think that I am capable of succumbing to such charms as those!"

"I certainly *did not* think so, Basil. But it seems to be the general opinion. What is my own humble one, against the Princess's, who actually was present? But I do not mind that so much, you know. It is only that I thought you trusted me enough to tell me of it yourself."

The Baronet was thunderstruck.

"Come, Diana! Give me a little credit! How long have you known me?"

"Not long enough, it seems. Either that, or you have changed a good deal in France. I certainly thought you were incapable of—well, never mind."

"What! What! Out with it, Diana."

The Countess turned away a little and stared in the general direction of the fireplace with a bored look.

"It is of no importance now, Basil. Only I do wish you had not drawn me into it. It has already caused me the most extreme anguish. It shall very likely continue to do so."

Sir Basil gaped. "How could I have caused you any anguish, my dear lady? You know there is no one I admire so much as you. I should never cause you the slightest pain, much less anguish!"

Lady Cardovan tapped her finger against the cup for a moment and said nothing. For a while there was no sound to be heard but the ticking of a clock and the faint drone of a north wind in the trees of the park. Sir Basil continued to stare at her with a combination of horror, disbelief, and rather boyish panic. At last, however, the lady chose to unburden her soul, and when she did so, it was with a suppressed fury that cut right through his shock.

"How *could* you, Basil! I have loved you as I should have loved my own brother, nay as much as a son! And trusted you—trusted your honour above everything! I did not know that all the while you were posing as such a virtuous, selfless man, giving all for King and Country, you were in fact no better than any of the others! No better than the worst of them, indeed! For at least *they* do not pretend to spotless virtue! It was a very clever ruse, to be sure—but not clever enough. Even I should have seen through it at once, had I not been so blinded to your weaknesses! And now you are

180

prepared to marry anyone, only to rid yourself of the burden of your past mistakes. And to think that it took Livvy's sly little eyes to see through it! The only trouble is, my dear Basil, that now you have got me entangled in your horrible little web. And you must untangle it yourself."

"Web . . . web?" Sir Basil was utterly baffled. He had no conception of what she was talking about. "Come, Diana— try to be calm. You are evidently overwrought about something, but how am I to help if you do not tell me what it is?"

Whereupon Lady Cardovan turned upon him a look of withering contempt. "Livvy believes," she said slowly, "that I am the child's mother. Well, don't look so shocked. I am not *that* ancient. Of course you and I know that isn't true, but it is what all the world shall shortly believe, if I know Livvy. She has got so many things to hide herself that she cannot rest until she has uncovered everyone else's secrets."

Sir Basil gaped at her. "Good God, Diana! Don't tell me that all this time you have been hiding a *child*! By Jove!"

"Don't be idiotic. I am not the one who has been hiding a child."

"Well, then, please be so good as to tell me whose child we are talking about."

"Nicole, of course."

"Nicole! Why, is she your child?"

"No! Is not she yours?"

"Not to the best of my knowledge. I believe you know as much as I about her parentage."

Lady Cardovan eyed him suspiciously for a moment. "You are not trying to put me off the scent again, are you?"

"You know I despise hunting, Diana. Pray find some other metaphor. But no, if you insist—" seeing her disgruntled look—"I am not trying to put you off the scent. Rather to the contrary, I am trying to discover some trace of your own. I wish you would not all be so baffling."

Now Lady Cardovan put back her head and laughed, a long, delighted laugh that infected the Baronet, though he did not know what all the mirth was about.

At last, having recovered herself sufficiently, however, and wiping a tear out of her eye, she was capable of speech.

"Oh, dear! I ought not to laugh, of course! I am sure my reputation has been ruined for good, and yet I cannot help admiring Livvy for her imagination! Only fancy inventing such a tale! She had practically convinced me that we *had* been lovers for years, and hidden away a child in the country, only to take her back, under the guise of your ward. My dear, it is too delicious!"

"I do not find anything delicious about it," returned Sir Basil at last, understanding dawning upon him. "I find it disgusting and horrible! What a loathesome creature!"

"No, no—she is not loathesome. Only Russian."

"Half French, which must explain it. In any case, she has succeeded in damaging your reputation, which is intolerable. I ought to challenge Anastasy to a duel."

"Really, Basil! You men are extraordinary. What good is that supposed to achieve?"

Sir Basil grunted. For once, he was at his wits' end.

"Well—what else can I do? I am damned if I shall let that sort of lie spread about, only because Livvy has nothing better to do with herself than invent rumours about other people."

"I do not care about myself so much," said Lady Cardovan thoughtfully. "At my age, that sort of gossip is more complimentary than insulting. But for Nicole, I do fear it may be very harmful at last. You have not had any hint of it?"

Sir Basil paused to think. "Why, now that you mention it! I hadn't given it any thought, but I have been getting some rather queer looks at the Foreign Office. Strange remarks— Lord Devon winked at me in the corridor only yesterday! Dear me! What are we to do?"

Lady Cardovan looked grave. "I do not know. But something must be done to stop the gossip. I should hate to think of Nicole living under a shadow for the rest of her life, only because of an idle woman's amusement."

The case was indeed grave, and was discussed at some length. The only sensible course seemed to be to approach the Princess outright and endeavour to persuade her to stop the rumour just as she had begun it. How that was to be accomplished, was for the moment a question neither of them could answer, but at last an idea was agreed upon: Sir Basil should go directly to the Princess and confront her openly. She who loved deceit so much would be incapable of avoiding the truth, when put so plainly.

Sir Basil went, as he had promised, to Grosvenor Square, straight away upon leaving Lady Cardovan. The Princess was at home, by great luck, and the Baronet went promptly to see her. At first she could not be put off; she delighted in twisting about the truth so much, that she could not be persuaded to think plainly at once. But at last even she saw the grimness in the Baronet's eyes, and having at least a grain of common sense, could not dispute his argument: She had too much to hide herself to risk enraging him. His argument was not so bluntly put as his plea, but it did its work. A much more sober Princess sat that afternoon before her glass, watching her maid dress her hair. If there was a sulk in that smile, held up so brightly before the world on her drive about the Park, it was hardly visible, and the Princess was as skilled at damping out a rumor as at igniting one. Her innuendoes could do as many twists as she liked, and when anyone hinted to her that the Sir Basil Ives possessed a natural daughter, now living beneath his own roof as his ward, she threw up her hands in disbelief. The rumour was not completely smothered, of course, but the worst of the damage was prevented. It was, at least, enough to spare the honour of the imputed figures. As to Miss Newsome and the rumour that Sir Basil was soon to make his declarations of love, the world was very soon put to rest upon that head.

Sir Basil returned to Regent's Terrace with the chief part of his business dispatched, but by no means all of it. The most difficult part seemed yet to be ahead of him. He had left the house that morning in high spirits, for a sleepless night, a long night of examining his heart, had rendered up some knowledge which could not be disputed. He had gone on purpose to Lady Cardovan, hoping to seek her advice upon the subject, but of course he had been prevented by her own news. And now that news, having already caused so much anxiety, must cause him still more, for it very clearly made his own course twice as difficult. Miss Calder, naturally, must be told, if only in order that Nicole might be protected from any gossip. And what would she think of him then? Her good opinion, he did not deceive himself, had yet to be won. It was the greatest wish of his heart that she should think well of him. He did not require any more.

He went, therefore, very gravely to his library upon returning home, and required a footman to seek out Miss Calder. He then poured himself a rather large glass of port, downed it with one gulp, and poured another. It was in this frame of mind that he heard a knock upon the door.

Chapter XXII

When she was summoned by a footman to go to Sir Basil, Anne was sitting at her writing table composing the most difficult document she had ever been called upon to execute. It was, in point of fact, a letter of resignation to her employer, though resembling the commonality of that sort of missive in nothing more than name.

Certainly the feelings with which she set down the few and simple phrases—born out of thoughts anything but few and simple—were a far cry from the feelings with which most governesses, submitting the news of their departure, compose their final words. In a few short weeks—hardly more than a month—Anne had undergone so many transformations that the young woman bent in concentration over her paper was almost a different creature from the one who had first sat at that same desk, writing with the same implements a letter to her brother from London. So vast was the metamorphosis, indeed, that she herself could scarcely recall that girl. In her heart she thought she must have been no more than that—for only the events of the last weeks had taught her to be a woman. And what good, indeed, had it done her? Only forced her to retreat from the happiest life she had ever known; only made her understand with awesome fullness the innocence and arrogance of that past self.

For seven and twenty years, Anne Calder had lived upon the earth indulged by her family, admired by her friends, the happy recipient of everything that love, and a reasonable fortune, and beauty, can provide. And yet she had been bored with her lot; bored, nearly, to extinction. Tedium had been her hourly plight, and only the habit of scribbling, formed at an early age and brought to maturity with the help of her brother, had eased that burden. But had she not been the luckiest girl in all the world? No, she had not: for her very good fortune had been her greatest bain, and the gifts which others might have envied, had only made her more acutely aware of what she lacked. Only the last weeks had truly opened her eyes to that vacancy in her life, which in the humblest existences is sometimes full. Only the last weeks had taught her that the real meaning of good fortune has little to do with wealth, or position, or beauty, but with the sense of fulfillment which is granted to those who are dearly loved and whose service is appreciated by their loved ones. Strange, that in her first taste of humility, had also come the first taste of that fulfillment.

To all outward appearances, Anne must have gained tenfold in the last month, for it was hardly more than that since she had first set foot in Regent's Terrace. She ought, by having seen the work of her hand and brain brought forth by a noted publisher, and admired by everyone who had seen it, felt a sense of triumph. Even had she not gained such a feeling from knowing herself capable of self-support in a strange city and amidst strange people, *that* triumph ought to have sufficed to fill her with pride. But whatever of triumph was in her heart, was overshadowed by a new sensation of humility, such as she had never experienced in the whole course of her life. Odd, that such a sensation should come now, when she was most prepared for the exact opposite, when all the world would have expected, even condoned, a trace of arrogance.

But what the world expected, or condoned, had never touched Anne very deeply. Her own ambitions were so far removed from the common run of human endeavour that one of the greatest sources of amusement in her life had been to observe the strivings of her fellow beings for riches, admiration, and social position. What others had fought for, she had never valued very highly. Her own ambition had been to achieve a place amongst the great satirists of the world, which she considered a company far more elite than any group of duchesses. And just at the moment when the first step seemed to have been taken toward that goal, she had found it unworthy. Her whole view of things had been transformed, in fact, and she now struggled helplessly to discern her new values, as if she had been a fish swept up upon the shore.

For Anne had undergone a transformation of the heart and soul as profound as any metamorphosis of fish to mammal. She had fallen in love, against all her best instincts, desires, and sense of right, and she now found herself changed beyond all recognition. The process had thrilled her as much as it had startled her—let there be no doubt about that. But it had also left her stunned and shaken. And now, just when she was learning to enjoy her new view of things, she must give it up. It was with the most immense reluctance that she now prepared to return to her old life, with only the achievement she had set out to conquer, and none of the whole new world of light and laughter she had just begun to glimpse.

Let us not, in the words of Ben, "digress from the action overmuch, nor philosophize our heroine into an unnatural, and early extinction. That Sir Basil Ives was the object of her sentiments can come as no great surprise either, though it may amaze the reader a little to discover it, given her former prejudices against that gentleman. The progress from dislike to ardour had been neither neat nor couth, as is generally the case in life. In a novel we may contract it a great deal, and lend it that degree of lucidity which reality usually lacks, much to the dismay of us all. As we have seen, Anne Calder had first found the gentleman "handsome, gentlemanly, and elegant" to the point of stiffness. He had lacked in amiability everything which he possessed in achievement, recognition, and stature. A little later, she was put off by his undue coolness, and then amazed by his spontaneity. She had pitied him his awkwardness with Nicole and every other female he was ever put in contact with: Here was the first sign of her regard for him as a regular human being rather than a character to be satirized in a book. But the dawning of her awareness had come at that moment when she had read over the extent of her first draft of what might have been called "The Determined Bachelor," and found that where she had always considered herself more than adequately wise, she was here sadly naive. That Sir Basil could not be made a mockery of was evident: at least by one of her own short-sightedness.

Naturally, the dilemma had made her think, for it threatened every supposition she had ever made about human conduct, and her own in particular. It was the opening of her own eyes to her own soul, and the first hint to her heart that she was not the self-possessed young woman she had always thought herself.

It had been only two days after this that she had had the suspicion, from the Princess Lieven, about Nicole's parentage implanted in her mind, and that, more than anything else, made her aware of what she might otherwise have avoided for some time. It was the pang of jealousy and rage (so foreign to her nature heretofore) which had given her the hint. And no matter how she argued with herself, saying that her own situation prevented her even regarding the gentleman in any other light but that of an employer, or the lady as anything more than a kind and condescending patroness, she had not been able to resist the calling from within. And it was in direct proportion to the growth of the suspicion that she had begun to view her true feelings. As it became more apparent to her that she was in danger of losing her heart, Sir Basil had helped along the process by unwittingly (or so she thought) beginning to reveal himself to her. Here was a very different man from the one she had first glimpsed and, with a toss of her head, supposed she might sketch in one or two lines. Complex he most certainly was, and far surpassing everyone she had known before for obscurity. But what she had thought before arose from an icy heart, had begun to seem as if it might really come from a surfeit of feeling. In his own way, Sir Basil struck her as nearly as sincere in his sensibilities as her own dear Ben, a man whom none other had ever approached in her esteem. Certainly he was more passionate: But this new side of his character, revealed as it has been, did little to cheer her. On the contrary, the increasing awareness that he was just that sort of man who might have won her heart—the only man, perhaps—had come jointly with the belief that his own heart was already taken. Even had there been less difference in their stations, that prevented any further thought upon the idea.

Anne had resolved all this in her own mind—with a good deal less simplicity than that with which we have set it down—and concluded that she had but one choice. Leave she must, at once, before she did any more damage to herself, or risked damaging some others by her conduct. Nicole was here regarded first: She would not endanger the child's happiness more than she already must. Would not Nicole feel her loss twice as strongly at some later date? No. The decision, having once been made, must now be acted upon and without any delay. And so the letter was written to her father, and no hint given to Ben of the true reason for her return. She expected that Mr. Calder, contrary to his first admonition, would allow her home. She had duly expressed her shame at having thought herself up to the task she had taken on, and declared herself fully prepared to return as a wiser, and a more dutiful, daughter. She suspected what elation *that* might cause at home—but for the moment she was too preoccupied with her own more pressing dilemma to care.

She had set it down upon paper already, in preparation for the letter she expected hourly from Devonshire, that there might be not a moment's delay in her flight. She had not told Nicole as yet: Let that awful scene come at the last possible moment. It was just as she had appended her signature upon the letter that the footman knocked.

Nothing could have been more ill-timed. Anne, still distraught, could hardly compose herself sufficiently to greet the servant, much less the Baronet. But go she must, and so, quickly taking up her shawl, she went toward the door, only at the last moment stopping and going to retrieve her letter. There would not be any more fortuitous time, she was sure. What must under any circumstances be a heart-rending chore had better be dispatched at once. And so it was with the letter in her hand that she stood in the doorway of Sir Basil's library—as always, uncertain whether she ought to come boldly in, or stay close to the exit.

Sir Basil regarded her with a smile. Silly goose—would she never take it into her own hands to come and take possession of what was rightly her own in any case? He supposed that would be one of the tasks which lay ahead of him—a by no means unpleasant one, indeed. But (as he reminded himself in a moment's time, having invited her to come in and seeing the look upon her face of reluctance) he was getting ahead of himself. The only task *now* was to ascertain what was in her heart. And first of all, he must dispatch his most unpleasant errand. It was to this subject which he now turned, when the young woman was ensconced in her usual place and he in his.

"I am afraid I have disturbed you, Miss Calder," said he with a look which was as much a plea for a contradiction as anything else.

"Oh—no, Sir."

She seemed to be hiding something between the folds of her shawl—he tried to get a glimpse of it, without seeming to do so, and was unsuccessful.

"Are you certain? I have not awakened you from a nap, or interrupted some business?"

A shake of the head, rather too abrupt, was his reply.

"Well, then, I shall be as brief as possible. I am afraid it is not a very pleasant thing I have to say."

Miss Calder seemed startled, but said nothing.

"It concerns my ward, which is why I wished to ask your advice. Well—not exactly. It concerns, in point of fact, both myself and Lady Cardovan." Now the young lady looked really uncomfortable. Could she have had any hint of it before?

Sir Basil rushed on:

"I wished especially to seek your advice, Miss Calder," said he, growing more red every moment, "as you have always been good enough to council me, and in a most generous and wise manner. I hope you shall do so again, for I am more in need of it than ever. The matter," said he, after pausing to cough and glance quickly at her expression, which was impassive, "has come to my attention only this afternoon. Lady Diana has been ill, and has not before been able to give me the news. It is not exactly news. I do not know what you would call it."

It would have been very difficult to judge, at this moment, which of the two of them was most uncomfortable—the gentleman was absolutely scarlet, and the lady white.

Miss Calder broke the momentary silence with, "Dear me, Sir Basil. Perhaps you ought not to go on. If it is some private affair of your own—"

"No, no! That is, well—yes, in fact. It is extremely private. That is, I hope it will remain so. But perhaps it will not. Gossip is such in this city, my dear lady—ah, well, you would not know about that, I suppose. In any case, suffice it to say that there are *some* women who have not your fine sense of decorum."

Miss Calder blushed and stared at her hands. His effort to make her look up was abortive.

"Please, Sir Basil," murmured she, "do not tell me anything I had rather not know five years hence. Do please consider *that*—for I shall have to live with it, as well."

"I hope not," returned the Baronet with immense gravity. "I most certainly do hope not, Miss Calder. It is just for that reason that I wish to tell you now, to clear the air, as it were. To clear it for my ward, as much as for you."

"I am glad you are thinking of Nicole," Miss Calder almost whispered. "You need not think of *my* comfort."

"Well, I choose to think both of your comfort and hers," replied the Baronet rather primly. Realizing how he must have sounded, however, he gave her a pleading look. "Please hear me out, Miss Calder. *Then* you may judge me. Only do not judge me first."

"I would not judge you, Sir Basil. Very well, then."

She seemed immensely resigned, which was hardly the attitude he would have chosen to proceed, but having very little choice, he blurted out the following:

"I went to Grove House today, Miss Calder, on purpose to consult with my friend upon another subject—" this with a little glance at her, which went unnoticed— "and also, to find out why she had refused to see me, or indeed, to recognize my existence these last few days. Lady Cardovan was good enough to come downstairs. She would not speak to me at first—at least not in any kind of amiable way—and it was soon apparent why. She had happened to be informed at her own soiree, on Thursday last, of a piece of news which, though interpreting it falsely, must by now be common news about the town. I shall not tell you who was the source just now—only let me tell you what it was. It was, in short, the far-fetched notion that Miss Lessington was in truth born my own child, and herded away to the country in order to obscure her true identity. The death of her real guardian, then, must have resulted in my coming into her guardianship as a sort of *double farce*, a joke upon the world in general, for, in fact, that would make her my *own* child, would it not?"

Miss Calder nodded dumbly.

"Naturally, I did not take the news at first. In fact, I thought the point was that she was Diana's child—only fancy! I nearly accused her of hiding away a natural child and then pretending she was an orphan! Well, of course, as it turned out, we were both wrong. The rumour was started by an idle woman who has nothing better to do with her time than suppose the rest of the world is engaging in her own narrow intrigues. Lady Cardovan was actually pleased at the idea—fancy being accused of having a nine-year-old child at her age! She was almost delighted. And when it came out that Nicole is nothing more than she has ever seemed, or been, or been suspected of—well, you can imagine our mirth! Only, of course, it was not really very funny—half of London may suppose just that at this very moment. That is, suppose Nicole to be our joint child. Only fancy!"

"She—she is not your child, then?" Miss Calder was exceedingly pale.

"Heavens, no! But of course that is not the point. The point is, that Nicole must be protected from any rumours to that effect. I have already been to see the Princess Li—— the person whose idea this all was. And she has promised to stifle it for us, as well as she can. But gossip is like fire, Miss Calder—it generally spreads a great deal faster than the objects of it would like. I have no illusions as to what the effects of that might be upon Nicole, should she ever get a hint of it."

Miss Calder nodded. "I understand you perfectly, Sir. Of course she must never hear about it."

"Do you indeed? Why! I knew you would. And so, Miss Calder—what ought we to do?"

"I don't imagine there is anything we *can* do. Of course, if she ever got a hint of it—if some ignorant and unkind person were to mention it, even in passing—it will be your duty to stand beside her."

"I doubt not but that she should rather have *you* stand beside her," replied the Baronet with a little smile, which was meant to speak volumes.

Miss Calder flushed a little, and looked down at her lap again.

"But," said Sir Basil, "do not you think one of us ought to prepare her for it—just in the eventuality——"

"I can see no reason for it. I think Nicole has got about as much sense as either of us. She would not be thrown much by it."

"Not even for a moment?"

"I think not."

"Well! That settles it, doesn't it?"

"I hope so."

Sir Basil was rather at a loss for where to go from here. He had hoped that the subject might lead naturally enough along, if indeed it was cleared up at all (although he had had less of an idea of preparing Nicole, if the truth be known, than of forearming her governess), to another subject altogether. But Miss Calder was not at all herself tonight. She seemed restrained, tentative, even aloof. She had not even seemed much shocked by the news, once he had let her know it, but rather, relieved. Suddenly the thought struck him that she had had news from home of an unhappy kind, and questioned her about it.

"I hope you have not had any letters from home to make you unhappy?"

"No!" She seemed amazed at the suggestion. "No, Sir, I have not."

"Good, good." Sir Basil was literally bursting to tell her that she might any day now have news of a very happy kind from that quarter, but restrained himself. Let it come in a natural way, of itself. He could wait yet a while.

"And Nicole—her lessons are going along well?"

"She is having some difficulty with her drawing, Sir, but otherwise, she is a clever as possible, and applies herself diligently."

"Ah, well—what a good child she is, to be sure."

"A wonderful child, Sir. I hope—that is to say . . ."

"Yes?"

Sir Basil had leant a little forward, as had the young lady, but she stopped and would not continue.

"Nothing, Sir—that is, nothing of any importance, now."

That "now" struck Sir Basil as a little odd. He should liked to have known what had been of some importance before, which was not now. Anything of importance to Miss Calder, it struck him suddenly, was important also to him. But he could not show it without threatening her own delicacy, a thing he dreaded doing.

"Ah! Well! Tell me, Miss Calder, have you had a moment to look into that little book I gave you?"

Miss Calder seemed not to understand.

"*A Country Parson*—did you determine in your own mind whether or not it was written by a man?"

Miss Calder seemed to smile a little.

"Why—yes, Sir. I read it quite thoroughly—acquainted myself with it as much as possible—and have decided that in fact you must be correct after all. It could not possibly have been written by a woman."

Sir Basil was delighted. At last he had convinced her to see something in his own way. The triumph of the moment made him beam.

"Aha! Far too clever, was it not?"

Miss Calder looked grave, considering for a moment.

"No Sir, that is not what I would say. I would say it was not clever enough."

Sir Basil gaped. Miss Calder, amused, only stared back and nodded.

Chapter XXIII

Mr. Calder, having read over his letter several times, at last made up his mind what to do. The decision was not born solely out of consideration for Sir Basil Ives, for he had very little reason to wish to be kind to that gentleman. The letter had been so pompous that it had made him laugh, until he had considered what spirit had moved the author to write it. That, combined with a little gnawing desire of his own (not wholly becoming in a man of the cloth) to find out what all the fuss was about which his wife and daughters were continually wailing over, put the final stamp upon his resolution: He would go to London himself upon a dual mission. The first, of course, was to collect his daughter, and the second, was to disillusion the Baronet.

The minister set forth at once, for he was not a man to sit about having once made up his mind, nor did he desire to be encumbered by the company of any other member of his family, which he knew was a strong likelihood if the news of his departure was allowed to get about. Setting forth that same afternoon, therefore, he took stages to Grimley and, passing the night at one of the larger and more commodious inns upon the highway, arrived the next morning in London at about twelve o'clock. He went immediately to the house of his sister, a Mrs. Norton, who lived in Curzon Street, and whom, by dint of having married a well-known solicitor, he could depend upon to advise him, as well as giving both himself and his daughter beds for the night. Mrs. Norton had not been told of her niece's residence in London, for Anne had not wanted to be obliged to her, nor had Mrs. Calder relished the idea of her sister-in-law's reaction to the news of Anne's governessship. Mrs. Norton was rich and well connected, but she was equally an expansive and devoted aunt. Mr. Calder was positive he could depend upon her to help him.

His sister met him with some amazement, but a great deal of geniality. Her amazement was, of course, destined to grow sharper when she heard the reasons for her brother's mission, and the background of the story.

"Oh, Lord!" cried she, delighted, when she had heard the whole business narrated. "I always thought Anne was of a class by herself! What a plucky thing she is! And now, you say, Sir Basil is offering you charity?"

"A thousand pounds, to start!" smiled Mr. Calder. "With the offer of more when it is needed. Can you fathom it? I am almost tempted to keep it, only to teach him a lesson."

"But it is not his fault, you know."

Mr. Calder looked grave. "I know; and that is the worst of it, for Anne has now caught me up in her web of untruths, and I cannot let the man throw about his money in such a heedless sort of way."

"Sir Basil has got plenty of it, however," responded Mrs. Norton. "And it is exceeding odd, you know: for while his brother, Lord Hargate, has got the reputation of a complete bamboozle with his funds—forever in debt from cards and the excesses of his Countess—Sir Basil is known for quite the opposite characteristic. He is a famous skinflint. I don't know either of them personally, of course, but they are so well known, each in his separate way, that I am positive of the fact. I heard not long ago that he would not put up the funds to redecorate the Embassy, and the House of Commons was forced to raise them for him."

"Clever fellow," murmured her brother, for he had a more pragmatic view of the distribution of one's money than his sister.

"So it is exceedingly odd that he has chosen this moment to commence so much generosity," continued Mrs. Norton. "He must be very fond of Anne."

"And so he ought to be. But, however, I do not think she thinks as well of *him*—for she wishes to come home at once, and has hinted that she dislikes him amazingly."

"Really? Well, how odd. I know Sir Basil is meant to be tight with his money, but otherwise have heard nothing but good of him. It was he, you know, who put us upon such amiable terms with the French, after Wellington had pretty well ruptured them."

Mr. Calder did not know this, and listened with interest to some other of the Baronet's accomplishments. It was a very long list, and after hearing it, he felt a conflict between his original prejudice against the man and the proof which this new view afforded of his being a diligent and illustrious diplomatist. The sister and brother conversed a little longer, and when it happened to come out that Anne had had her book published, Mrs. Norton exclaimed in delighted amazement.

"What a girl!" cried she. "What is it called, Arthur? I shall get a copy as soon as ever I can."

"*A Country Parson*," replied Mr. Calder, adding, "It is meant to be a satire. I hope it is not all aimed at *me!*"

"Why!" cried Mrs. Norton, "I cannot believe it! It is being talked about everywhere, you know! Sir Walter Scott has called it brilliant, and the Regent is clamoring to know who wrote it! Heavens, and it was our very own Anne! I cannot believe it!"

Mr. Calder could believe anything good of his daughter, and having once accustomed himself to the notion that she was an authoress, even the notion that she was thought brilliant by such figures as Walter Scott and the Regent did not amaze him.

"That so?" he inquired. "Well, well! She is a very clever girl, you know."

"Clever! She is being called everywhere a genius!"

"Well, that is putting it a little strongly. Let her produce another book, first."

Mrs. Norton was amazed. She had ever held a high opinion of her eldest niece, and had always had a special fondness for her. But to think she was an authoress! And one so highly thought of! Well, it really was an astonishing thing.

Mr. Calder was very glad to hear all this, but his chief purpose in coming to London had been to fetch his daughter home, and to return the check to Sir Basil Ives with an explanation of his daughter's conduct. Having passed a few more minutes with his sister, therefore, and promising that he should return a little later with the prodigal child, he set off on foot for Regent's Terrace.

His thoughts had come full circle since he had set out, and now, walking through the city streets, he endeavoured to collect them a little. He had initially intended to confront the Baronet with the check, apologize for his daughter's conduct, and enjoy the spectacle of befuddlement upon the supercilious fellow's face. Now, however, he had come to review his ideas a little. He was unsure how he should go, and, having reached the house on Regent's Terrace, knocked tentatively at the door.

He was soon admitted and, having offered the butler his card, saying he was "Miss Calder's father," was shown into an elegant drawing room. There he waited for several moments, until a step was heard in the corridor, the door opened, and in stepped a tall and personable gentleman.

Mr. Calder rose from his chair and extended his hand.

"Your Excellency—I am afraid I have disturbed you. No doubt you are very busy."

Sir Basil Ives took in the dignified figure before him, a little amazed, inquired if this was really Miss Calder's father.

"Yes, I am afraid so! And I am afraid we have caused you a great deal of trouble."

"Trouble! Nothing like it! It is only that—well, to be frank, I expected something else."

Mr. Calder raised a comical eyebrow. "Ah! How so?"

Sir Basil hemmed and hawed a moment, taking a chair and inviting his guest to resume his own.

"I expected something rather different, Sir. Miss Calder led me to believe——"

"That I was an impoverished little old clergyman from the country?"

Sir Basil looked uncomfortable. "Well—yes, I suppose, if that is how you must put it."

"My daughter has deceived you sadly, I am afraid. She is a very naughty girl. This was all a whim of her own devising, and had I any suspicion of how far it would go——"

Sir Basil, looking exceedingly shocked, held up his hand.

"Pray, Sir! Do not belabour the point. Only tell me how far I have been led astray. You are not a clergyman? What, in Heaven's name, is the point?"

Mr. Calder smiled at his host's confusion, and felt a knot of sympathy for him. Having four daughters and a wife had taught him to regard the caprices of womankind a little more indulgently than he might have otherwise. A bachelor must certainly be appalled to find the whole sex so scheming and frivolous. As clearly as he could, therefore, he attempted to tell the story right from the start. Sir Basil, as may be expected, listened with profound amazement.

"So you see, Sir, she has led us all right down the primrose path. I need not tell you how sorry I am for having been any party to this ruse. I ought to have forbidden it right from the start. But how could I have known how far it would go?"

Sir Basil was sitting very pale in his chair. He said nothing for a moment.

"Then she has no need to be a governess? She has, you say, thirty thousand pounds of her own? Excuse me, Sir—but I cannot fathom it! Why should she have wanted to masquerade as a poor girl?"

"To escape her own life for a little, I suppose," replied Mr. Calder, smiling. "Who can ever say what gets into these women's heads? She did not wish to marry, and her mother loathes the idea that one of her daughters might be a spinster. She had several offers, you know—none of them brilliant, but then we live in a remote part of the country. Besides, she has always had a fanciful mind. I am exceedingly sorry, Sir, to have put you in such a position, and have come to take her away and to give you back your check. My son is perfectly all right. He shall never recover completely, I am afraid, for the effects of his illness are permanent. But now he has got something to amuse him—now that the book seems to have had so much success, well, I am sure he shall content himself perfectly with helping Anne to write her little books."

"Book . . . books?" repeated the Baronet, baffled.

"Why, you know, she is an authoress—ah, I suppose she has not told you that, either? She wrote a little novel—something to fill her idle hours in the country—and now it seems to have become all the rage. I have heard it is a very good one, too! I mean to read it as soon as I can. It was really on account of that that she wished to come to London. She said she had exhausted the resources of our little part of the world, and wished to see the Great One. Only now, I suppose, she finds it is really too much for her. She has led a very sheltered life, you know."

Sir Basil was looking flabbergasted. "Excuse me, Mr. Calder, if I seem to be having some trouble getting my breath. So much news all at once . . . dear me! She is an authoress, and has thirty thousand pounds! Her father is a gentleman, and *she* desires to be a governess!"

"It is all rather odd, is it not? But women are like that, Sir Basil. You have not seen as much of 'em as I have. I dare say. I am dreadfully sorry to have inconvenienced you in this inexcusable fashion. But I shall attempt to make it up as soon as I can. First, by returning your check, and second, by taking my daughter away. You shall resume your normal life as soon as possible, I hope."

"Oh, Sir—I hope not!"

Mr. Calder regarded him in amazement. "Why, what do you mean, Sir?"

"I do not see how I can do without her! She has made herself invaluable here, both for my ward and for myself! I depended upon her coming to Paris with me!"

"I do not understand you, Sir. Surely you cannot still wish her to be in your employ! I do not think she will like to be, in any case! And, Sir, I have made up my mind. I think this prank has gone far enough."

"Will you, Sir, allow her to make up her own mind?"

Mr. Calder looked uncertain. He thought perhaps he ought to inform his host that Anne already *had* made up her mind, but having already caused him so much chagrin, he did not see how he could refuse.

"Very well, Sir Basil. Why do not you send for her at once?"

The bell was pulled, and a footman sent to fetch the young lady from the schoolroom. Having not been informed of her father's presence in the house, she opened the door quickly, unsure why she had been sent for. The sight of the two occupants of the room almost made her jump.

"Father!" she exclaimed. "What—what on earth are you doing here?"

A nervous glance between the gentlemen was sufficient to tell her at least part of the story. The one was staring at her crossly, the other with an imploring look.

"I have come on purpose to attempt to undo some of the damage you have done Sir Basil, my dear."

Anne looked inquiring, and then guilty. "Oh dear!"

"And to take you home."

Mr. Calder paused. "Sir Basil, however, is such a charitable man that he seems to wish you to continue in his employ. I have attempted to make him see the true light of your character, but he seems blinded to it. We have therefore agreed to leave the decision to you. Well, my dear—do you wish to come home with me at once, or to go to Paris as the Ambassador's governess?"

Sir Basil coughed. "Ah—Miss Calder. I hope you will not make up your mind just yet. I should have preferred to do this in another way, but I seem to have no choice. I do not wish you to come to Paris with me as a governess."

Miss Calder, already startled, looked doubly so. "Sir?"

"Not as my governess—that is to say Nicole's governess—but as my wife."

Now it was Mr. Calder's turn to look flabbergasted. He stared back and forth between the two other occupants of the room, wondering if he had heard correctly. Had Sir Basil said "wife"? What on earth was going forward? His daughter's face had gone perfectly white, and then perfectly red. She was staring at the Baronet in shock. Sir Basil himself was utterly pale.

"I know this is not how it is generally done, Miss Calder. I have not much experience with this kind of thing, and hope you will forgive me. Perhaps we ought to walk out into the garden, where I can fall upon my knees—only I am not much good at that sort of thing. I only know that I shall be miserable if you tell me "no.""

Anne had raised a hand to her forehead, and was swaying slightly. Seeing that she was any moment in danger of fainting dead away, her father rushed to her side, just in time to catch her fall. Sir Basil, too, had jumped forward, and now struggled to help move her to a sofa. Here the two gentlemen bent over her, chafing her wrists and looking rather idiotic, under the circumstances, since neither of them had ever been in this situation before. It was some moments before either of them was composed enough to speak. By that time, Anne's lids had begun to flutter, and she gazed up into the face of Sir Basil Ives, bent in utmost sympathy above her.

"Did you really ask me to be your wife, Sir?"

Sir Basil nodded emphatically.

"You do not hate me?"

"On the contrary, I am in love with you. I wish you would say something."

Anne did.

Chapter XXIV

"Never," murmured Sir Basil Ives in a wondering meditative tone, "could I have imagined that I should find myself so happy to be so much in the company of women."

Some few days had passed since the enactment of the last scene, and so much had occurred to fill them up that neither the Ambassador nor Anne, who now sat next to him upon the drawing room sofa staring absently into the flickering fire, could account for their passage. The Baronet had indeed been subjected to an almost constant barrage of female company and conversation. No sooner had the news of their engagement reached Devonshire than Mrs. Calder and her two next eldest children had descended upon the Capital to oversee the couple's plans. Anne had been instantly transported out of Regent's Terrace to the more appropriate environment of Curzon Street, for now, as her mother declared, that she was no longer Sir Basil's governess but his intended, she could scarcely remain beneath the same roof. Sir Basil failed to see the logic of this argument, for as he quickly pointed out, he had fallen in love with her beneath that roof, and beneath that roof they had already passed one blissful month of solitary peace, enjoying each other's company in the most proper and civilized fashion, without the aid of any chaperone. Mrs. Calder would have snorted upon hearing this, had she not fallen so much beneath the Baronet's spell the moment she clapped eyes upon him that it was sometimes difficult to tell whether mother or daughter was more enraptured with that gentleman. She could scarce bring herself to contradict even his most facetious remarks, which were made on purpose to tease her, and found his circumlocutions of her arguments only a little more charming than they were frustrating. Still, the ladies had had their way in the end, as Sir Basil remarked now, leaning back against the pillows of the sofa and heaving a deep sigh of contented indolence. His hand searched out the fingers of his companion, which lay an inch or two away from his own, and gave them a gentle squeeze.

"I think you really ought to congratulate me, my darling girl, on my admirable stoicism in the face of it all."

Anne replied with a wry little smile, which quickly melted into a gentler look as she caught his eye.

"I think you have been admirable indeed, Basil! Much more than *I* have been! I really thought you might take flight the instant you saw my mother descend upon us. And I should not," she added, softly, "have blamed you much."

"What!" The Baronet looked shocked. "Take flight just when the object of my heart was nearly won! Leave my poor love to the tender mercies of that tribe of ministering angels? I may not be Wellington, dear girl, but I hope I have got a *little* spine!"

Anne laughed softly at the expression of ill-usage upon her lover's face.

"Don't laugh at me. I shan't have you laughing at me," retorted he.

"I wasn't laughing at you!"

Sir Basil gave her a little sideways glance and pouted "Very well, then. You may laugh at me if you like. Only see what an imbecile I am become for you!"

"On the contrary," responded Anne, with an equal degree of mockery in her grave look, "you are only become a little malleable. It is an excellent quality in a diplomat."

Sir Basil grunted, and there was a brief silence whilst the lovers stared into the fire and only the ticking of the clock disturbed the utter tranquility of the moment. After a little the Baronet stole a look at his companion's profile, which, touched as it was by the firelight, looked even more composed and lovely than he had expected. He could not tear his eyes away for a moment or two, and Anne flushed a little beneath their gaze.

"Are you—" commenced she after a moment— "are you *quite* sure of what you are doing? I shan't hold you to anything, you know, even if you change your mind at the last moment."

Sir Basil gave her a sharp look, and then exclaimed, "Why,

I am mightily glad you asked, my love! For as it happens, I have just discovered a most extraordinary weakness for a certain young lady—a most wrong-headed and silly girl, to be sure, but nevertheless quite wonderfully enchanting. I suppose you will know her—and I wish instantly to be released, that I may marry her!"

Anne, who had looked startled at first, and rather dismayed, now burst out laughing.

"*Do* be serious, Basil! I am perfectly in earnest. I mean, you really ought to consider what you are doing. I may be an immense disappointment to you. I have no training for diplomacy, none of the qualifications expected of an ambassador's wife—I may disgrace you abominably. Once we are settled in Paris and you are returned to your own world, you may look at me one day and regret most bitterly what you did in the passion of the moment. I should far rather you scrutinized your heart now, than discover a contempt for me *later!*"

"I would far rather, my love, scrutinize *you*," replied the Baronet, turning her face gently toward his. "For I never in all my life supposed a face could be so lovely, nor hold so much fascination for me. Look at me, Anne, what do you see?"

Anne turned her eyes to meet the Baronet's, and quickly glanced away."

"A man infatuated, perhaps, only for the moment, and for the first time. A wholly wonderful, remarkable man—but still, perhaps, only carried away for the moment, and blinded to his true sense of right."

Sir Basil smiled. "And are *you* similarly blinded?"

Anne shook her head gravely. "Only in so far as I am happier now than I ever imagined possible. But I know when the novelty has worn off and I am grown quite accustomed to being the luckiest creature on earth, that I shall still regard you as I do now. For I have weighed in my *mind*, no less than in my heart, what we both are, and though I find *myself* sadly lacking, you are more than I could ever require in a man."

"And do you think, only because I am a man, and therefore incapable of this sort of deep thought which you have described, that I have not myself engaged in a little similar contemplation? Do you suppose I have simply fallen prey to a tantalizing witch? Dear me! And I thought your opinion of my sex had improved a little."

"*Do* be serious, Basil. You know that is not what I meant."

"I never was more serious in all my life, my dearest Anne," responded Sir Basil, still gently holding her chin and gazing deep into her eyes. "I have weighed the matter most carefully—for no one, I think you will agree, could fault me for being unmeticulous—and I have concluded that no two people upon earth could be more admirably suited. That is, if you will have a little patience with me, and continue to instruct me in the art of happiness as successfully as you have done thus far."

"You don't think I will shame you through some thoughtless act or remark?"

"Only," said Sir Basil, smiling, "if you insist upon lecturing King Louis as you do me!"

"I shall try to learn to hold my tongue," replied Anne, flushing.

"Oh, I hope not, indeed! But perhaps—perhaps just a *little* more restraint with some of the French would help. They are not endowed with my vast store of self-mockery and humility."

"Hmmph!" snorted Anne, laughing out loud.

"Hmmph, indeed! No—will you do me one great favour?"

Anne looked puzzled. "Anything, Your Excellency."

"Will you hold your tongue long enough to let me kiss you?"

Anne, without much trouble, obeyed this command, and the lovers were much immersed in this fascinating activity when a soft knock sounded at the door. Lady Cardovan appeared a moment later, smiling indulgently at the pair upon the sofa, who both rose quickly to their feet, looking slightly guilty. Her ladyship had lived upon the earth for several years, and was not much fooled by their sudden show of interest in the arrangement of logs upon the fire. She had come to chaperone the dinner party, and being a sensible woman, had removed herself as soon as the repast was finished, ostensibly to read a story to Nicole. In fact, the child had fallen almost instantly into a deep and happy slumber, leaving Lady Cardovan to amuse herself for half an hour with a book.

The engaged couple had been given hardly a moment's peace since the arrival of the party from Devonshire. Between plans for the wedding (which Mrs. Calder was determined to make a very grand affair, despite the protestations of her daughter and future son-in-law), between fittings, and visits, and the innumerable balls and breakfasts which were suddenly being held in their honor, barely a moment could be found for such a *tête-a-tête* as this. Lady Cardovan, seeing the expressions upon her friends' faces, judged that the half an hour she had given them alone had been well accounted for.

"Well, children," declared she, coming into the room and assuming the expression and stance of a prim old spinster, with her lips pursed and her hands clasped against her waist, "I hope you have used your time wisely."

"Oh, very wisely, Diana," responded Sir Basil, with what was almost a sheepish grin. "But I do wish you would remove that expression from your face. You make me feel like a child of twelve. Have *you* no mercy upon us? I should have thought you at least would be a little more kind than the others!"

Lady Diana looked offended and, giving up the pose, moved to an armchair.

"Really, Basil, I think you are most unjust! I have just passed the most grim half-hour. I do wish that whoever owns this house would put something more fascinating upon the library shelves than *The Complete Erwin James*. A most pedantic and insufferable fellow, and one could very well get along with less of him. Indeed, I am delighted that I managed to live so long without making his acquaintance at all."

"Why," exclaimed Anne, turning about, "I thought you were upstairs reading to Nicole!"

Lady Cardovan smiled. "She, poor lamb, had no more use for me than you did. She was fast asleep as soon as her head touched the pillow. I make no doubt but that the exertions of the last week have been quite as trying to her as to you."

"I doubt it," retorted Sir Basil, taking Anne's arm and guiding her back to the sofa with him. "For she is a female, and constitutionally immune to such goings-on. I believe all women are born capable of any amount of strenuous activity, so long as it is centered principally about the dressmaker's and the ballroom."

"Well, she is certainly very happy. She asked me about a dozen times if it was not marvelous that you were going to be married."

"Sweet girl!" exclaimed Anne. "I do hope she will have as little trouble adjusting to life in Paris as she has had here."

"I make no doubt of it," said Lady Cardovan. "I never knew a child who had so little trouble making friends. She is the most charming little creature I ever saw."

"By Jove! There's an idea, Diana!" exclaimed Sir Basil with an inspired look. "What a genius you are!"

Lady Diana looked puzzled. "Why, what have I said, Basil?"

"I shall send her to the Tuileries ahead of me, to argue with King Louis over the Slavery Question. I don't doubt but that he'll be twice as entranced with her as the Regent, and in any case, her chattering is bound to confuse him so much that after an hour he'll be eager to do her every bidding."

There was a burst of laughter from the ladies, and Anne remarked, "Well, at least if she cannot solve your slavery dilemma, Basil, perhaps she shall succeed in improving the King's manners. I cannot imagine he will be able to hold out very long against her little lectures on hospitality and etiquette after she has been kept waiting all day in the antechamber!"

"Oh, perfect!" concurred Lady Diana, adding with a grave look, "I hope you have warned poor Anne of what is in store for her. I do not much envy you, my dear, being subjected to all those tedious Court rituals and endless breakfasts in the kitchen!"

Anne looked a little startled upon hearing this, but was quickly reassured that although the French King was indeed very fond of pomp and circumstance, his guests were not usually required to take their meals in the kitchen. Lady Diana had been referring to the Bourbon habit of leaving the royal family's guests to dine alone in a state dining hall whilst they took their own meals in another part of the palace.

After a little more of this kind of banter, Sir Basil, who had been silent for some minutes, interrupted:

"In any case, my dear ladies, I do not think Anne will have to tolerate this sort of thing much longer." Seeing the surprised looks upon the faces of the other two, the Baronet continued.

"I have been doing a bit of serious mulling lately, whilst you ladies have been gadding about racking up bills at the dressmaker's, and I have concluded that now I am to be a happily married man, and with the attendant responsibilities of a guardian, I will not long remain in the Diplomatic Corps. I think I should like to come home once and for all and reap the rewards of my labours."

"Why, Basil!" exclaimed Anne, "I hope you are not thinking of giving up your career on my account! You have still an illustrious life ahead of you. I should never forgive myself if I was the cause of your giving it up. In any case, the whole kingdom depends upon you!"

"Oh, I shan't retire just yet, my love. But in a few years' time, when, perhaps—" with a twinkle in his eye— "our little household may be further increased, I believe I shall have had enough of this vagabond's life. We are still young, and have some years left to wander about, but I should like to see my children grow up on native soil."

"Well," declared Her Ladyship briskly, "it is early days yet to be talking of such things. Really, Basil! Poor Anne is not yet a married woman, and already you are talking of your dotage and a whole houseful of children! Do you at least wait a fortnight, until you are man and wife!"

"Indeed," breathed Sir Basil fervently, "I wish that fortnight would hurry up and pass!"

Lady Cardovan looked fondly at the couple upon the sofa, who seemed already to be so much in harmony with each other that they might have been married already for several years. She inquired if there had been any news of Miss Newsome since their engagement had been announced.

"I believe she has taken herself off to Scotland for a little medicinal hunting," replied Sir Basil. "I have no doubt but that she will recover soon enough with the aid of a little riding to hounds, and some other of the horsey delights to be found in that part of the world. My sister-in-law, alas, will not speak to me, however."

"I am sure an invitation to Paris would have an instant effect."

"Good God, Diana! Don't mention such a thing, I beg of you! We should never be rid of her! Anyhow, I shall not allow my wife to show her any hospitality, after the treatment Anne received at *her* hands."

"Oh, I am sure that now she is to be Lady Ives, your sister-in-law will be friendly enough," returned Lady Diana. "But I suppose you shall have a constant stream of visitors to the Embassy in any case. Your whole family, I suppose, will be there, will they not, Anne?"

"Oh, no! Papa has strictly forbidden them to come! He says we are to have a full year of peaceful married bliss before the barrage begins."

"Sensible fellow!" breathed Sir Basil.

"But," continued Anne, "we are expecting *two* visitors at least, and *they* are to stay as long as they please."

"Ah! And who are they?"

"Why, yourself, of course, and my brother Ben."

"Oh," exclaimed Lady Cardovan, "I should not think of intruding upon you."

"Nonsense! You are quite one of our little family—indeed, had it not been for you, there should *be* no marriage—and Ben is my coauthor. He is to come after a month or two to help me get a start upon my next book."

"And what is that to be, my dear?" inquired Her Ladyship with great interest.

Anne smiled a little slyly at her betrothed, and put on a mysterious look. "Why, it is a bit of a secret at present, but you shall both know presently."

Chapter XXV

As commander-in-chief of the staff at Number 23 Grosvenor Square, Rutgers considered it his duty to apprise the newest members of that staff of the goings-on amongst the occupants of the neighbouring houses. It was not, in fact, the least enjoyable of his many duties, nor did he count it as the least important. A good footman, like a good major domo, must know when to bite his tongue, when to stare impassively ahead despite the wildest sort of high-jinks, and (not least) when to pass along any little bits of gossip acquired during the course of his duties, that his elders and betters might interpret their true import. It was, therefore, his habit, at the time of any new arrival into the household, to follow the first regulation tour of house and grounds with a brief monologue upon the neighbours.

Some years after the events which have just been recorded, the old retainer (who by now had served half a dozen Russian ambassadors, and was more master of the house than any of them) was stationed before his favourite window—that giving out from the pantry upon the whole of Grosvenor Square—delivering his customary lecture to a young footman. The fellow (for he was, as yet, too recent a member of the staff to have earned a name) was much impressed by the butler's voice and manner, and stood quietly by, a modest half-step behind the elderly Rutgers, eagerly taking in every bit of slander and ogling each house in turn as it fell beneath the old man's scrutiny.

"Ah, lad," sighed Rutgers, having successfully laid to rest half the reputations of the *ton*, "it is not what it once was.

The Square was a grand place in its heyday! But it has seen more common goings and comings than Haymarket by now. A dozen years ago, my boy—the Princess Lieven lived here then, you know—Grosvenor Square was the finest address in all of London. Still is, by most counts, I'll warrant. But for those of us who *know*, lad, for those of us who know. . . ."

The butler's voice trailed off, as in a paroxysm of despair at the very thought. The footman gave a sharp intake of breath, and tried to summon up in his slender imagination some picture of what it might have been like in those glorious times. Since he was already so much agog at the splendour of the houses in that part of town and the great beauty of the streets, which now shone brilliantly beneath an early summer sun, he did not have much success. Nothing, he supposed could be much more awe-inspiring than this little square, with its rows of vast mansions and noble old trees, its continual swarm of elegant carriages, and the stream of fashionable ladies and gentlemen who continually alighted from them before some one or other of the doors.

"The Princess used to give balls regular, then, lad—half a dozen a week at the very least. Breakfasts, dinners, houtdoors fêtes—you never saw the like of it! 'Twas a very different place in *those* days, you can imagine! Hah, well. Now, then . . ." Rutger's eyes surveyed, rather critically, the houses in the Square, in search of someone whose history he had forgotten to reveal. Almost instantly, his eyes brightened. "*Now* then," he repeated, in a brisk voice, "there is *one* house that has fared better than some others. I am speaking of that large stone edifice catty-corner across the way, lad. Hargate House."

"Yes, Sir," murmured the novice, peering in the indicated direction. "A very grand house, Sir. Nearly as grand as *this* one!"

"Well, not quite, lad," returned the butler with a derogatory little sniff. "It *is* rather larger, but in appointments and luxurious haccommodations, I assure you, it is nothing to touch it. But, however, it is a great deal improved since the days of the Princess. Then, lad, it was the repository of the vulgarest family in London. One could scarcely dignify it by any other name. A very rubbish bin of humanity. The Princess would not speak to 'em."

The young footman's eyebrows shot up expectantly.

"Why, Sir—who on earth lived there?"

"Lord Hargate, of course," sniffed the butler. "Lord Hargate and his lady, and their three small brats."

The footman digested this information. "And who lives there now, Sir?"

"Why, Lord Hargate, of course. Lord and Lady Hargate."

The young man pondered how this could have changed the tone of the place much, and could not think of anything to say.

"Not the *same* Lord Hargate, of course. Another one," remarked Rutgers after a moment. "The late Lord Hargate's younger brother. A very different sort of gentleman, however. One could scarce imagine how they belonged to the same family. This one, lad, was once called Sir Basil Ives. You will have heard of him, of course?"

The footman looked blank.

"Sir Basil Ives, later Lord Ives, our Ambassador to France, and, more recently, Chancellor of the Exchequer. Now retired to private life."

The footman looked illuminated.

"Well, his elder brother, that is to say the one who was Lord Hargate *last*, departed this life a few years ago. Long before his time, of course, but then he was so much given to eating and drinking that one would not have expected him to live half so long as he did. Monstrous fat fellow. Don't *you* go about eating and drinking too much, young man," warned the butler with a suspicious look. "A young man of your age ought not to drink at all, and scarcely to eat anything. Healthier that way."

The footman looked a little shocked at this advice, but nodded his head fervently nevertheless.

"Anyhow, as I was saying, the late Lord Hargate died, and now Sir Basil has come into the family title and family mansion at once. It is a great improvement, not only for him—which it no doubt is—but for all of us. Lord, how I used to grow nervous, watching the goings-on in that household!"

The footman looked curious. "Was it so very bad, Sir?"

Rutgers snorted. "Eh? Bad! You never saw such a place! Butler always asleep, coat unpressed, marketing at all hours! And the nurse! You ought to have seen the nurse!"

"But now it is much better? The new Lady Hargate runs things more—er—smoothly?"

Rutgers had drifted into a reverie, and did not hear the question. After a second he let out a chortle, and declared, "What a comical thing it was, to be sure!"

211

"What, Sir?"

"Very comical," repeated the butler sternly. "It was very comical. Are you deaf, lad?"

Rutgers regarded the footman severely. "No, Sir. I don't think so, Sir. But what," inquired he timidly, "if I may be so bold, Sir, was comical?"

"Why, the manner of their marriage, lad! The marriage of Lord and Lady Hargate! The *present* Lord and Lady Hargate. She was his governess, you know."

The footman puckered up his brow at this idea.

"Why, is she so much older than he, Sir?" inquired he mildly. He had seen the elegant Lady Hargate once or twice, driving about the Square in her fashionable curricle, with her two little sons beside her. She certainly did not look old enough to have been Lord Hargate's governess. If she was, indeed, it would be a minor miracle of nature, for she was certainly very comely, and did not appear to be so very ancient.

"No, no, no!" exclaimed Rutgers impatiently. He eyed the footman with some suspicion. Had he inadvertently employed a dimwit? "She was not *his* governess, lad! She was governess to his—to his—well, adopted daughter. An orphan, actually. She is now Lady Ormsby-Thwaite. But, anyhow—that can be of no concern to you, young man. As it turned out, in any case, she was not a governess at all—not a governess as you would commonly think of one, at any rate—but a young lady of good family, and an authoress besides. You will perhaps have heard of her—Miss Anne Calder, who wrote *The Determined Bachelor* and some other distinguished volumes. A most erudite young woman. Of course, some will say that Sir Basil married beneath him, but I always felt that though she *was* only a clergyman's daughter, she possessed more hactual refinement than many of your so-called haristocrats. But we must not question the ways of the haristocracy, lad," continued Rutgers with a sudden shift of tone. "It is not our business to judge them, but to serve them. They are our betters, and so, of course, their ways are different from our own."

Rutgers regarded the footman sternly, having delivered what was, after all, a rather curious finale to his little lecture, which had successfully destroyed half the reputations of that very class.

The footman, shifting nervously from one foot to the

other, and still endeavouring in his mind to untangle the knot of relationships which had just been laid out before him, nodded humbly.

"Yes, Sir. I see what you mean, Sir."

About the Author

Judith Harkness was born in San Jose, Costa Rica, the daughter of parents in the diplomatic service. After a childhood spent in eight countries in Europe and South America, she attended Brown University in Providence, Rhode Island, where she studied literature and theater. Six years as a starving actress and a successful fashion model led unexpectedly to a free-lance career in journalism. She currently lives in Providence, where she divides her time between writing fiction and magazine profiles of artistic personalities.